Before We Leave

Before We Leave

Chronicles of the Maca III

Mari Collier

Published 2015 by Creativia

Book design by Creativia (www.creativia.org)

Cover art by http://www.thecovercollection.com/

http://www.maricollier.com/

Contents

Lorenz and Antoinette: The Early Years 1869 to 1878   **1**

1   A Family Divided   2

2   Flight   5

3   The Welcome Home   10

4   Wedding Plans   15

5   Marriage   19

6   Anna's Last Stand   25

7   Rescue   30

8   Father and Son   34

9   Truth and Concepts   37

10   A Summer Day   45

The Family: The Middle Years 1886 to 1899   **52**

11   Father and Sons, the Next Generation   53

12   Young James Conducts a Service   62

13	The Grandmother	68
14	James Confronts the Unknown	72
15	Blizzard	79
16	A Frozen World	84
17	Der Pastor Becomes The Shepherd	88
18	The Bargain	97
19	Christina in Love	102
20	A Hanging	105
21	The Telegram	114
22	Mad Maggie	118
23	Rescue	123
24	Anna's Boys	128
25	Christina in Exile	141
26	Escape	145
27	Panic	148
28	1892: The Rolfe's Anniversary	153
29	Love and Marriage	158
30	Death in a Frontier Town	164
31	The Fugitive	168

32	Justice Texas Style	175
33	A Visit to the *Golden One*	185
34	Patriarch of the House	191

Last Years on Earth 1921 to 1950 **199**

35	A Death in the Family 1921	200
36	Smashed Dreams	206
37	Texas: September 1, 1939	212
38	House Call	217
39	The Organization Investigates	221
40	Time to Leave	229
41	Plans	235
42	General MacDonald	237

Lorenz and Antoinette:
The Early Years 1869 to 1878

Chapter 1

A Family Divided

Daniel turned from the stallion he was breaking for his employer, Jeremiah "Red" O'Neal, with a wide smile on his face and his grey eyes alight with pleasure. "That is one fine horse..." The smile died as he saw the set look on Red's face. Daniel's sixth sense signaled danger and this time danger came from his employer and half-brother, if his white mother and MacDonald were to be believed. The Comanche raid when Daniel was eight had broken all ties with his white family.

When his Comanche family was captured by the U.S. Army, he was recognized as white and sent to a fort in Kansas. There he had taken the surname Hunter. He refused to acknowledge his white mother and that reputed stranger from a planet among the stars named as his father. He couldn't explain the two hearts his brother Lorenz, sister Margareatha, and possibly half-brother, Red, possessed while he did not. He simply ignored that fact.

Red stopped in front of the young man. "You stepped over the line, boy. Now you'll get a lesson." Red drove his fist into the young man's stomach.

Daniel twisted his body out of the way, not sure why the attack was under way, but knowing his chances weren't good. He whirled back, his left coming up towards Red's chin. He missed by less than an inch, and felt a fist smash into his nose. Desperately, he swung into Red's rib cage driving the older man back. Red shrugged and dove in again, his fists slamming into Daniel one after another.

Neither Red nor Daniel heard Margareatha screaming. "Let him alone you barbarian, or I'll blow your head off, so help me God!"

It was the sharp thud alongside of his head that made Red step back and lower his fists. Then he saw her standing there, shotgun in hand. He spread his hands out. "Miss Lawrence, this is a private matter."

"Private, be damned. He's my brother." Her mind raked into his, scalding and scathing him with anger as she used mindspeak.

'And he's yours too, if you have wit enough to remember we have the same father. Do you want Mac pounding on your head like you've pounded his?' The shotgun remained pointed directly at his chest. The men at the corrals were shifting uneasily, not knowing whether to draw against a woman or let the boss play this one out on his own.

Red considered. Daniel was on the ground and bleeding from the nose and mouth. He had executed several well-placed kicks and knew there were broken ribs. Margareatha was right. Any more and he would have MacDonald as an adversary. Lorenz, he discounted as too young to be any more of a threat than Daniel. "Someone put him on a horse and get him out of here."

"Wrong. They bring him to my house." The shotgun never wavered. "He doesn't leave here until I say he's well enough to travel."

Red glared at her. Both stood an even six feet and their gaze was level. "This is my ranch."

"Just who do you think you are Red O'Neal? Your books can rot if that's your attitude."

Red blanched. He needed her. There was no way he could explain to another bookkeeper the shipments of grain to nowhere on earth or the sudden disappearance of certain people within his businesses and the regular changing of gold and silver into currency.

"Very well, take him to Miss Lawrence's house." He turned and walked away.

Margareatha did not appear in the office for almost a week. When she did, she flounced in and put both hands on her hips, her tall frame almost reaching to the top of the door and the sun flaming her red hair into a fiery glow around her head.

"Daniel's better, but it will be another week before the ribs heal enough that he can leave. Now suppose you enlighten us as to what you thought you were doing."

Red threw down the pencil and looked up. He knew his efforts at the accounts were slow and clumsy compared to Margareatha's neat columns. "Margareatha, Daniel and Antoinette were planning on getting married. My mother has been crying for weeks and spending even more time on her knees in front of the Virgin's shrine than she has done previously. Her fingers are almost bleeding from the number of times she's said the rosary. What did you expect me to do? Tell Daniel he couldn't go near her again? They would have devised someway to disgrace us all."

Margareatha regarded him with a look reserved for the insane. "You are totally mad. Antoinette doesn't give two whoops about Daniel. He's too crude and too poor."

Red stood up. "I'm afraid you don't have the same information from Antoinette's private quarters as I do. Antoinette will be leaving for the convent in New Orleans within the next two days."

Margareatha smiled to herself and let the perfect revenge play out in her mind. She knew exactly what Antoinette was planning. Aloud, she said, "Suit yourself. I may return when Daniel is well enough to travel." She spun on her heel and walked out, steadfastly refusing to let Red mindspeak to her. Red was blinded by his own male prejudices, she thought. Let him continue to delude himself.

Four weeks ago Antoinette had brought a letter addressed to Lorenz, pleading with her to mail it. Margareatha had done so. She remembered all too well the convent life that she had been confined to so long ago.

Chapter 2

Flight

For once the trunks were minimal when Antoinette traveled. Consuela would be her companion all the way to New Orleans and have control of the money. Red made sure that Antoinette's horse and saddle were securely kept under guard. Both he and the Senora heaved a sigh of relief when the stage rolled out of Wooden. Daniel was just barely able to sit up and the men had orders to shoot if he left within the week. Red was confident he'd covered every possibility. Right now, he needed Margareatha back at the books as he had another grain buying trip to complete before heading to Galveston to arrange the shipping to a South American warehouse.

They had been in the stage for four days before Antoinette began to be anxious. They were but two days away from Houston and the boat taking her to New Orleans. She had been praying to the Virgin, the Saints, and the Holy Trinity that Lorenz had received her letter in time. He should have, but where was he? She couldn't see him riding up and stopping the stage, and she certainly didn't want anyone to be injured. Consuela sat prim and perspiring in the summer heat, her dark clothes drawing in more heat. Antoinette dabbed daintily at her brow with her hanky as they bounced and jolted over the roads.

The driver pulled the horses into the stage stop as close to noon as possible. "Everybody out. You all have thirty minutes to eat while we get the horses changed."

Antoinette stepped down and brushed the dust from her clothes and swallowed. A tall, young man was standing by the corrals with a saddled horse. He tugged at the front brim of his hat and walked the animal behind the wooden stable. "I believe I need to use the facilities," she whispered to Consuela and noted the look of relief on the older woman's face.

Consuela tried to keep up with the long strides Antoinette was taking and failed. The outhouse for women was set off to the side and Antoinette scooted in first and locked the door. She hurriedly did what nature demanded, exited, and let Consuela in. She nodded at the other woman waiting and walked briskly to the back of the stable.

Lorenz smiled at her, his grey eyes glowing; the scar on his right cheek dragging the lip line upward, and her heart went to her throat. Strange, that was all he had to do, smile.

"Let's go." He boosted her up onto the horse before swinging up behind her. He held his horse to a trot until they were over the rise and then kicked it into a gallop. They rode into a small, hidden gully and Lorenz collected two more horses; one carefully laden with camp goods, the second equipped with a regular saddle and bridle for her. She hooked her leg around the saddle horn as sitting astride would have shown too much leg. Later, when she had time to think, Antoinette would wonder how he knew to wait for her at that stage stop with the extra horses and equipment hidden away.

They rode steadily for an hour and then walked the horses. Lorenz seemed to be deep in thought, but his eyes kept searching the surrounding landscape. Finally as the sun began to set, he found a small, wooded area and they dismounted.

"I'm afraid this will be a grueling trip for y'all." His concern showed in his eyes. "We'll have to keep a steady pace for days. I don't think anyone is following us, but we'll eat a cold supper tonight just in case."

"Ah'm a Texan." Antoinette smiled at him. "Were y'all able to bring me anything in the way of clothes?"

"I didn't have time to find anything for ladies." He looked at her doubtfully. "I threw in an extra pair of my trousers and a shirt. Y'all can roll up the trousers. There's also a regular hat. It's a little beat up, but it will be better than that doodad on your head."

Antoinette considered. "Ah believe ah'll try your clothes for the journey."

Lorenz started to pull the saddles and turned back to her. "Uh, Antoinette, y'all aren't going to change your mind, are y'all?

She stared at him, disbelief spreading over her face. "Never! They were going to lock me away in that convent." For one brief moment her drawl had disappeared. Then she smiled. "Besides, ah'm a marked woman now."

"Antoinette, I won't do anything to hurt y'all, and I promise we will be married before..." Lorenz started to redden and turned to the horses, lips compressed. He'd promised himself that he would conduct himself as a gentleman in word and deed.

His resolve almost broke the sixth night after they'd eaten. Antoinette was bone weary from the days of riding, sleeping on the ground, and quickly prepared camp food. Her movements were listless and the laughter gone from her violet eyes. Lorenz took her in his arms to comfort her and suddenly she was holding him tightly and he was tasting her lips, the dusty cheeks, his tongue seeking hers, and his hands starting to move over her while he kept whispering, "I love y'all, Antoinette, Antoinette."

He never knew how he managed to break away, but somehow he was walking rapidly uphill to the small crest above their camp.

Antoinette found herself blinking, her breath coming in and out of her mouth as she stood stunned, watching him move away from her. After a few moments, she followed him upward and found him sitting cross-legged, his arms crossed in front of him as he sat rocking back and forth. She could see his profile, so perfect, so clean in the moonlight, his face drawn taunt from pain. Should she approach him? She had no other clothes except her dress which she intended to put on the last day. She had listened to the servants' chatter in Spanish and remembered that they talked about the "blood." That was frightening, but the married ones had spoken of it with a certain satisfaction. Obviously, there were things she didn't know. There was no bed, basin, or clean rags here.

Antoinette could not stand the agony stamped on his face and as she drew nearer she reached out her hand to touch his shoulder. "Lorenz?"

"Antoinette, go away."

His words were sharp, and she turned on her heel, fled back to the camp, and pulled the thin cover over herself, a small smile playing on her face. It was a heady experience to discover just how much he loved and respected her. She knew they had by passed the town of Arles and it would be just a couple of days before they were at his ranch. Briefly, she wondered what Red was doing and decided sleep was better than needless worry.

* * *

Consuela realized Antoinette was gone when she walked into the restaurant portion of the stage stop. No one paid any attention to the excited voice of a middle-aged Mexican senora until she started screaming. Finally the driver confirmed that the young woman was gone. There were no spare men to send out on a search party and a schedule had to be kept.

Her attempt to telegraph Mr. O'Neal involved the same mindless fight against the prejudices of the white men running the telegraph office in the next town. Consuela finally prevailed by paying double the price of the regular telegram and was left short of funds.

It took another two days for the telegram to be delivered to the plantation turned ranch. One of the maids timidly knocked on his door. Red's satisfied mood shifted to absolute fury. Rapidly he wrote a note to sheriff in Wooden about an abducted female. He hurried to find his Mother, soothe her, and then it was time to confront Margareatha.

"Where are they?"

"You are shouting, and which 'they' do you mean?" Rita's face was bland; her copper eyes with the gold circle around the pupils were cloaked.

Red put his hands on the desk. "Daniel and Antoinette. Where did they go:"

"Daniel's in Wooden and leaving in the morning. He hasn't been able to ride until now. As for Antoinette, I have no idea. Isn't she safely locked away in that horrid convent?"

Red stared at her. "Then who took her?"

"Took? Red, no one 'takes' Antoinette. She does have a mind of her own."

"I went into her mind when Consuela told me she was planning a wedding. I saw Daniel."

"I believe you are mistaken." She smiled. "You made an incorrect assumption and acted on it. Now you've alienated Daniel, Antoinette, and in all probability the entire MacDonald House." Deliberately she used Mac's Thalian word for family.

"I'm telling you, I saw…" He hesitated and continued. "If it was Lorenz, there was no scar."

"I'm sure she sees him as perfect. You did encourage them to correspond, remember?" She smiled in satisfaction, but a nagging doubt implanted itself. Daniel continued to insist that Antoinette loved him.

"You knew." His accusation was laced with disbelief.

"I guessed."

"He has abducted my sister, and I'll have the law on them."

"You'll make a fool of yourself, Red." Margareatha was shouting at his back. "She's nineteen and can prove it."

Red turned back to face her. "She took her baptismal certificate? Did you tell her?"

Margareatha smiled. "No, I merely mentioned that proving who you are is sometimes a necessity in a strange locale."

"Why? Why have you bothered to stay here?"

Her smile softened, but her eyes remained hard. "I stayed because I need a decent paying job, and you need me. You don't dare trust anyone else with these books and the Slavey grain accounts. You can't explain it rationally to anyone on Earth, and anyone dishonest enough to not want a reasonable explanation would try to rob you; however, I will not permit you to hurt someone in our family and then ship off a young girl to a nunnery like you are some medieval liege lord. This is 1869, not 1269."

He glared at her, his copper eyes with the golden circle around the pupils almost in flames. "Just how do you think a young girl is going to handle the fact that my father isn't hers? What if she finds out we're half-brother and half-sister?

Margareatha's smile grew colder. "She'll handle it just fine. It might even make the Senora human in her mind."

"Do you think I'll let Lorenz get away with this?" Rage laced his words.

"First you'd have to go through Mac. As it is, you already have a problem the next time you meet him. He has a very narrow view of anyone who attacks his House."

Red stared at her for a moment and left. Words were useless. Worse, she could be right. Lorenz, he knew, he could still take, but Mac? Not a chance. The Mac-Donald's might decide this was a bad match and prevent an actual marriage, but his own actions were effectively blocked. There would be no telegram to Wooden or Arles. He pulled out a cigarillo and inhaled. Now he would need to console the Senora and hope that her weeping, praying, and incense burning didn't last for months. He'd write a note to Margareatha in the morning for her to transfer to Nevada. Books could be done from there, and the Senora would have one less thing to rail against.

Chapter 3

The Welcome Home

Red's hope of MacDonald stopping the marriage matched Anna MacDonald's hopes. Almost one month ago, she had found the note Lorenz left on the table informing one and all that he had gone to claim his bride. In the note, he reminded them that he delayed the wedding only until Papa healed from the gunshot wound and operation. Every day she watched for him to reappear, praying that the young woman would refuse him on religious grounds. Miss O'Neal was Catholic and Catholics weren't permitted to wed Lutherans. Thank God Lorenz had been confirmed by Pastor Wentz two years ago. Surely they would come to their senses, and then Anna remembered what it was to be young and would fear for the worse. Whenever she kneaded the bread, it was with angry blows, and when she did the laundry, she pounded at the clothes in the tubs with a vigor unmatched by the younger Armeda Gonzales.

Anna was on the last tub of clothes when Mina appeared at the corner of the house, her darkening reddish-brown, sun-streaked curls as unruly as ever. "Mama, two people are coming. I think one is Lorenz."

Anna straightened and smoothed the escaping wisps of white curls back from her face with wetted hands. "You stay here with Armeda and watch Roman for her." She looked at the toddler playing on the blanket shaded by the eaves of the washhouse.

"Armeda," she called to the young woman hanging clothes, "these things need to be pounded until they are clean."

Rather than go through the gate, she cut through the house before going directly to the front porch. Two of them, Mina had said. Were they mad? Anna stopped in the kitchen and sipped at a cup of water from the bucket while looking out the window. She watched the riders draw nearer. She did not want them to see her outside waiting with hands on her hips and tapping a foot. Confrontation without warning would be more effective. She felt, however, she and Zeb would need to acquiesce to the wedding simply to keep a scandal from erupting. Zeb, Anna suspected, would offer complete support for a wedding, or a bedding. His attitude toward the necessity of the same religion did not match the fervor of hers or the beliefs of others; nor did his thoughts on the need for marriage match the beliefs of this world.

Anna moved away from the window and stood in the doorway between the kitchen and the main room until she heard them pull up and dismount. She strode out onto the porch without slamming the door behind her and looked into the faces of two handsome young adults coming up the steps and smiling at her.

"Mama, this is Miss Antoinette O'Neal, and she is going to be my wife. We need you and Papa to go with us to Arles and sign for me to get the marriage license." His grey eyes were alive with love and determination, his arm wrapped around the young woman's shoulder, completely protecting her from the world. The young woman was about five foot four inches tall, and dressed in a traveling outfit of light, cotton fawn. Her black curls were crowned by that old hat of Lorenz's and set at a rakish angle that somehow added a bit of exotica to her appearance.

Anna felt her hand go to her throat as she looked helplessly at the young people. If she screamed and yelled, she would lose her son for the second time, and she could not bear the thought. Lorenz was still speaking with that strange, adult authority his voice.

"Antoinette, this is my mother, Mrs. Anna MacDonald."

Antoinette gave a quick, precise curtsy and spoke with the proper courtesy as though there was nothing extraordinary in their arrival in dusty attire, or that her mother-in-law to be was almost as tall as Lorenz.

"Hello, Mrs. MacDonald. This is such a pleasure." Her southern accent made each word sound as though sweetness and music were part of her core, and Anna's stomach twisted. This child/woman was a formidable opponent. Anna knew she was left with but one objection to their marriage.

Anna swallowed and said in a measured tone. "Miss O'Neal, du must be exhausted." She turned to Lorenz, her fears propelling words from her mouth. "Du haven't ved yet? How long vere du…"

Lorenz stepped forward. "Mama, nothing happened. I promised you. Of course, we haven't married. It wouldn't be legal without a license. That's why we need to go to Arles, but right now Antoinette needs to get out of the sun and have a nice, cold drink of water."

Anna stepped back and opened the door, her mind working rapidly. "The O'Neal's vill have the authorities notified."

"Red won't. He doesn't want to put his sister or his mother through dealing with Southern customs and Union control. He has too many other things to worry about right now, and one of them is staying out of Papa's way. Even if he has contacted them, Antoinette is nineteen. She can legally wed."

Anna frowned, not sure what Lorenz meant about staying out of Papa's way, but she persisted. "The county officials vill ask for proof that she is old enough before issuing a license."

The young people preceded Anna into the room as Lorenz continued to speak. "Antoinette thought of that. She has her baptismal certificate with her."

"The Catholic priest vill not marry du and Pastor Heidenstram von't be here again until November."

Lorenz turned to her. "Mama, we'll have the Justice of Peace in Arles marry us."

Anna fought the impatience in her voice. "Then Miss O'Neal vill not be able to go to Mass." She saw Antoinette's eyes widen. Good, she thought.

"Ah didn't think of that." Antoinette turned to Lorenz.

"Would y'all mind being married by a priest?"

Lorenz's eyes narrowed. "I reckon it doesn't matter that much. I can still take communion when der Pastor comes through."

"Ja, das ist true," Anna conceded. "But do du vant to raise your kinder as Catholics?" She was still fighting to control her voice, her accent becoming heavier, the German words slipping into her English.

"I reckon we'll cross that bridge when it happens." He smiled at them. "I'll go get us some of that spring water. You all rest a minute and get acquainted."

"Der priest vill make du sign a paper dot du vill raise them Catholic," Anna snapped the words out. Her words stopped Lorenz at the door and he turned back, a quizzical look in his eyes.

"Is that true, Antoinette?"

"Why, yes, ah do believe they need to have assurance that the children would be raised Catholic if y'all do not convert. Does that matter?"

Lorenz was looking at Antoinette and then at his mother. "Y'all knew this. Why did y'all wait until now to say something?" His grey eyes were darkening and his voice was almost an accusation.

Anna did not allow herself to smile or look satisfied, but felt she was winning. She knew Lorenz, MacDonald, and LouElla had spent long hours in that spaceship and she wasn't sure how much of their science and their philosophy he had absorbed. She was certain, however, that the beliefs of Catholicism were not compatible with Llewellyn's or his mother LouElla's beliefs, and she steadied her voice.

"I did not believe du vould just go off like du did, and I could not believe that Miss O'Neal vould discard her beliefs. I thought du two vould discuss religion in your letters." Her words were not exactly a lie.

Antoinette stepped forward and laid a hand on Lorenz's arm and looked up at him. "Ah believe we can be married by the Justice of the Peace and then settle everything." Her laugh tinkled into the stilled room. "After all, my penance wouldn't be more than a few extra Hail Marys."

Lorenz bent and hugged her. "I'll get that water." He spun around to head towards the kitchen when Anna's next objection stopped him.

"Ve are Lutherans. They vill consider him a heretic." Anna was glaring at Antoinette. "The penance vill be far more than a few Hail Marys."

"Mama, Antoinette is correct. We will need to discuss this between ourselves." His eyes were like frozen water and his mouth was stiff. "Did y'all want us to leave?"

"Nein! This ist your home."

Antoinette smiled at her. "Why thank y'all, Mother MacDonald. May ah call y'all that?" She did not wait for an answer, but continued.

"Lorenz and ah love each other, and he is right. We'll need to discuss this by ourselves, but more important, we do need to get married. Ah'm sure y'all see the wisdom of that."

Anna could only stare at her. She knew that usually the woman ruled when it came to teaching religion and manners. MacDonald did not interfere with her raising Mina, nor did he object to Lorenz being confirmed. "I know vhat du are doing."

"Of course, y'all do. Y'all are a very beautiful, intelligent woman, and according to Lorenz, y'all are married to a very powerful, intelligent man."

Lorenz grinned at them both and grabbed the bucket in the kitchen. Anna heard Mina's delighted welcoming whoops and felt her world spinning. Antoinette broke the silence.

"Mother MacDonald, ah do not wish to be your enemy. Ah know Lorenz loves y'all dearly. Ah have a letter in my purse from Margareatha. Ah hope it will help explain the situation and why ah needed to run." She removed one of the pieces of paper from her lady's handbag and extended it.

Anna took the proffered letter, but before looking at it, she tried one more time. "Your mother must be opposed to your marrying Lorenz." She did not embellish her reasoning with information about Red's parentage.

"Why ah should imagine she's even more devastated than y'all." Antoinette removed her hat and smoothed at her hair while Anna read rapidly.

Finally Anna looked up, her eyes wide, her voice almost a whisper. "Ist Daniel really all right?"

"Why, yes, he is. Margareatha somehow managed to circumvent all the people guarding me when she brought me this letter for y'all. She assured me he'd be fine. Ah can't imagine why Red thought ah was going to marry Daniel. Ah never, ever, let anyone think that. Ah'd managed to get away once before with the letter for Lorenz when ah found out they were shipping me to that covenant for refusing to marry that disgusting old man. Can y'all believe that? Why the very idea is disgraceful."

Chapter 4

Wedding Plans

MacDonald tried to comfort Anna that night, but she would have none of it. "They are not thinking," she whispered in German. "Can't you convince him this is madness?"

MacDonald smiled into the darkness and leaned down towards her. "Anna, my love, they wish to wed and to bed. Ye can see it in their eyes. Tis yere culture that says they must wed ere the latter."

Anna put her lips together and turned over, offering a cold shoulder to MacDonald. He sighed and tried again.

"Anna, let me be yere counselor this eve. They are both set on this. The more we oppose a marriage, the more they twill insist. I dinna wish to lose our laddie. Let them wed and build their home here. They twill be close by. She has already surprised me with her stamina and insistence on staying out of the covenant. Most would assume she would willingly wed a rich, older man rather than risk what she did." MacDonald admired a lassie that could look at his three hundred pounds of muscle set on six feet nine inches and not blanch or be struck dumb.

Anna's thoughts were dark. It had been a point of contention between them. MacDonald had advocated taking Lorenz to a high-class brothel for his "first bedding." She had vehemently protested such sinful behavior, and MacDonald had relented. Why hadn't the woman wed the wealthy man of her own faith? Antoinette's twinkling laugh at the dinner table came back to haunt her.

"La, they had me all engaged to this sixty-year-old man. Why he didn't even have all of his own hair left on top and the most repulsive, stained mustache y'all would evah want to see." Anna wanted to believe it was the bald head and stained mustache that repulsed Antoinette, but somehow suspected it was more than that.

They all planned to leave for Arles within four days. Anna and Antoinette had taken a rushed trip into Schmidt's Corner to purchase enough chambray and linen to make the needed undergarments and dresses. Anna had also managed to cut down an old dress for Antoinette and Lorenz had hired Armeda to wash, iron, and perform other duties for his fiancée. Both young people were discussing plans as to where their first house would be located on the property and who should be hired to complete it.

Two nights before they left, they were all seated at the kitchen table relaxing after the chore of washing up the dishes when Antoinette smiled sweetly and asked, "Is there a suitable hotel in Arles to spend the night after being married?"

Lorenz looked puzzled, Anna's eyes widened, MacDonald sat his coffee cup down and looked at Anna before replying. "That twould depend upon what ye mean by suitable."

"I would like a certain amount of privacy and decent quarters with clean linens."

The amused look in MacDonald's brown eyes grew and the left corner of his mouth tugged. "I fear the hotel in Arles is like too many others in the small towns of this land. Ye twill nay find the lavish accommodations available such as in Hays City, Sedalia, Saint Louis, or San Antonio."

Antoinette set her cup down. "Then I believe that all we should do in Arles is get the license and wait for your Pastor, isn't that what y'all call him, to arrive in November. That's only about two months away. Y'all did say it took about ten days to go to Arles and back, didn't y'all? That means it would be just six weeks. We do need to find someone in Arles to design a house and order the materials. Heaven knows when they would deliver everything or how long the building takes."

"Why the wait?" demanded Lorenz, his face flushing and the grey eyes beginning to glint. Neither he nor Antoinette noticed the look of satisfaction on Anna's face.

Antoinette remained grave. "I do not wish to spend my wedding night in some non-descript hotel with dirty sheets and a bunch of carpet baggers listening; nor, do I wish to spend it out under the stars. The alternative is to wait and have the wedding here where we will be living until our house is built."

Lorenz looked at her and realized this soft, petite woman was as determined as his mother and a bile taste rose in his mouth. He'd waited for this a long year's time while Papa healed and now it would be wait again.

"Why don't y'all and Mama just pack the things we'll need? We'll get a room towards the back and Papa and Mama can get the room next to us. Hell, I'll even pay for a d…uh, sorry, Toni, Mama. I'll pay for a room in-between the two or rent the whole floor if it makes everybody feel better. Arles isn't going to be crowded this time of year."

Anna was speechless. MacDonald's tried unsuccessfully to keep the silent laughter from shaking his shoulders. The laddie twas ready for his first bedding and nay they could say twould stop it. It twould be best, he thought, to let Lorenz have his way. He looked at his wife.

"I believe Lorenz has offered a solution." Laughter edged his words. "Tis an expensive one, but one we can all live with. Now, ere we go to bed, here tis something to consider. It may be best to be wed by the Justice of Peace in Arles as I am nay certain the Pastor twill marry ye when he arrives."

"Why ever would he refuse?"

"Ye are Catholic and ye dinna have yere parents' approval."

"I am nineteen." Indignation rose in Antoinette's voice. "Wouldn't I just be required to sign a paper saying that I agree to raise them as Lutherans? It seems such a simple matter for two people in love."

MacDonald smiled inwardly as he noted how quickly Antoinette could switch from a thick drawling, helpless Southern lady's voice to a voice laced with decision. He looked at Anna standing by the door.

"Nein, I mean no. Der Pastor vould have to believe that du are converting by studying to show that du are sincere in vhat du say before he vould agree. There vould be no paper to sign."

"Well, how do y'all expect me to study if everything is in German? Ah can't think of a better way to discourage someone."

"We twill buy the King James Bible while we are in Arles. That tis a simple matter. Do ye nay agree, Anna?"

Anna's eyes had brightened and she bit her tongue to keep from saying Deutsch was the better translation and much clearer. "Ja, and I can help her. So can my brother Kasper until he goes back to Austin for the next session of the Texas legislature."

"He twas elected and needs to go. The Reconstruction Act requirements must be implemented ere Texas can rejoin the Union. I am nay certain all those nay-reconstructed rebels who are part the Texas legislature wish to do so."

Antoinette was wide-eyed. When did men let women hear their political views? This family was a family and they had accepted her as member. She stood.

"Ah do believe ah'll turn in now."

Anna remained at the doorway. Her mind was still on the last conversation.

"Du love him so much du vould give up your religion?" This time she bit her tongue to keep from saying false religion.

"We rarely went to mass at a church. Periodically, the priest would arrive at our house and father would always find something else to do. Even before father had the fit of apoplexy and couldn't move or talk anymore, Mother spent most of her time on her knees in front of the Virgin's Shrine praying for more children. Just how they were to have more children when they weren't even speaking to each other was never explained. My parents didn't have a marriage. You all do. I've seen that in the short time I've been here. I don't want to have a marriage and be alone."

She moved towards the door for the last trip to the outhouse and Anna stepped aside. "Du are very wise."

"Thank y'all, Mother MacDonald, but ah'm sure ah have much more to learn."

Chapter 5

Marriage

The hotel room was dark except for the half-hearted glow of a turned down lamp, and Antoinette was fussing about the bed, her hair, fiddling with her buttons, flitting towards the window, and then jerking away from it. Finally she spoke, her voice slightly exasperated. "Aren't y'all supposed to leave and let me undress?"

Lorenz smiled, his grey eyes sparkling. He was sitting on the edge of the bed, pulling off his boots. "I reckon that depends on the couple." His voice dropped to an almost gravely rasp as he stood.

"I'd rather stay and help y'all."

Antoinette's eyes opened wider as did her mouth. She couldn't say someone will hear us as Lorenz had rented the whole floor and the elder MacDonald's and Mina were at the other end.

Lorenz walked over to her and put his arms around her and pulled her close. "It's all right, honey. I'll help y'all." He could feel the heat rising and his right thigh tingling. It would, he hoped, be a very long night.

His father had been very explicit about techniques and pressure points. What most men assumed was straightforward was evidently an art to Thalians. In his rush, he forgot the first time, but by the second he blessed his father. Antoinette was moaning and straining against him.

As her last shudder subsided, Antoinette closed her eyes, her thoughts jumbled, and fear stalked her mind. What was Lorenz going to say? Would he leave her? Her body had betrayed her. She must have behaved exactly like one of those women people talked about. Surely Lorenz would think he had married a loose woman and never treat her like a queen again, and now she could feel something escaping from her inmost being. Oh fiddlesticks, it couldn't be. It wasn't time.

Lorenz was slumped over her whispering, "Antoinette, Toni, my sweetheart, my love," and she knew she had to move or the sheet and mattress would be forever ruined.

Antoinette took a deep breath and said stiffly, "Y'all will have to move now. I need to take care of something." Her heart was racing. What would he say?

"Huh, oh, yeah, sorry," he mumbled and rolled over to watch her. "I reckon you're right. We both need to clean up." He remembered Papa's admonition. He had brought in an extra basin when he rented the whole floor. He also made sure the ewer and basins were clean and the ewer full of clean water before retiring. "I forgot I must be pretty heavy. I didn't hurt y'all, did I?" His voice was full of anxiety and concern.

Antoinette stood and wrapped her robe around her and moved towards the washstand. She stared with surprise at the stain on the washcloth and the water turning a different shade in the half light. How did she tell Lorenz about this?

She heard his steps behind her and his arms slipped around her and held her tight. "What's wrong, honey? Y'all haven't said anything. Did I hurt y'all? I didn't mean to. I've just been waiting so long; ever since I saw you in Saint Louis three years ago when we were sixteen."

Antoinette closed her eyes. She had to say something, anything, but women didn't talk to men about these things, did they? Anna's words came back to her. "Men and vomen in a good marriage talk about everything. Sometimes it takes years, but in the end, they know there is no one else." Her throat felt constricted and she found herself whispering, "No, no, ah'm fine. Ah think ah just need some rest."

He picked her up and carried her to the bed. "That's all right, Toni. We've got the rest of our lives."

He crawled in beside her and drew her close, smelling the faint perfume of her sweat and it was good. There's the morning, he thought to himself.

Morning did not go as he planned. He awoke after the first light of dawn. Muted sunlight slipped through the windows lighting the dark corners, and he reached for her. At first she slipped willing into his arms, and then something changed.

"Ah think ah need to rest a bit more, if y'all don't mind." The whisper was almost choked, urgent, and he could feel her drawing away from him.

Lorenz was baffled, but did not argue. "All right, I'll go have breakfast and then come back." He didn't use the porcelain chamber pot, but went down the stairs and out the back. Lorenz felt Antoinette would shudder in disgust if she saw his leavings.

When he returned to the front of the hotel, he headed to the restaurant with the word EATS painted across the front. As he walked in, he saw his parents and Mina already seated at one of the tables eating. He drew up a chair and greeted them. "Good morning."

MacDonald raised his eyebrows and Anna's smile was still fixed. This wasn't like he planned, but he was young and he was hungry. He motioned to the waiter.

"I'll have an order of hash browns and gravy with a slab of ham, if y'all have it, and coffee."

The waiter nodded and dashed to the kitchen in a show of unnecessary importance. There weren't that many townsmen in the place and business was slow after the cattle drives. Most of the townspeople of Arles might hold the MacDonald family in contempt as damn Yankees, but he knew MacDonald always left a sizeable tip.

Mina stopped eating long enough to ask. "Where's Miss Antoinette?" She was thrilled at the idea of another sister. Maybe there would be babies before long. After all, Uncle Martin and Aunt Brigetta had one baby, and they'd only been married for two years. "Should I go up and help her?"

"Nein, Mina," admonished Anna.

"Uh, she's still sleeping." Lorenz figured it wasn't exactly a lie. He'd have to get Papa alone. If he used mindspeak here, Mama would know and raise a fuss. Right now it was another thing he didn't care to explain to Antoinette. What the hell went wrong?

The waiter hurried in with Lorenz's coffee. "I'll be right back with your vittles." He rushed back to the kitchen. Two of the drummers at the other table rose and left.

Lorenz sat glumly staring at the wall, and MacDonald looked at Anna and inclined his head toward Lorenz. She shrugged and continued eating. The waiter returned with his food in less than ten minutes and he fell to, scooping up the hot food and gulping the scalding coffee.

Finally Mama and Mina rose. "Should I check in on Miss," she hesitated, "on Antoinette?"

Light came back into Lorenz's eyes. "Would you, Mama?"

She nodded. "Vhen do ve leave?"

"We plan on going to the lumber yard and see about house plans," replied Lorenz. "If Clifford will do business with us, that is. We could be ready to leave before noon."

Anna nodded, and held firmly onto Mina's hand as she led the way upstairs.

'Tis something amiss?' Papa's mind entered his and Lorenz continued to eat as he answered with mindspeak.

'Yeah, and I don't know what it is. Everything was fine last night, and now this morning she, well, she's acting like everything is wrong.'

MacDonald finished his coffee and spoke aloud, "Mayhap we should check the horses ere we go back up. Twill give yere mither some time to freshen up."

Lorenz nodded and sopped up the last of the gravy. "Let's go."

Anna marched up the stairs and deposited Mina in their room. "Du are eight and du vill vait here vhile I go talk with Antoinette."

Mina could think of all sorts of reasons why she shouldn't, but knew Mama would be angry if she argued. She decided to be very quiet and maybe she would hear something.

Antoinette's voice quavered when she answered Anna's knock. "Who is it?"

"Antoinette, it is your mother-in-law. May I come in?" She heard the key turn the lock and the door swung open to reveal a very distressed Antoinette.

"Oh, Mother MacDonald, thank goodness. I don't know what to do and you are the only other gentlewoman around. Please, come in. Hurry, please, I want to shut this door."

Anna stepped into the room and heard the door click behind her. It was difficult to believe that Lorenz would have hurt this woman. She took a deep breath and turned to face her new daughter-in-law. She never got her question out.

"Oh, Mother MacDonald, what am I to do? I've started the curse. Is it a punishment? It shouldn't have. I counted. I don't even have anything with me and ah can't, can't do that with Lorenz now, can I? The sheet is ruined." Her words rushed out in a torrent.

Anna blinked her eyes and shook her head. "Ach, is that all? I have some scissors in my bag. Ve'll cut up the good part of the sheet and use some safety pins." She smiled at Antoinette. "It's not a punishment. It's a common thing to happen to a new bride. Du should be all finished by the time ve reach home. Vait here. I'll the scissors and pins go get."

Anna hurried to their room. Why, she wondered, was she helping this woman who stole her son? Other people, however, Anna had to admit, would say Lorenz had stolen Antoinette. She realized that Antoinette had closed the door to her previous life and now depended upon them. Anna could not forget how abandoned she felt when the Comanche had taken her away from all that she knew.

Anna entered the room to find Mina hastily backing away from the wall. "Ve are too far avay to have been heard," she said firmly and opened her bag to extract the scissors and safety pins.

"May I go see Miss Antoinette now?"

"Nein." Anna turned to leave, but saw the crestfallen look on her daughter's face. "Du are not old enough. This is about vomen things. Soon enough du vill be a voman. Then I vill tell du, I promise."

Back in the other room Anna handed the scissors and pins to Antoinette and began to reassure her. "Ve'll leave for the ranch by this afternoon. It vill take almost five days to get there. Du vill be done, or almost so. Things vill be fine between du and Lorenz. Du vill have to tell him though, or he von't know."

Antoinette didn't stop plying the scissors as she asked, "How can I do that? My goodness, I couldn't even talk to my own mother. It was Consuela who showed me how to do things when, ah, well y'all know what ah mean." Antoinette's cheeks had turned a light pink. She finished the last snip and looked up.

"This sheet is ruined. Ah am so sorry."

Anna shook her head. "Du vill learn to talk with each other. As for the sheet, ve vill buy material for more. I go now, and if du like, Mina and I vill join du at your breakfast."

"Yes, thank y'all. It'll just take me a minute.

"Mother MacDonald, can't y'all tell Lorenz? It would be ever so much easier."

"How could I ever talk about that to mein sohn? I vould Mr. MacDonald have to tell." Anna was horrified.

"Oh, no, please don't tell Father MacDonald." Antoinette swallowed. "I'll find someway." She began to dress rapidly hoping to hide her now flaming face.

They were at breakfast when MacDonald and Lorenz returned. Antoinette looked up and saw Lorenz looking at her. His grey eyes were puzzled and filled with misery. He carried himself so straight and so tense. Antoinette smiled at him, her eyes trying to convey how much she loved him.

Suddenly the smile was back on his face and he was beside her, reclaiming his territory and seated in the empty chair. Antoinette could not believe how rapidly he could change when he smiled. His face was transformed as a light seemed to come over him, making people wanting to draw closer, forgetting that he was known as a dangerous man.

"Do y'all want to do some shopping before we leave? We just met Clifford from the lumberyard and he refuses to do business with Yankees. We'll have to send a telegram to Fredrick Reichmann in Houston. He's the Master Journeyman who built our church in Schmidt's Corner. He'll be able to draw blueprints from the drawings we send him, and buy the lumber we need there. He'll bring everything with him and any carpenters he might need when he's ready to build."

"Well, for heaven's sake, such nonsense. Money is money. Couldn't I as a Southern lady appeal to Mr. Clifford? I could cry real tears for y'all"

"No! The man can rot."

Antoinette set her cup down. That she was not pleased with the outcome showed on her face. "How long will it be until we have our own home?"

Lorenz thought about what he could do with his mind controlling Clifford, but the look on his parents face forestalled that notion. "Well, I reckon it would be like four to six months. I don't know. I'm a rancher." He was becoming as exasperated as his wife.

Antoinette noticed the waiter and two men dressed in suits and ties were looking at them. She reached over and patted Lorenz's hand. "Well, in that case, ah think ah'm going to need some really nice material for a new dress, don't y'all?"

Chapter 6

Anna's Last Stand

Anna's sour mood worsened as the morning progressed. All her instincts, kenning ways as Mr. MacDonald called her premonitions, kept screaming that Antoinette and the babies should have stayed home. Toni, as they called Antoinette, had ignored her three months' pregnancy and brought their two boys and Mina with her in the buckboard to the Rolfe ranch. They were there to help Anna and Brigetta with the wash and to visit. Mina was put to work watching Lorenz's sons and Martin's two boys.

"It does become so boring with no one to talk with, Mother MacDonald." Antoinette did not count Armeda as someone to talk "with." Armeda was hired help. "The men should be back this afternoon."

Zeb and Lorenz were with Herman and Martin Rolfe and the hands branding cattle. Anna had arrived one week ago to keep an eye on a very pregnant Brigetta as the birth should be soon. She was directing the washing of the Rolfe's laundry. She had already shooed eleven-year-old Mina and the boys up to the porch. "It's too varm for out in the sun to be. Keep Brigetta company."

Mina was spending her time chasing three of the boys back up on the porch to play with the blocks Uncle Kasper had made. Randall, Lorenz's two-year-old, contentedly stacked the blocks and then would start all over when Kendall or one of the Rolfe boys would knock them down.

Anna tried not to think of how much Randall looked like her first husband: the copper eyes with the golden circle around the pupils, the red, coppery hair, and the two hearts hidden inside his slim body. She always felt uneasy when she looked at him. He was far too solemn for a two-year-old and he spoke

English and German as well as a four or six-year-old. Lorenz had at least been boisterous, a trait she was sure the Justine children did not possess.

Anna's stomach contracted and she felt the urgings that occurred when her premonitions began to come true. She stopped pounding the last of the clothes and looked around. The road that ran more-or-less north to Schmidt's Corner and then on to the German farm communities farther north was empty; its rutted lanes waiting to jolt the bones and rattle the teeth of any passerby riding in a wagon. The small river by the side of the ranch house ran low and languid, severely low for the middle of September. It was still summer hot and no rain, just passing clouds that whispered of moisture and then fled.

She wiped the perspiration from her forehead and temples, glancing to the east at the gentle hillocks beyond the river rising to meet the foothills. Leaves on the oak trees were drooping, wilting, waiting like the brown prairie grass for rain, their whispering leaves sounding like a soulful prayer. Anna looked towards the house where Mina played with the boys and Brigetta sat in the rocker listless and drooping like the leaves. Brigetta was swollen of face and body and in complete misery. Why hadn't Martin taken her and the boys into Schmidt's Corner or brought her to our ranch? Anna looked at the barn and corrals laying to her left beyond where Toni was hanging clothes. It was then she noticed the horses had their heads up, one sniffing the air.

She dropped the wooden pole with the metal flange and cone inside that they used for pounding the clothes and screamed for Toni and anyone outside to go into the house, meanwhile screaming within her mind at Lorenz. He had to hear her.

Toni was hanging the colored clothes on the line and stopped long enough to look at her mother-in-law as though she had become a woman possessed.

"Didn't du hear me? For the love of Gott, get into the house!" Anna ran for the porch and disappeared through the door. She reemerged carrying her shotgun, and then shooed Brigetta and the children into the house.

Puzzled, Toni left the clothes and went towards Anna. Perhaps Mother Mac-Donald was in that "phase" of her life, she reasoned to herself. After all, she must be nearing fifty. Toni had heard the whispers of some women going mad. If so, she was certain she could soothe the woman. She moved rapidly to placate Anna, her pregnancy not yet a hindrance. Toni hugged the thought that, maybe, just maybe, this time she would have a daughter.

The sounds of hoofs interrupted her thoughts. Were the men returning early?

"Run," came Anna's sharp command.

Toni looked briefly over her shoulder and ran. Indians, she thought, dear God, where did they come from?

She pounded past her mother-in-law who looked as though she were going to stand outside and fight them. Folly! Toni had seen the flash of an arrow. Some of them probably had guns, but they were notoriously bad shots. Inside the doorway, she turned. "Mother MacDonald, come inside. Hurry!"

Anna let loose with a blast from her shotgun and ran under the porch roof and into the house. Toni slammed the door. Both of them lifted the bar and lowered it into the metal prongs set into the wood on either side, and then Anna began to issue orders.

"Mina, take all the children into one of the bedrooms. Now!" She didn't wait to see if Mina obeyed. "Brigetta, do du know vhere there is any ammunition in this house?"

Brigetta stared at them, her eyelids almost devoid of lashes blinking over her pale blue eyes, her breath coming in short pants, and her right hand supporting her protruding belly. "I think my water broke," she said in German while water ran down around her feet.

"Down," screamed Toni. "Get into the bedrooms. An arrow flew through the window and thudded into the opposite wall.

Anna thanked God the Rolfe house was dug into the river bluffs. The only wooden room was the long one used for the kitchen, eating, and sitting areas. The furnishings were minimal: a black stove, a table and chairs for eating, a daybed, and a desk. The only windows were on either side of the door and they were small. The porch roof sloped upward over the porch and the long room. The roof was secured into the bluff with beams driven into the soil and calked every year with mud, stones, and willow boughs.

Toni was busy pushing the desk against the door while Anna dumped the table over on the floor. Then she pulled it closer to the arch doorways dug into the bluff. "Check the drawers for ammunition," she ordered Toni.

Outside they could hear the horses whinny and heard the banging of tubs being overturned and men laughing and whooping. They're probably amused by the white men's clothing thought Anna. Toni scooted behind the table with a box of bullets, and Brigetta let out a scream. This set the children to screaming and more whoops could be heard outside as someone jumped onto the porch and started for the window. Toni pulled the rifle trigger and they heard a grunt before the man disappeared from view, his blood splattering against the window sill.

Brigetta and the children were still screaming and Anna longed to slap them into silence. They heard the men outside bang at the door, then hatchets crashing into the heavy oak timbers, but the door held firm, and the Indians stayed far away from the windows set on either side. For a moment there was silence. Then a flurry of arrows sailed through the windows, most of them went downward into the floor while others struck the tipped over table top.

"Antoinette, scream in your mind for Lorenz," Anna said through set teeth.

"Why, whatever for?" Toni had heard of Anna's kenning ways, but never that Lorenz possessed any.

"Sometimes when two people love each other and something is not right, they sense it." Anna closed her eyes. Lorenz had not told her! Something was wrong, her stomach was still making her dizzy and she fought back the nausea. "Mina, stop screaming. Keep them quiet. Hide them!" She was shouting at her daughter.

"Mina, honey, toss me my purse," Toni called.

"Vhy?"

"There is a revolver in it. I'm a good shot with that and it is not as heavy as this for close quarters."

"Mina, take that revolver and if the Indians make it to the bedroom door, shoot for the middle of the door. Du can do it!"

"Mother MacDonald, that would mean they'd kill them all."

"That vould be better than them taking them." Anna's voice was grim.

Both were taking cautious peeks around the edge of the table while they talked. Toni noticed the arm sliding through the window on the left side of the door. She lifted, then shifted her rifle into a better position. Anna realized the same was happening at the window on the right side and gripped her shotgun with both hands. Dear Gott, she prayed silently, let me kill them.

As though synchronized, two Comanche started to slide through the windows. Had either woman bothered to look, they would have seen these were young men still in their teens. Neither woman looked at the Indians as men but as demons, and both shot as the torsos appeared. Antoinette's bullet crashed into one's head, smashing it and blowing out the back. The youth's body fell, draped half inside, half out, his blood staining the floor. The other man yanked back and slid to the porch. Anna had not missed, but the shotgun's pellets had not killed him. The pellets had his left blood splattered over the sill. What they didn't know was the shot had blinded the man.

Anna sank back to the floor; dizziness, then gray started to blank her eyes. For some reason her head was incredibly light and she had sense enough to put her head down.

"Mother MacDonald, are y'all all right?"

Anna slowly straightened. "Ja, I just felt so strange." She set her lips and reloaded the shotgun. The aching in her left arm started to descend and the nausea threatened to release itself. She fought to keep from vomiting or be-fouling her linen, petticoat, and hose.

From above they could hear someone starting to chop away at the shingles. Someone must have pulled the stove pipe out as the cast iron stove burped smoke and ashes, and Brigetta broke their concentration on the ceiling by screaming again. Toni blinked and swung the rifle back to the windows and fired.

"Mother MacDonald, shoot! Ah have to reload." She did not look at Anna, but opened the breach and methodically put in the cartridges and snapped it together. She fired one shot upward where she could hear some sort of noise and then fired around the table edge, hoping it went up towards the window. She had not heard Anna's shotgun and now she turned to look at the older women.

"Oh, dear God, no," she half-whispered.

Anna was sprawled backward on the floor, her grey eyes wide-open and her tongue out. The shotgun rested on her long legs, pointed at the table. Above the sounds of chopping had stopped, but now a crackling was heard and smoke began to seep downward.

Toni closed her eyes momentarily praying. Her survival depended on a run into the dug out bedroom where the children and Brigetta were screaming. She took Anna's shot gun and aimed it at the two windows before firing. She knew that running upright in her long skirts was her only chance. Then she stood and fired the rifle, turned, and ran.

Chapter 7

Rescue

"Stay away from the doorway!" Toni screamed and then grabbed Mina before she could run to her mother. "Blow out that lamp. We'll need the air."

Brigetta stopped screaming long enough to whisper. "Ve'll all die. Gott uns mitt us."

"Mama, Mama!" Mina was screaming and stamping her feet, trying to pull away from Antoinette.

Toni couldn't tell whether she was hearing Mina's screams, her own children's or the Rolfe children's. Tears were streaking down Mina's cheeks.

"You left Mama!"

Toni pulled Mina away from the doorway, making soothing noises. Kendall was pulling at her skirts crying, "Mama, Mama."

It was then she realized gunshots were still being fired. "Do you hear that?" she screamed. "The men are here!"

Quiet seemed to fill the room while more shots echoed and horses screamed. The silence was broken by Lorenz pounding on the door.

"Antoinette, lift that bar. You all have to get out of there!"

"I can't do it by myself. Mother MacDonald is gone." Toni yelled back. She realized Mina had rushed to her mother. Toni scooped up Kendall and grabbed Randall's hand. "Children, follow me. They'll carry your mama out of here."

She swept out of the room and did not see the oldest Rolfe boy, Marty, grab his mother's hand with a determined look in his blue eyes. "Kumen, Mama, kumen."

Lorenz climbed through the window, looked at her to satisfy himself that she and the children were all right, ran to the door, dragged the desk to the side, and flung the bar out of the way, and stepped back as the door crashed inward.

MacDonald rushed in and looked at Lorenz and Toni. "Where tis she?"

"Papa! Mama won't talk to me!" Mina was sobbing and screaming at the same time.

Lorenz stopped long enough to pick up Randall and two-year-old August, the youngest Rolfe boy. Then he and Antoinette carrying the children ran out the open door. They didn't see the huge form drop to his knees and pull his dead wife up into his arms rocking back and forth while Mina threw her arms around her father's neck and continued to cry and scream. From the bedroom came the sound of Brigetta screaming again. Fire ate away at the roof line.

"She's having her baby. Y'all will have to carry her out," Toni managed to yell at Martin as he ran pass them through the door.

Lorenz kept Augie from rushing after his father. Once they were outside he heard his father's mindspeak in his.

'I am taking her to the *Golden One*. Mayhap there tis a procedure there.'

'Papa, she's dead,' his silent mind-cry went out. 'She died before we rode up'

He went back to the door. MacDonald was moving toward them, his Anna cradled in his arms and Mina hanging onto his neck. Lorenz doubted if his father even realized she was there.

Martin appeared in the bedroom doorway carrying Brigetta. Young Martin was behind them, then scooted ahead to run out the door. They left the porch, hurrying away from the smoke and the embers that were starting to fall.

"We need the mattress for Brigetta." Antoinette was issuing orders. "We'll put it under the shade of the willows or the wagon by the river if we have to." A quick glance had told her the Indians had fired the barn and wagons.

Some of the hands must have pushed one wagon into the river and then pulled it back. Like the others she ignored the dead Comanche warriors lying on the porch and the ground.

"We'll also need sheets and blankets. I can use the tub from the wash if someone will fill it with water. It should be warm, but right now we need to be ready."

Martin looked at them both, panic edging his voice. "I'll go get Olga."

"Martin, your wife is having a baby. Y'all are staying right here. Your father or one of the hands can go get Olga." Lorenz looked at his friend in disgust. "Y'all are just going to have to hold her hand or look after your boys."

31

He looked at the senior Rolfe dismounting, rifle in hand. "Uncle, would y'all or some of the men get the mattress and sheets out of there? Brigetta's going to need them. We can't take her anywhere until she's finished."

Rolfe looked away from MacDonald and nodded. His blue eyes were hard and his face set. He spat and farther befouled his white mustache. It was hard to tell what the natural color had been. The old mountain man was still dressed in his buckskins and moccasins and he ran into the house.

Lorenz bent over Antoinette and asked, "Can y'all handle things here, honey? I've got to talk with Papa."

Toni nodded and watched him hurry over to MacDonald who was trying to mount his huge horse while cradling Anna and ignoring Mina clinging to his neck and dangling down his side.

Lorenz used mindspeak and made it sharp. 'Papa, Mina is alive and needs you.'

Aloud he said, "Papa, let me hold Mama. You and Mina can mount and I'll hand her to y'all." The water in his eyes and the huskiness of his voice surprised him.

MacDonald's dark eyes were guarded as though he refused to acknowledge those around him. Grudgingly, he handed his burden to Lorenz. "My wee one," he whispered, "climb onto my back as ye did when ye were truly wee, and we twill take yere mither home. Hang on tightly."

Mina continued to sob into his neck but gradually changed her position. Lorenz waited until both were seated and lifted his mother towards MacDonald.

"Papa, I have to stay with Toni and the children. Martin can't be trusted to deliver that baby alone with all those other babies running around. It may be late when we get back. Will you all be all right?" He laid his hand over MacDonald's knowing how much a Thalian needed the touch of another being.

MacDonald's mouth was set, the eyes like obsidian, and he nodded his head. In truth, he did not trust himself to utter another word. He clucked his tongue while snapping the reins and the big stallion trotted off.

Lorenz hurried back to Antoinette and the children. The group had utilized the wagon that had been shoved into the river, dunked, and hauled back up. The one side was charred, but the wagon was intact. Someone had placed the mattress, still with its bed coverings in the partial shade of the wagon and Brigetta was lying on it. Toni was directing that a saddle be placed at her back while she added saddle blankets and a pillow to brace Brigetta. The elder Rolfe was standing to the side folding the grizzly pelt he'd rescued from the small den that served as his bedroom when and if he slept there.

Martin looked up as Lorenz approached. "Everything's gone." His blue eyes were bewildered as though the enormity of the day's events were beyond his comprehension. "We'll have to start all over."

Toni looked at him in surprise. "Martin Luther Rolfe, you have thousands and thousands of dollars in the bank. You can just take some of that money and build your wife a decent home with two stories for all of the bedrooms that you all are going to need if you keep having children every year! Do you hear me? Brigetta deserves a home with a real kitchen and dining room. She needs a place for company, and you need an office." She turned her back on the two men and knelt beside a sobbing and moaning Brigetta.

Lorenz was smiling. "Martin, I wouldn't argue with her right now. Did y'all send someone for Olga?"

Brigetta screamed.

"Lorenz, Martin, hold up something to shield her. The baby's coming! And somebody watch those other babies." Toni knew she was yelling to hide her own fright. What did she know about delivering babies? Mother MacDonald, Tante Gerde, or Olga had always served as the midwife.

Chapter 8

Father and Son

Wisps of daylight lighted the way when Lorenz made his way to the main house and hung his hat on the peg by the kitchen door. His mother never allowed men to wear hats in her house.

He had left Antoinette and the children at their house. Toni insisted the children be bathed before dressing for bed. Before heading to the main house, Lorenz gave instructions to Ramon to have a couple of the younger hands bring in water for her. Ramon was then to take the bundle of baby linens to Brigetta. The Rolfe's had chosen to take Brigetta and children into Schmidt's Corner to stay with Olga and her family. They would be crowded, but it was family.

Lorenz walked through the narrow kitchen, smelling the smells of his mother and the food she had cooked; vinegar, vanilla, roast beef, yeast breads all vied with each other to bring back memories and constrict his heart. He found his father sitting at the table, sipping a brew as the big man called his beer, while cradling a sleeping Mina.

MacDonald looked up as Lorenz approached. Lorenz lowered his head on one massive shoulder, then the next, as he made the tsking sound in MacDonald's ear that was the standard Thalian greeting. On Earth, it was a greeting done in the privacy of home. The sorrow deep within the big man hit his mind and spread through his body like herd of stampeding cattle running over him. It was sorrow that engulfed and almost took him to his knees. With an effort he was able to straighten and begin speaking.

"Papa, my heart sorrows with yours."

"Aye, my laddie."

MacDonald's free hand almost crushed his. Damn, he thought, but held his tongue. He knew telling him that she was with the Lord would not make Mac-Donald feel any easier. Right now it wasn't helping him that much except to make him feel guilty for the hurt inside. He put up his mind walls and spoke aloud.

"Papa, y'all want me to put Mina to bed?"

"Nay, I canna sleep. I dinna wish her to wake and start to scream. I had to have Armeda watch her whilst I cleansed and dressed my Anna for the funeral tomorrow. Tom Jackson tis making the coffin for her."

"How tis Brigetta?"

"She's fine Papa. It was a little girl this time, no bigger than a mite. They've named her Christina Anna."

MacDonald's big chest heaved and Lorenz saw moisture forming in the brown eyes. Lorenz decided to keep talking.

"Martin was acting like he was going to live in a cave when Toni lit into him about the thousands of dollars he has in the bank and how he should build a decent home for his family. When Brigetta started screaming and giving birth, Martin gave in."

Both men smiled at the thought of tight-fisted Martin letting loose of his money.

MacDonald took a deep breath. "We twill give them a suitable housewarming gift. Ye can attend to it. After the funeral, I twill take Mina with me to Arles. There I twill order a marble headstone for the two of us with her dates on them."

"And just what are y'all going to put down for your birth date? The year, whatever it was in Thalian reckoning isn't going to look right on Mama's tombstone." Lorenz deliberately kept his voice low.

"I had nay thought of that. I shall give them a false one based on Earth years. Something a few years younger than hers should be fine. After I make those arrangements, Mina and I twill visit mither in Galveston. She can verify the space navigational math I've done and start me on the next segment. Then we twill travel to Europe. I'll arrange for a tutor and governess for Mina to travel with us while I'll study, and mayhap, attend to other things in the evenings. Occasionally, we twill return here so that I can study at the controls of the *Golden One*. Mither twill do likewise. We may even consider moving it as it must be flown in the sunlight within the next thirty years. Ye and Antoinette may have this home. I canna live here again. The hurt tis too deep."

Lorenz stared at his father for a moment. "Papa, are y'all sure? Y'all might change your mind in a couple of years. This is all Mina's ever known. She may wish to come back."

"Aye, for myself I am sure. If Mina does return when she tis of age, are ye going to turn her away?"

"Good Lord, no."

"There tis one more thing. Ye have nay told Antoinette about yere abilities or yere biological fither, have ye?"

"I've told her that y'all adopted me, but she knows that; has since we started writing."

MacDonald looked down at the sleeping Mina and then at Lorenz. "Ye ken what I mean. She tis nay stupid. She has been bedding with ye for nigh four years. She can hear, and I'm sure she kens that Randall also has two hearts. Ye canna put it off any longer."

"I know, but I'll wait until she has this baby…"

"Ye Gods, ye mean she tis expecting a wee one again!" MacDonald's huge voice rumbled out and Mina stirred in his arms.

He bent his head and whispered, "Shh, my wee one. Yere fither tis here." He rocked back and forth and watched her quiet.

"Lorenz," he whispered, "ye canna keep having wee ones every year. Ye twill kill her. Ye must do what I did for my Anna. Visit the Golden One with her and go to the Medical Unit. Weigh her or yereself and enter the information that twill prepare the dosage to stop her eggs or yere sperm from developing. Promise me ye twill attend to this."

"I will, Papa, but right now she's upset enough over the Indian attack and Mama's dying. We all are. What happened? I didn't see an arrow."

"Twas nay a mortal wound, but like her twin, Kasper, her heart just gave out. Mayhap it twas the thought of her or her family being captives again. I dinna." The pain was back in his face and in his voice. He looked up at Lorenz.

"Laddie, ye must be honest with yere true love. If she truly loves ye, she twill nay run."

Lorenz nodded and swallowed. He could not admit the emptiness he faced if Toni left him. He bent and laid his head on MacDonald's shoulders again. "Goodnight, Papa."

Chapter 9

Truth and Concepts

Toni burped three-week-old Melissa Angelique and cradled her in her arms. She knew she should put the baby in the cradle, but it was cozy sitting here in bed with covers drawn around them and the heat coming from the stove. Unlike Martin, Lorenz had not quibbled about money when she began adding to and rearranging the original MacDonald homestead.

"I do want a real dining room, a sewing room, a music room, and a spiral staircase, and, honey, y'all know y'all need your own office where y'all can close the door on the noise of the household." She had rehearsed and rehearsed her speech for the enlarged home. It was all unnecessary preparation. Lorenz readily agreed. The building was rapidly nearing completion, and she could order the furnishings for when they moved. She had two complaints. The staircase was not a spiral one, but it had a certain sweep to it with an upper level landing before it turned to the upstairs bedrooms. The music room did not exist. Tonight, however, he might become angry with her request.

Lorenz had promised to return by dark. The early dark of a January night had fallen, and it was cold. Where was he?"

She felt the baby wiggle and looked down. She realized she had gone into the automatic rocking motion of a mother holding her baby and her soft smile faded as she heard a closing door and Lorenz's footsteps.

Lorenz walked into the room and smiled broadly at his dark-haired wife dressed in a white, frilly nightgown of some kind, surrounded by mounds of white lace coverlets, holding a dark, curly haired baby dressed in white, and wrapped in a white, lace shawl. How, he wondered, had the good Lord brought him from a half-starved, half-clothed kid in so few years?

"Sweetheart, y'all look like a perfect painting." He moved over to the bed and bent to kiss her.

"She's beautiful, just like her mother. Y'all want me to put her in the cradle?"

Antoinette's face became grave. Suddenly she needed the baby as security for what she had to say. "No, not just now, but we have to talk."

Lorenz saw the serious look on her face and straightened. "Why, sure, but wouldn't y'all feel better if the baby were in the cradle?"

"Lorenz, it is this baby we're talking about; this baby, Randall, Kendall, and y'all. Did y'all know she and Randall have two hearts just like y'all? Why? How does that happen? Is Kendall the only normal baby we have?" Her mouth was set and puzzlement was in her violet eyes.

Lorenz wet his lips. "Well, it's probably because my biological father has two hearts."

"I thought y'all didn't know him."

"I've not spoken to the man since he arranged that Comanche attack on us when I was four. He came back twice to finish the job, but Papa stopped him the first time, and Grandmère helped me the second time. It was Mama and Papa who told me Toma had two hearts."

"I still don't understand. Does it affect one's health? What about our babies? Why didn't y'all tell me sooner?" Toni was still rocking back and forth with Melissa in her arms.

"Well, I did, sort of." He was growing more and more uneasy, knowing he was in the wrong and still wracked with the fear of losing his wife.

Her eyebrows went up. "Sort of? How on earth does one 'sort of' tell another?"

"It was when I told Mina's Story at Christmas time. Randall's old enough to hear it for the first time and become familiar with the concept of two hearts and being different. Fairytales have long been used to tell an essential truth. There really wasn't a Prince or Princess, and the Princess wasn't named Anna. Mina was just allowed to name her."

"Mina's Story contains something that's true? Which part and what essential truth?" She looked at him in exasperation. "Lorenz, that tale had people with two hearts living for "long year spans" and flying around the stars, other people with magnificent builds, and people with scales..." her voice died away and she took a deep breath.

"Why was that part in there about the people with two hearts having copper-colored eyes and red hair?" She was looking directly at him and her teeth were almost clenched.

"It had to be there so that any of our children or Papa's children will not panic when a child is born with copper-colored eyes and two hearts, or just the two hearts like Papa and I have."

"Father MacDonald has two hearts too? Isn't he supposed to be the one with the magnificent build and be a Prince?"

"Well, he has the magnificent build of a Thalian, but he also has two hearts like his Justine father; and, he isn't a Prince. He's the Maca of Don. It seems Grandmère's titles were Lass of Don and Captain of Flight"

"Lorenz, y'all better start at the beginning and explain everything. Then I'll see if I can believe anything y'all are saying which right now doesn't make any sense at all, and I still don't know if there's anything wrong with my babies."

"Fair enough, I'll tell you what I've been told and seen. And, honey, there's nothing wrong with any of our babies." He held up his hands as though to stem any more questions as he saw her brow start to wrinkle.

"It seems my biological father left his home planet to explore for research purposes and somehow became stranded here. In the meantime, war broke out in the star system inhabited by the people, beings as Papa calls them, in the tale. The Thalians were thoroughly beaten. Grandmère was taken prisoner and sent into exile. Her guards were one elderly Justine and several Kreppies, that's the ones with scales. She used her feminine wiles to seduce the Justine (Toni's eyes widened at the thought of the muscular woman she had christened Grandmère having any feminine wiles). When they finished, ah, being together, he relaxed against her, and she snapped his neck."

He paused at Antoinette's gasp.

"She then killed the rest of her guards, flew the Kreppie starship into the bay of the *Golden One* (it's what the Justines call all of their starships), and took off. Grandmère spent several months becoming familiar with the new starship and plotting revenge against the Justines. To her surprise, she realized she was pregnant. Somehow she had Papa alone, managed to get near enough to Thalia to leave Papa with a friend and instructions for his care before taking off into space. When she next appeared, she aimed the *Golden One* into the Justine planet and used the Kreppie ship to fly out of the *Golden One* just before impact. She killed over a million Justines that day, but didn't know how many still lived or how many ships the Kreppies possessed. She started hunting for a livable planet in another star system. She spotted this Earth before the Kreppie ship gave out. That ship had been slightly damaged when the planet exploded, and was almost out of fuel. She buried it in the Adirondack Mountains of New York where she landed. That's why Papa, Mama, Mina, and Grandmère took that trip to New York last year. Papa made sure that the land is now in our possession.

"Anyway, on Thalia, Papa's Uncle pretended Papa was from one of the important people of Don and wished to raise him. His wife approved the subterfuge. When Papa turned twenty, he wanted his first bedding. They think it's like a religious rite and arranged by the main Houses or political groups."

Toni's mouth dropped.

"Since this would have resulted in someone hearing two hearts thumping away, his uncle tried to dissuade him. By this time conditions were harsh on Thalia as there were enough Justines left to impose their idea of a new rule, but not enough left for enforcement. They used the Kreppies to guard the Thalians and turned the government over to a newly created House called the Sisterhood. Papa challenged a young woman from the ruling House to a fight in the Arena for a bedding. It's another of their customs. After a Guardians Council meeting, people from the Houses can challenge for a fight. The winner can claim a 'bedding.' Uh, that means going to bed like you're married only you're not. To the horror of everyone, he won."

"I hardly find that surprising," came Antoinette's icy voice. Inside she shrank at the idea of such a custom.

Lorenz's smile was more of grimace. "I know, but men weren't supposed to win under the rules of the Justines and the Sisterhood. They had Papa medically examined to see if he had taken any drugs. Of course, they found the two hearts and notified the Kreppies and the Justines. Papa was taken to where the Justines lived and put under isolation. He was allowed to study and exercise, but he nearly went insane. Thalians need contact with other beings."

"Since the Justines were down to about two dozen people..."

"How in the world did they control others if there were so few?"

"I'm not sure of all the details, but their technology enabled them to destroy all of the Kreppie warships. They are able to control the Kreppies with their minds."

"What?"

"Yeah, well that's the Justine's ability that other beings don't possess. Let me finish, please." Lorenz was desperate to avoid the whole truth as long as possible as he wasn't certain how well any of this was soothing Antoinette.

Antoinette looked up at him and then down at the curly haired, sleeping baby. For some reason she noted the perfectly formed little hands and pink nails. It took her a moment to raise her head and nod her assent.

"The Justines decided to risk one Justine to search for Toma, my biological father. His presence would increase their ability to procreate. They knew the area he intended to search. The crew consisted of six Kreppies. They sent Papa because they meant for him to be left on a suitable planet. To the Justines he is a mutant: beings that aren't biologically able to exist. Their teaching is that beings from different planets cannot procreate. If for some reason they do, we are presumed to be like mules and incapable of reproducing. That obviously is not true." He nodded at the child in her arms.

"They found this planet, and what Papa called traces of a previous visitation, and investigated. The Justine selected an area with a red haired populace and used a smaller craft to land. He left two Kreppies in charge of the landing craft and took Papa with him as a servant. It never occurred to him they might be attacked. When they were, he stood there trying to control a mob with his mind. It was a harsh lesson. The Justines can't enter everyone's mind on this planet. Papa had the sense to run. The Justine was killed." By this time there were lines in Antoinette's brow and her eyes were opened far wider than normal. Lorenz continued with his recital.

"Papa went back to the landing craft. He'd been here long enough to decide Earth was a far better place to be than isolated on the Justine refuge. He killed the two Kreppies, returned to the *Golden One*, and killed the remaining Kreppies. Then he searched for a quiet, unpopulated place to hide the *Golden One*. It's buried up in the hills to the east. I'm not going to relate how he and Uncle Herman fell into each other's company, but Papa went with him to hunt furs. Over the years they became friends and business partners. It's why their ranch is next to ours.

"I've been meaning to tell you this since Mama passed away. Papa insists we need to decide which one of us will suppress the ability to have children until we decide to have more. We both should go to the *Golden One* and prepare the necessary medication. While we're there, it will give you a chance to see that everything I've told you is the truth."

Antoinette's eyes were still wide and her mouth partially open. She closed her eyes and shook her head.

"Y'all still haven't explained completely about the red hair and strange eyes. My brother Red fits that description. So does your sister Margareatha and our son Randall. Are y'all saying we're related, and they can go into people's minds?"

Lorenz took a deep breath. "Yes, they can go into people's minds. So can I, and Melissa and Randall will probably be able to do so. That's why y'all are so important. Y'all have to help me teach them how to behave around people. Remember, in the story the Justines can go into another being's mind and control them."

"Is that what y'all do? Have you been into my mind?"

"No, not into your mind, but I did locate your presence when you were on that stage to the nunnery. Y'all would know if I actually went into your mind, but, yes, I can go into people's minds just like the Justines in Mina's Story." He let out his breath.

"Can Daniel do the same thing with his mind?"

"No, he's a normal human being. He doesn't accept the fact that Toma and Papa are from different planets. He refused to go see the *Golden One*."

"What about Kendall and Mina? Does Mina do that?" Her voice was almost shrill.

"No, Mina can't mindspeak or enter another's mind, and I don't believe Kendall will. He's like Mina and Daniel, a completely normal Earth human."

"Are you and Margareatha somehow related to Red?"

This time Lorenz had to swallow before answering. "Uh, well, yes, we are. Toma is also Red's father. Red is our half-brother."

"I'm your sister?" Toni screeched out the question.

"No! Red's our half-brother. Our biological father is Toma; the same as Red's. Your father and mother aren't related to us at all."

"You cannot tell me that my mother committed a venal sin!" Her face was becoming as hard as her voice.

"Honey, I'm not saying any such thing. Y'all can't blame your mother. She couldn't have been much more than sixteen or seventeen, and who knows if Toma went into her mind or not."

"Mother MacDonald knew all of this. That's why she was so opposed to our marriage, isn't it?" She noted that Lorenz winced at the accusation.

"Yes, she felt I should tell y'all everything before we married and had children."

Toni's chin went out. "Why didn't y'all give me that chance?"

At least her drawl is back, thought Lorenz.

"Toni, I swear to the good Lord above, I was afraid I would lose y'all; that y'all would turn away from me in fear…" He stopped as he saw how hard her eyes were.

"Well, Mother MacDonald was right. Y'all had no right to presume I am so childish." She stopped.

"Y'all said I'd know if y'all had been in my mind, but how would I? If he controlled my mother so easily, why didn't he do the same to Mother MacDonald?"

"He couldn't go into Mama's mind. It's how she fought him later. She was only seventeen when she married him. Later she felt she had to obey the vows she made before God's altar. It's why she took all of us and went to Texas with Toma when he insisted on moving here. Y'all know about the Comanche attack."

Toni still looked troubled. "Did Mother MacDonald know whether your father or Father MacDonald had two hearts before she married them?"

"She didn't know about Toma, but she knew about Papa. Papa hugged her when she agreed to marry him. As soon as she heard the two hearts, she refused. That's when Papa explained everything to her. Since he believed the Justines about not being able to have children, he told Mama what he had been taught: that there would be no children. Mina is another Justine teaching proven wrong. Just like our children. The Justines are wrong about a lot of things."

He took a tentative step forward, his voice pleading. "Toni…"

"I need to know why y'all didn't tell me before. Didn't y'all believe my letters?" She derived a certain amount of satisfaction from the pain on his face and in his eyes.

"I was afraid y'all would react like Daniel, and then maybe y'all would have thought it was safer to choose Daniel or that rich, old man Red had chosen. I was wrong, but I can't change that now. I'm sorry I didn't trust y'all."

"Why on earth would I choose either one? That old man was revolting, and Daniel didn't smell nearly as good as y'all, and he's still nothing but a hired gunny; and another thing Lorenz Adolph MacDonald if y'all ever, ever, not tell me what is going on, I am going to be so angry with y'…"

Her words stopped as Lorenz moved swiftly across the floor, gathering her and the baby into his arms, hugging them both.

"Lorenz, y'all are going to squeeze us to death," came Toni's muffled protest.

He kissed her ear, then her cheek, and then the baby's cheek before releasing them and stepping back, a wide smile on his face.

"Will y'all put Melissa in the cradle now?"

Lorenz gladly took the child and gently placed her in the cradle. He pulled the blanket upward and rocked the cradle back and forth; hoping Toni would listen to the rest of what happened so long ago; listen and decide to stay here. He smiled down at the little girl and turned back to Toni.

She was watching him while settling things in her mind. The man could be so gentle and yet, he was so strong. It was like a tiger lurked beneath his surface. Her decision was right. Her words to him when they were sixteen were true. She had no intention of living like an Indian or being poor. Daniel would never provide for her like this man.

Lorenz dug into his pocket and pulled out a vial. "Here, this is what I was working on all afternoon. I used the instructions Papa wrote down, and followed the directions in the medical unit of the spaceship. It's what Papa called a "strengthening potion." It contains all the nutrients our body system needs. Toni, when y'all are stronger, we'll ride up there and I'll show y'all the starship. We'll go inside and y'all can see how other beings live."

Antoinette eyes grew larger. "I cannot imagine such a ship with sails strong enough to go into the sky."

"Uh, it doesn't have sails."

Antoinette's eyes grew hard again. "Lorenz, I will not take something called nutrients, whatever they are, if y'all don't answer my question. How does a ship sail without sails?"

For a moment the light went out of Lorenz's grey eyes as he thought of the huge golden, ovoid craft buried in the earth. This was going to be a very long night of explanations.

Chapter 10

A Summer Day

Six trail hardened men looked down at was left of their companion, Taylor. Farley had sent him ahead to check out the Rolfe spread to see how vulnerable it was to a take over. Michael Walton, the husband of Shelton's oldest daughter, had warned them that Rolfe was old, but still dangerous. He suggested they hit the Rearing Bear Ranch instead.

"There ain't nothin' there but women, Mexicans, and one old man that might be a mixed breed."

Taylor had sneered at the thought of an old Dutchman being dangerous. Now his ant covered head, neck and top of his shoulders were mostly eaten away. Animals had torn his clothes to get at his flesh. Someone had shot him, possibly scalped him, and thrown him into the willows along the river.

"I don't believe we'll give the Rolfe ranch a visit. The other one sounds like easier pickings and we'll be ready when the men come back."

Farley wheeled his horse and the others followed suit.

* * *

Antoinette returned to the house after leaving Armeda in charge of the laundry. Her dark hair was pulled up and coiled at the top, looping around to brush the neck. Curls carefully made to look rebellious framed the sides of her face. Her cotton dress implied that this was a work day. Summer had set in and the grasses were drying, waiting for the late summer and fall rains that would sweep up from the coast. The day was warm, but not unbearable. Lorenz wouldn't return from the cattle drive until sometime in August. Perhaps there would be an opportunity to work on her watercolors later. She held three-year-old Melissa's hand firmly in hers.

Kendall could stay with the laundry workers' children happily building his forts to fight off the Indians, wrestle with the others, and devise ways to shoot a missile or rock somewhere. He'd already been warned that one more rock landing near the wash tubs meant he was in his room until dinner. At five years of age Kendall needed to roughhouse with boys his own age or there would be a fight between him and his studious brother. A situation Antoinette would not risk with Lorenz away on a cattle drive.

She entered the back door through the covered porch and went to the kitchen. When they enlarged the main house they built the side of the kitchen out to butt against the springhouse. Now the door to the springhouse opened from the coat area. This technique had widened the kitchen by ten feet and it was now a spacious room for the huge cook stove, sturdy table, and cabinets. A veranda wrapped across the front of the house.

By adding five feet to the original great room, Antoinette had gained her dining room. True it was a bit narrow, but it was large enough to hold her fancy rosewood dining set. The sweeping stairway in the entrance and grand hall was her pride and joy. The hallway between the bedroom, the old stairwell and part of Mina's bedroom was now a bath. By widening the east side of the house and using the rest of Mina's bedroom she gained a parlor for the rosewood piano, fancy sofa, and needle worked cushioned chairs. Lorenz had painted a lovely portrait of her and hung it on the wall behind the piano.

They'd left the fireplace along the south wall of the hall. When one entered the front, the view ran straight to the French doors opening to the garden. She had laborers install a low, paved with stones, veranda between the French doors and garden. It was more like a Spanish patio or court area where one could catch the breezes. Lorenz's office door was on the other side of the fireplace. She had disliked the original great room and modernized everything by eliminating the old dining and seating area and creating specific rooms. It was a shame there really wasn't space enough for a separate music room, but she had conceded that he needed the office. The sewing room she located upstairs with the bedrooms for the children.

Six-year-old Randall was sitting on the fireplace hearth bent over a Dickens's novel. She really didn't think he could understand much of it, but was secretly afraid he understood far too much.

Melissa looked at Randall and then at her mother. "Why can't I go back outside and play with Kendall?"

"Because he plays too rough for a young lady like y'all. Let's find your colored chalk and y'all can draw something. Maybe Randall will help y'all with your numbers or alphabet."

Antoinette didn't think other children learned as rapidly as her first and last born. She wasn't sure a governess would be sufficient this fall. Miss Ambrose was to return in September. Lorenz had mentioned he would look for a teacher after the drive. One was needed. Antoinette felt the Rolfe children would benefit as much as her own. It seemed Marty Rolfe was the only one receiving any instruction and that was in the ways of the wild from his grandfather. She shuddered at the thought.

The clatter of hooves, gunfire, men's shouts and women's screams interrupted her thoughts. Randall looked up at her, and his eyes widened.

"Mama, do y'all want me to find Pawpaw's rifle? It's danger."

Antoinette looked out the huge front window and saw six horses. Two were heading for the house and four were racing for the barn and bunkhouse area.

"No, come with me both of you!" She picked up Melissa and ran to her bedroom and put Melissa and Randall in the closet.

"Don't move. Randall, take care your sister. Be still, very, very still. Shh. Don't come out of there until I say it's all right!" Her voice was stern, insistent.

There wasn't time to grab one of the larger guns from the office and she pulled her derringer from her purse and ran to the rocker by the window. From the table beside the rocker, she picked up her embroidery and covered the derringer with the linen scarf she was working on. Thank goodness the bed is made ran through her mind. She heard the man coming up the porch steps and wished she had had time to be sitting in the parlor. She did not want Randall to come out to protect her. Thank God it was Randall in the closet and not Kendall. Kendall would be arguing with her.

The man didn't really knock at the door. He kicked against it and walked in. Julia had been in the kitchen, but must have run.

Antoinette walked to the open bedroom door with the linen strewn with a field of pink and blue flowers draped over her right hand and the needle in her left hand.

The man was clad in denims and a dirty, sweat-stained calico shirt. His grey hat was wide brimmed and two guns hung on his hips. Obviously, someone had told him the men were gone. He needed a bath, and Antoinette stilled a gag from the stench of him.

"Hallo, pretty lady. Greet the new man of the house. We're taking over..."

Antoinette pulled the trigger. The first shot hit his gut and the second his heart. He splayed out on the floor, his blood running in both directions, staining the wooden boards. She quickly stuck the empty derringer in her pocket and grabbed the light wooden, caned bottom chair by the bedroom door. If he moved, she would bash him with it.

She walked to his side and bent over enough to pull out one of his pistols. From outside came the call.

"Farley, y'all okay. What's going on?"

She could hear the man mounting the steps and ran back to the bedroom doorway. There she turned and aimed the revolver at the open front door as the man tried to come in sideways. He held his revolver at shoulder height, trying to see who was on the other side by the downed man. Antoinette pulled back the hammer and fired, then repeated the process. At least Red had taught her to shoot straight. She knew she had hit him, but didn't think it was a fatal.

This revolver held a much heavier caliber and the man was slammed backwards and out the door. He began scrabbling across the porch, desperate for a way to out of here and safe.

Toni ran for the office and pulled down the rifle hung over the doorway. This one she knew was loaded. Then she opened the drawer of the gun case and took out the shells and put them in her apron pocket. She peered around the edge of the fire place. To her horror, Randall stood in the open bedroom door with lips set in a straight line, his slender body held straight, the red hair neatly in place.

"Go back, go back." She was yelling. She didn't want him hit by a stray shot. That man might shoot through the door.

Outside she could hear other shots and men yelling. Oh no, she thought, one handyman and two Mexican hands and all of them too old for the trail. She doubted if they even had guns. She ran to the front window, knelt, and peered over the sill. The wounded man had managed to regain his saddle on his horse. The stains on his shirt and one leg told her she had hit his right shoulder and one of his legs. He turned his horse toward the barn and bunkhouse area. Antoinette ran for the back door. She could fire from behind the tubs or the washhouse itself; anything to keep those men away from the children inside and Kendall who was outside somewhere. Dear Jesus let him be safe with one of the Mexican women.

As she emerged from the back porch door and looked at the scene below, she saw that two of the men were off their horses and had the Mexicans kneeling and they were raising their rifles to their shoulders. The other two men were on their horses and started for the house. Antoinette took careful aim and fired. One of the men coming towards her slumped over his saddle and his horse shied and danced at the sudden smell of blood. The other horse reared at the shot and the man turned it and headed for the lane. Antoinette aimed one shot at his back and one at the two with the rifles, fired, and ducked down behind the back steps. Mentally, she counted: four shots fired; two shots left. This time there was no Anna to back up her down time.

"Senora, is that you?"

The words came softly in Spanish. Antoinette looked up. Armeda stood at the far side of the washhouse. Miracles of miracles, she carried Anna's old shotgun. Armeda had requested the weapon when they had given her the right to choose something of Anna's. Like Anna, the shotgun gave her comfort when her man was gone.

Antoinette took a deep breath. "Armeda, I'm going to fire two more times and then I'll need to reload. If someone starts toward us while I'm reloading, fire that at them." Then a frightening thought came to mind.

"Armeda, is the shotgun loaded?"

"Si, Senora."

Antoinette didn't ask if she could hit anything. In this situation, it didn't matter. A shot from below got her attention.

"That's one of your hands. Give up now and we won't shoot the other two."

Antoinette stood and ran for the open door of the washhouse. They fired, but their shots were hurried and their aim bad. She hadn't given them time to get her uphill range. Once inside she broke the south window with her rifle butt and ducked knowing that their next shot should come in there. She ran to the east window and broke it, ducked again, and walked bent over to the south window and fired. Like the men, she hadn't taken time to aim and the shot went harmlessly into the ground and the next trigger pull clicked harmlessly. Antoinette jacked out the shells with a rapid motion to reload.

The remaining horseman whooped and started for the washhouse at a run. Armeda must have suspected something. She stepped out and ran forward, fired the shotgun, and ducked inside the door.

The horse screamed and reared, nearly sending the man out of the saddle. Behind him he heard another scream. He turned and saw one of the men guarding the Mexicans on the ground with a pitchfork impaled in his back.

"Let's get out of here." He wheeled his horse and followed the other man.

Antoinette finished loading the rifle and peered out the door. The one remaining man shot at the Mexican he was guarding, mounted his horse and started for the house.

This time Antoinette took careful aim before firing, and the man tumbled from the saddle. His horse bolted and headed for the open prairie.

A strange quiet seemed to descend on the ranch yard.

Antoinette stood clutching the rifle, her stomach heaving, her hands trembling, and water filling her eyes.

Armeda emerged from the shadows in the washhouse. "They are gone, Senora."

Antoinette turned. "Armeda, I, I can't tell y'all how wonderful y'all were."

Armeda's eyes were wide and serious. "You are strong; just like Mother Mac-Donald."

Toni was having a terrible time trying to control her emotions. "No, Armeda, Mother MacDonald would have still been angry. All I want to do is cry." She choked back the tears.

"Kendall, where is he?"

"He is with my Conchita, Senora. She has all the little ones."

From below came a holler. "Hey, Missus MacDonald, Pedro needs to be bandaged." It was Bill, the man hired as a handyman. "That feller I got with the pitchfork ain't going to make it."

"All right, Bill, I'll get my medical bag and be right there."

Antoinette turned to Armeda. "Y'all are getting a brand new sewing machine and Conchita is going to learn her numbers and also how to read and write a fine hand. Please have her keep Kendall long enough for me to tend to the man below. Conchita is ten-years-old now and if she is as smart as her mother, I think she'll make a wonderful lady's maid." Just what Armeda might think didn't concern her.

Antoinette hurried back into the house for her bag and her babies; she had to get them out of the closet. That man had to be removed from her hall, the floors bleached, sanded, and refinished. Coffins needed to be constructed. *Now where did Julia go?* She opened the door to the springhouse and deep, full screams from Julia.

The Family:
The Middle Years
1886 to 1899

Chapter 11

Father and Sons, the Next Generation

The year 1886 started pleasantly enough for the inhabitants surrounding Schmidt's Corner. There were no wars affecting them, the nation was slowly healing from the dirty, bitter 1884 campaign waged by Democrats for Grover Cleveland and the Republicans for James G. Blaine. The West heaved a sigh of relief when the news of Geronimo's capture in March spread throughout the region, and even the most hard-hearted political opponents warmed over President Cleveland wedding the lovely Frances Folsom in the spring. Most of the concerns in Texas were over using barbwire for fencing or not fencing at all. Lorenz and Martin argued over whether they should allow a railroad over their land for a station at Schmidt's Corner. Martin was against a railroad; Lorenz felt it necessary to avoid the railhead in Arles where they shipped their beeves rather than trail them. Their argument waxed back and forth as spring left and summer began to spread its hot and humid heat.

Randall and Kendall raced their mounts up to the front porch, flung their reins over the hitching rail, and pounded up the steps each trying to beat the other into the door. Sixteen-year-old Randall beat his brother by inches; his legs were longer and he wasn't impeded by spurs. Both ran to the office where they knew their father was working.

"Papa, Uncle Martin needs y'all," shouted Kendall at Randall's back. Randall might be older and taller, but he rarely spoke as rapidly.

Lorenz looked up from the papers neatly arranged in front of him and saw an angry Randall and an excited Kendall skidding to a halt in front of his desk.

Randall had fulfilled Anna's foreboding. He looked exactly like his Justine fore bearers: tall, slender, red hair slightly wavy, and copper colored eyes with a golden circle around the pupils. Lorenz had been surprised that Randall had accompanied Kendall over to the Rolfe ranch. Normally, Randall ignored anything to do with the ranches, but it was still three weeks before Randall would leave for the East and college. Boredom probably drove him to associate with the others.

Kendall resembled his father. He was two inches away from six feet. His black hair wasn't as curly as Lorenz's, his eyes blue instead of grey, and the cleft in the chin less pronounced. He continued his nonstop message. "One of Uncle's hands brought word that there's a homesteader family almost here, and they've already made their claim at the county office in Arles for that land up by the spring near the foothills, and they've got pigs, scrawny cows, and maybe sheep, and Uncle's going to run them out before they can settle, and he wants y'all there."

"Where are the homesteaders and where is Martin?"

"The homesteaders just drove by our place, and Uncle's getting his boys and some of his hands. He says y'all need to take a stand and not let such filth mess up our land." The Texas drawl was thick on Kendall's tongue.

"Father, there are no sheep and but one skinny hog, along with two miserable looking cows. You cannot seriously consider being a part of..." Randall stopped as Lorenz rose.

"Come with me. I'll need to saddle."

"I will not be a part of this."

Lorenz looked at his white-faced older son before he spoke. "Kendall, go see that my horse is saddled. Now!"

Kendall grinned wickedly and left the room as rapidly as he had entered.

"Randall, I want both of my sons there."

"Why? So we can see how you destroy people to increase your wealth?"

"It seems y'all have imbibed too much of the Easterners way of thinking. Y'all may choose between going hogtied or upright."

"Why bother with such physical means when you can use your mind?"

"Damn it, son, y'all know I will not use my mind on y'all, but if I did, y'all couldn't stop me. Now are y'all coming upright or not?"

Randall's gold-banded copper eyes blazed with hatred before he spoke. "I'll go, but if necessary to prevent bloodshed I'll stand in front of the homesteaders."

He clamped his lips together. Appealing to his mother, wherever she might be, would be of no use. She might stop any mistreatment of Kendall, a younger version of his father, but not for him.

"I suggest y'all remain on your horse."

Lorenz picked up his rifle setting against the wall and a handful of shells, and led the way to the front door. He decided against leaving a message for Toni. They should be back within the hour. He watched Randall stalk toward the barn without his horse. We're like two stallions in a stall, he thought. It rarely works. Kendall must have taken his own horse with him and he grabbed the reins of Randall's horse. He wanted no more arguments with Randall.

His horse was almost saddled when they reached the stables, and he stepped closer to finish the cinching. He dropped the extra shells into the saddlebag before swinging up. Both of his sons followed suit.

"I want both of you to stay behind me, no matter what happens. Neither of you all will ride ahead. Is that clear?"

"Yes, sir." Kendall was eager to agree to anything.

"Randall?"

"I believe that will depend on the situation." Randall refused to give an inch.

Lorenz kicked his heels and slapped the reins into the horse's sides, urging his horse into a fast trot. All of them moved out following the road that led towards the Rolfe ranch and Schmidt's Corner. The word road was a loose terminology. The road was used by any passerby on horses, cattle drives, and wagons. Deep, grooved ruts had worn into the ground since Lorenz first arrived.

Lorenz made sure he remained in the lead. Within minutes he could see the group ahead: one covered wagon in bad shape, a couple of milch cows tied onto the back, one pig being pulled along by someone on a lanky horse. He suspected the rider was young as the job wouldn't go to the man of the family. He rejoiced that Kendall's report about sheep was wrong. One pig wouldn't breed unless it was a sow all ready pregnant, but he doubted it. He nudged his horse into a gallop as he saw Martin and crew arriving, blocking the passage of the wagon.

Lorenz reined his horse up along side of the team of heavy work horses, and eased back into the saddle. Martin's face was flushed underneath the deep tan and he was roaring at the new arrivals.

"You all ain't welcomed here. Go back to where you all came from." He waved his rifle at the couple.

Lorenz swung a quick glance in the homesteaders' direction. The woman holding a baby was white faced. He heard Kendall behind him unleash his rifle. "Kendall, put that rifle up." He turned back to Martin.

"Aw, Pawpaw, I was just going to shoot the pig."

Lorenz ignored Kendall's protest. "Martin, don't y'all think y'all should put up your guns and tell your boys and men to do the same? These folks don't look like they will hurt anybody, and I don't see them holding any weapons."

Martin snapped his head in Lorenz's direction as did the rest of the men in the group. Lorenz wasn't worried about Martin. He'd taken his measure years ago. It was Martin's son, Martin Junior, who worried him. Marty, as they called him, had inherited Herman Rolfe's hard nature. He was the one that could and would kill.

"Are you defending them?" Martin was still roaring. "They're nesters. They'll ruin the land. Better to hang the man right now."

"Martin, y'all can't kill innocent people, and if y'all kill one, y'all will have to kill all of them: man, woman, boy, and child."

He let that one sink in as silence descended on the group.

"Then we take the wagon and everything destroy." Martin reverted to the German syntax, something he hadn't done in years.

Damn, thought Lorenz. He's crazy mad.

"Martin, be reasonable. Y'all will still wind up killing them. If y'all don't, the man will fight or somehow bring the law here. Leave it be. This part of Texas will never be fit for farming. The land will defeat them."

"By Gott, I ain't waiting. What's the matter with y'all? Are y'all going to help or not?"

"Martin, think. Y'all can't do this. Not without breaking God's law."

"Don't use scripture on me."

"Hell, y'all helped teach it to me! I can't let y'all do something y'all aren't going to be able to live with."

"Who are y'all to talk? Y'all killed three men before y'all were sixteen, and how many since?"

"Martin, those men were trying to kill me or my people. I'm the one living with it, not y'all."

Martin raised his rifle and shook it. "Just what are y'all going to do? We've got our guns out."

Somehow there was a revolver in Lorenz's hand pointed straight at them. Surprise flickered across each face.

"Last warning! These people drive away from here now. No one bothers them. If anyone tries, I will shoot."

"I thought y'all were my friend. Y'all do this, Lorenz, and no MacDonald is welcomed on my place; not y'all, not Mrs. MacDonald, and not your kids." He looked and saw that Lorenz had no intention of moving.

Martin knew too well that Lorenz did not bluff; not at poker, not in fights. He could not risk his son's lives. It was too much to ask of a man. He waved his rifle at the group and turned his horse towards his ranch. The rest followed.

Lorenz's face did not move, but his lips had whitened. Damnit, Martin, he thought to himself, y'all are my friend; my only friend. He sat there immobile watching the group ride away until they had ridden over a rise and reappeared still going towards the Rolfe spread. Kendall moved his horse closer.

"Uh, Pawpaw, shouldn't we go after them?"

"Why? We would not be welcomed." Lorenz slipped the revolver back into the holster and turned his horse toward his Rearing Bear Ranch. He did not look at the people on the wagon seat.

"Sir, we need to thank you, and ask some directions." The man on the wagon seat half rose as if to swing down, but rapidly resumed his seat as Lorenz whirled his horse, shouting at them.

"Didn't y'all hear the man? You all aren't wanted here. This land will starve you all to death if y'all try to farm it. There'd better be food in that wagon. There's no time to put n a crop this year. Go back to where you all came from." Lorenz swung his horse back towards the ranch and lashed at the hindquarters with his reins.

Randall moved his horse closer, and saw the stricken look on their faces. "You should be safe for now. What type of directions do you need?"

He noted the sweat pouring off the man, wetting his shirt, his face, even the forearms. The woman had her arms wrapped around the baby as though protection was still needed. The young man on the horse looked ready to vomit. None of their clothes were too clean, but trail dirt would account for that.

The man took off his hat and used his forearm to wipe the sweat away and then replaced the hat. "I'm Frank Gavin and this is my missus. According to the folks in Arles, after I passed that ranch back there I was to go about a mile or two and turn on a track toward the foothills. There's a spring up there that is part of our claim. We've gone about a mile, but there's no road." He did not say the six hundred and forty acres I filed on.

"Yes, that's true, just drive for the high ground and look for the spring. No one lives in that direction, so there's no need for roads. There are animals moving through there. You'll find you will need to build a fence to protect your crops. I'm surprised you didn't choose the land next to Schmidt's Corner. There is water there that's less likely to run dry at the end of summer."

"The man at the County assured me that it was cooler up there. My missus finds this heat bad for the young 'un. Thanks for the help, young man, and be sure to thank your pa."

He seated himself on the wagon and started the team towards the foothills. His woman nodded her head, but did not smile. The young man herding the pig mouthed a "thanks," and turned with the wagon.

"Why did y'all help them?" demanded Kendall of his brother as they rode toward the ranch.

"It seemed the Christian thing to do."

"Huh, and that's why Pawpaw did what he did?"

"Our father does as he pleases." Randall's words were terse. He was having a difficult time reconciling what he thought his father was going to do and with the outcome of today's encounter until he realized that his father was clever enough to know that the people in Arles had deliberately sent the homesteaders here. Like him, they figured his father would kill anyone that crossed his land. Instead, it was Uncle Martin that was going to destroy the homesteaders: a fact that didn't make sense. Randall had always assumed Uncle Martin followed his father's lead.

"When do y'all think Uncle Martin will cool down?" Kendall preferred spending any leisure time with the Rolfe brothers rather than with his own.

"Whenever our father tells him he made a mistake and should have joined him in killing four innocent people today."

The rest of the ride was silent. As they pulled up at the barn used for stabling the horses, they heard the sound of rocks crashing somewhere behind the washhouse.

"Pawpaw's really mad," commented Kendall.

"Whatever he planned didn't turn out like he wanted." Randall had regained most of his confidence in his belief that his father was the archetypical robber baron.

In silence the young men unsaddled and headed for the house. Supper would be served within an hour and their mother did not allow for anyone missing a meal when all were present.

Toni greeted them as they walked in. She was dressed in a blue, light cotton dress with a low collar. She was still slender and her face protected from the harshness of wind, sun, and outdoor work, remained unlined. She'd grown from a beautiful girl into a beautiful, mature woman, and her violet eyes still made men her slaves.

"What on earth has set your father off? He has been throwing those rocks since he rode in. I even had to have one of the hands care for his horse."

Kendall broke into an excited recital of the afternoon events. Randall tried to edge away, but his mother shook her head. "And right now, Uncle Martin won't let any of us come on his place and they can't come here, and all because of a bunch of homesteaders."

"One family hardly comprises a bunch, Kendall. Why do y'all suppose they sent them into the foothills? The ground isn't very good there."

"I'm assuming someone at the county courthouse thought of it. The sheriff will undoubtedly be out to see if they survived our father's wrath. They've hated us Yankees for years." Randall answered the question as Kendall just shrugged.

"Y'all are probably right, Randall. Otherwise only a Mexican family or a Negroid family could live on that land, unless they are poor white trash. Is that what they were?"

"Mother, your perception of humanity is worse than father's." He stalked towards the stairs.

"Randall Matthew MacDonald, y'all are impertinent. Y'all will apologize to me right now."

Randall turned back to her before speaking, his voice as stiff as his body. "My apologies, Mother. I should not have spoken in that manner."

"Very well, supper will be served at its regular time." She swept into and through the dining room to enter the kitchen. Lorenz would be upset over Martin and their friendship. She knew he would turn to her for solace and she needed to order a bath with perfumed oils.

Randall took the stairs two at a time. He was disgusted with his quick acquiescence to his mother's demand, but he knew his mother had to be placated or it would mean an angry father. Father angry was something the years had taught him to avoid. He spent the next thirty minutes with his law books. When the sound of rocks slapping into each other ended, he headed downstairs and into the washhouse. As he suspected he found his father there, the man was stripped and ready to pour cold water over his sweating body. For a moment, he was speechless. It was always difficult to realize his father was so muscular, and when Lorenz turned the scar running from the neck downward was far more visible than the one on his face. It was as though he had kept that portion of the scar to remind himself of the horrors when separated from his family.

Lorenz's grey eyes narrowed at the sight of his oldest son.

"Y'all want something?"

"I'm still not certain as to why you permitted the homesteaders to continue towards what you consider your land." It irritated Randall that he had arrived at the same incorrect assumption as those yahoos in Arles.

"And y'all need confirmation that I am evil incarnate." The words came softly into Randall's mind as his father dumped first one bucket of water and then another over his head.

Randall found he had no words. All the resentment he'd meant to unleash wasn't possible. He watched as Lorenz shook his head and grabbed a towel. Finally Randall spoke.

"You will have to admit that it wasn't exactly in character."

"It appears y'all know nothing about my character. What I said out there is true. The land will defeat them. They might have been able to hang on had they filed next to Schmidt's Corner, but up in those rocky hills? They'll be lucky to have one good crop in five years. Grandpa Schmidt had farming land in Missouri. He showed it to me. Ran it through his fingers and had me smell of it. That soil up there doesn't compare. To kill them would be a sin."

"The other times then, you don't consider sinning?"

Lorenz pulled on his summer linen underwear before answering and reaching for his shirt. "The other times were fulfilling my intent to continue living. Neither the senior nor the junior in that group are a threat to my existence." 'Unless they stumble onto the Golden One.' The last part was in mindspeak.

"Father, has it occurred to you that the people in Arles deliberately sent them here."

Lorenz buttoned his shirt before replying. "Very good, Randall, y'all have picked the exact reason they thought they knew where to go. When do y'all think the sheriff will be here?"

"Since they want to find dead bodies, I believe by tomorrow or the next day."

Lorenz smiled. "They won't bother. They're relying on the woman and youngster making it back. They don't believe I'd kill them too." He hastily pulled on his denims and then sat to pull on his boots.

'Is your mother very upset?' The words were in his mind again. Damn, his father insisted he practice the Justine skill.

'She didn't seem to be.' He used mindspeak to answer. To Randall, the mind-speak was a reminder that the ability came from his father; not his mother.

"Good, let's go eat." Lorenz spoke aloud. Then he switched to mindspeak as they started for the house, Lorenz carrying the guns he'd ridden out with. 'Have y'all changed your mind about my character?'

'I'm in the process of modifying it.' Randall answered in kind and both fell silent.

Chapter 12

Young James Conducts a Service

Tom Jackson, his wooden leg clunking against the floor, led the way out of the saloon and leaned on the hitching post railing to rest his good leg. It was becoming harder and harder each year to move with or without crutches. Thank God, his boy was big enough to do the iron work. Tom spent more and more time at Jesse's drinking away the pain: the pain of his missing leg and the pain of a controlling wife.

Tillman, a lanky rancher, and two of his hands brought their beer mugs with them and stood alongside of Jackson. Jessie Owens preferred standing near the door of his saloon. He'd taken off his apron and slapped a hat over his bald head. The September morning sun still beat down with a ferociousness that would not let up.

"Y'all sure this is when the fireworks start?" asked Tillman, tipping back his hat to look at the small church sitting catty-corner across the street. "Emily ain't never said much about how they do things."

"Yep, they're through with the sermon and what they call their liturgy music. Mrs. Jackson's quit playing the organ so she can take communion with the rest. That's when the Pastor serves the bread and wine."

Tom's stories of his wife's Lutheran faith and the goings on in the church where the preacher man spoke in German, the congregation sang in German, baptized babies, and served wine instead of grape juice made good conversation for everyone to speculate as to what really went on and what was being said.

"Olga told me that Pastor James was not going to serve it to MacDonald or Rolfe. I almost went just to see the expressions on their faces, but, hell, then I remembered. I won't be at the altar because I ain't Lutheran. I'd be watching their backs. Having a decent size drink the honest way seemed a lot better to me."

Jackson's memory of the service sequence was accurate. Pastor James Wilhelm Rolfe, once called Young James, stood in front of the congregation, clad in his black monk's robe and surplice, his hands gripping the communal plate. His sermon had been a long exposition of St. John's first epistle, Chapter Three, where the disciple admonishes all to "…love one another. He that hateth his brother is a murderer." His thinning blond hair was carefully combed, his slender body leaning forward when he expounded upon its meaning among Christians. He enjoyed the experience of watching his brother Martin's face becoming a deep shade of red under the tanned skin. Lorenz, he surmised, must be the better poker player as his face did not change. Only those strange grey eyes became colder and colder.

Pastor Rolfe was taking great satisfaction in knowing that he was causing both Martin and Lorenz to squirm inside. Those two were proud, stiff-necked men who continued to sit side-by-side in the front pew reserved for men. It was a custom their fathers started long before the quarrel and neither would sit behind the other. This meant they would be side-by-side when kneeling in front of him and he, James, as Pastor could deliver his edict. All their superior ways while they were growing up and lording it over him would be avenged.

As Pastor Rolfe finished saying the words of the Sacrament, he turned to face the small congregation. Like the rest of the service and the hymns, the words were in German.

"All who have prepared themselves are asked to come forward and receive the body and blood of our Lord, Jesus Christ."

He watched with intensifying anticipation as the men filed up to the kneeling rail curved around the altar while the women remained seated. He then bowed to the men.

As the men returned the bow to the Pastor and the cross, Olga Jackson (nee Rolf) moved away from the organ sitting by the north wall lined with a row of windows. It was time to be among the women. Her brown hair was parted down the middle and pulled into a tight bun, her face tanned by the Texas sun framed brown eyes and lips that remained a raspberry color. The grey taffeta swished around the floor as she settled her matronly figure on the pew next to her daughter, eight-year-old Bertha. Gerde Schmidt, dressed as always in severe black, looked like a dried walnut with deep wrinkles cutting across her face. Emily (Tillman) Plank was on the other side tending her two babies, three-year-old Arthur and one-year-old Mildred.

The total of women numbered six with the visiting Mina Rolfe, Lorenz's sister, and now her sister-in-law. Her other sister-in-law, Brigetta, had produced so many sons that it took two pews for the women and children which now included two-year-old Hans Rolf, Martin and Brigetta's last child. Toni's girl, Melissa, and her niece, Christina, Martin's girl, would tend to the younger girls and boys while the women were at the altar.

Olga kept her hands folded, but managed to look sideways at the men where Lorenz and Martin knelt. Kendall was on Lorenz's right side, and Marty and August, Martin's two oldest sons, on Martin's left side. Her own son Thomas knelt beside her nephews, and Gerald Plank completed the row.

James offered the bread to Kendall intoning the words, "Take eat, this is the body of Christ."

He straightened as he approached Lorenz and Martin and stood between them. "I cannot, in good conscience, give either of you the body and blood of Christ. You, as brothers in Christ, are living in sin by not speaking to each other. You have both brought shame on this congregation. To give the sacrament to you would be to your damnation and to mine."

Both ranchers' heads snapped back. Martin stood, his hand closing into a fist, his blue eyes cold. Gasps and rustlings could be heard from the women's section.

Lorenz was on his feet just as rapidly, his own browned hands closing and opening as a wild surge of anger raged through him. Suddenly Melissa was mindspeaking to him in screams.

'No, Pawpaw, no, y'all can't at the altar.'

He was forcing himself to control his temper as he turned towards Martin and put his left arm out over Martin's chest as he softly mouthed the words, "We can't hit him in here. Let's take this outside."

Martin swung toward Lorenz and gave a curt nod of assent. As one they turned and marched up the aisle, their boots clicking against the oak floor, each one throwing open their side of the double door. Neither noticed the group at the saloon watching them as they stood on the porch under the roofed stoop and faced each other, Lorenz taller than Martin by five inches.

Martin's face was still red, the veins were throbbing on each side of his throat, his hands clenching and unclenching. "Y'all stopped me again."

"Yes I did. Go ahead and hit me if it makes y'all feel better. Y'all have owed me one anyway since I got y'all into trouble over my trying to run away."

Martin hesitated. That incident occurred over twenty years ago and Young James had stopped the fight by intoning, "Seventy times seven."

"Ja, but Young James was right, then. Y'all were trying to apologize."

"I hate to admit it, Martin, but he's probably right this time too."

"Ja, hitting the pastor isn't too smart." Bitterness tinged his words. "What ailed y'all with them nesters?"

"I didn't want anyone killed. It's only one family and the county agent in Arles probably sent them here to make trouble for us. I still say the weather will eliminate them. They can't grow decent crops up there."

"Which means they'll turn to rustling. We've got enough problems with thieves."

"That man won't. He doesn't know how. I'll admit that doesn't mean the son won't when he gets a little savvier about horses and cows. If I'd known those people were on the way, I'd been over to talk with y'all before they got here."

Martin half-way turned towards the street and swung back to face Lorenz, his anger turning on the men who were suppose to be their friends. Instead, they were waiting for a fight.

"Lorenz, we got an audience. That means he was planning this all along. Young James should have said something when we signed up for communion. I say we wait for him when he comes out of the sacristy and dump him in the river."

Lorenz gave a low chuckle brought on by the relief that Martin was talking to him again. It meant the quarrel was over.

"Sounds like a good idea to me. I've wanted to do that to the sanctimonious little prig ever since he kept sticking his tongue out at me the day Papa insisted on taking me home to Mama."

"It would serve him right." Some of the anger went out of Martin's eyes as he faced his friend and remembered the bitter, dirty youth that had violently entered their lives. Was his anger worth their friendship? Martin was not one to contemplate past actions, but right now he felt he was in the wrong and didn't know how to repair it.

Lorenz was grinning broadly. "Yes, it would, but we'd still be in the wrong as far as the synod is concerned. I doubt if we'd ever get another pastor through here. It seems der Pastor has left us with one choice. We can shake hands and go back in there and tell him all is forgotten and forgiven. That we're friends again and demand he give us communion. He'd have to swallow his words in front of everyone."

"Ja, but then Young James will want us to apologize to the congregation." Bitterness still lingered with anger.

"Leave that part to me. Papa did a darn good job of teaching me how to apologize whenever I managed to break one of their rules."

The doubt left Martin's eyes and he stuck out his right hand. "Herr MacDonald."

"Herr Rolfe."

It was a ritual they had begun years ago. Lorenz broke the grip and reached for the door handle on his side when he realized both he and Martin had moisture in their eyes.

"After y'all."

Martin reached for the handle on his side. "No, together; just like when we went out."

Pastor Rolfe was returning the cup to the altar and the women were returning to their pews where the younger children were seated as the two men marched back down the aisle, their wide shoulders swinging in the bowlegged swagger of men long in the saddle. Since the congregants filed to the right and re-entered their pew from the wall side this did not restrict their movement.

Toni and Brigetta smiled at their mates and each other, happy at the thought of restored visits. The young men were smiling, thinking of the missed companionship. James turned, his gooseberry eyes reflecting shock. What had gone wrong with his plan? He could tell these two were once again as arrogant and determined as when they were seated in the pew. What were they plotting?

Lorenz and Martin stopped at the rise leading to the altar, clasped their hands and bowed towards the cross and their pastor. Lorenz spoke for both of them.

"We are friends again and ask that you give us the Lord's Supper for the reminder of his promised forgiveness. If we have shamed our family and friends of this congregation, we apologize and pray that they forgive us as the Good Lord has." Lorenz and Martin waited.

James considered. As a pastor he had to accept their announced repentance. There was only one other Elder in the congregation and Gerald Plank wasn't about to cross Lorenz or Martin with an objection. He turned back to the altar, swallowed his bitterness, and picked up the plate to return to the communal rail where he bowed to them. Once again they returned the bow and knelt.

As Pastor Rolfe he administered the bread and then the cup while he intoned Christ's words as recorded in Matthew 26:26 through 29. Then he made the sign of the cross, saying, "Go in Peace. Your sins are forgiven." He bowed to them. Both men stood and returned the bow before returning to their seats.

James replaced the cup and reverently laid the cloth over the plate and cup while Olga struck the chord on her organ before playing the Nunc Dimittis.

Pastor Rolfe was back in command. When the singing ceased he went into a long, closing prayer thanking God for his blessings and for bringing two sinners back into the fold. He then finished the liturgy while the congregation sang their responses and broke into the final hymn. It was perhaps the loudest the singing from the church had been since the elder MacDonald's booming voice had been absent.

Outside Tillman tipped his hat back. "Well, boys, here comes my missus and young 'uns for our Sunday dinner with Emily and Gerald."

He nodded toward a buckboard approaching from the north. "I'll let you all know if anything happened, but it looks like they settled it like gentlemen."

Jesse shrugged. He'd been hoping for an afternoon of high spirits over the two damn Yankees fighting. Beer would have flowed freely. Of course, everyone had bet on Lorenz winning. He would have collected his ten percent for holding the money, but now he had to pay them back. He wandered into the musty saloon, the two Tillman hands following. Jackson remained outside waiting for his family to emerge from church, wondering which family they would be joining for dinner.

Chapter 13

The Grandmother

LouElla raised her fist and banged on the door of the parsonage in San Antonio. The deep blue, tailored dress did little to hide her bulging arm muscles, although the despised clothing hid the rest of her physical structure. Something about Mina's latest letter and pregnancy alarmed her. She left Red to contend with the shipping business in Galveston and journeyed to San Antonio to check on her granddaughter. LouElla had avoided visiting them this last year as James always made clear how uncomfortable he felt in LouElla's six foot-three over-powering presence. He was also becoming puzzled over her continued youthful appearance as she made no pretense of coloring her hair grey.

Mina's letter, late last October, announcing her pregnancy was filled with joy: Joy at finally being in the family way and pride in her husband for healing the riff between Lorenz and Martin the month before. Then the handwriting had been firm, but in this last letter the writing was shaky. Mina simply apologized for not having the strength to write. According to the first letter the baby wasn't due until the end of May or the first of June. This was only the middle of March. What was wrong? She waited impatiently and then banged again, shaking the door in its frame. If someone didn't answer soon, she was going to tear the door off or break it down. What was her granddaughter doing in such a poor, mean dwelling anyway? The MacDonald House could afford better.

Inside she heard a man's cross voice and then a muffled sound that might have been, "Coming."

Finally the door opened and Mina stood there, her face bloated and her belly huge for someone in their sixth month. LouElla had been on Earth long enough to realize how the females of Earth beings looked in this stage of birthing.

Recognition surged through Mina's dull eyes. "Grandma! And the place is a mess. I'm so sorry." Tears started rolling down her cheeks.

To LouElla it looked like Mina was ready to fall.

"Are ye all right?"

"I, I think so. Oh, I don't know, Grandma. I'm so tired."

"Who is it, Frau Rolfe?" James voice came from within.

LouElla stepped forward and picked Mina up as though she were a child and walked into the house. "Ye have a visitor. Yere wife tis nay well." She stalked through the small dining area, turned towards the small bedroom, and carried Mina over to the bed.

She heard the chair scrape and realized James was probably behind them. In her arms, Mina was still sobbing, but there was no strength in her to demand to be set down.

In between sobs, Mina repeated over and over, "I really need to go finish the dishes, Grandma."

"Grandmother LouElla, to what do we owe this visit?" James shocked voice was behind her.

"To the fact that Mina's letter twas written by a sick woman. What tis the matter with ye, man? She needs a doctor."

"I'm the judge of that." James voice was stiff and filled with anger. "This is my house, and as Mina has told you, there is work to be done here."

LouElla looked at him in amazement. Twas the man blind? LouElla held a low opinion of the doctors on this planet, but most of them at least ordered a sick, pregnant woman to bed, didn't they?

"She tis in nay condition to work right now. She needs to rest. Slow walks twould be good, nay else."

"Since when are you a doctor, madam? As I said, this is my house."

"And hers," LouElla roared back.

"I cannot permit you to disrupt us like this. I'm preparing the sermon for Sunday and I need peace and order here. If you cannot abide by my wishes, you may leave."

James felt he had delivered this in a firm, manly tone. It was then that the fist connected with his stomach and then another with his chin as he bent over, and he remembered nothing of the next hour.

"Grandma, what have you done?" Mina's wail came from the bed.

LouElla ignored the wails and picked up James and carried him out of the room and dumped him out the back door. Then she stomped back into the bedroom where Mina sat on the edge of the bed.

"Ye get back into bed. Ye need to rest. Yere husband tis all right and should come to in a bit. I intend to find ye a housekeeper and then a doctor. I twill be back later, and in the meantime, ye sleep, my wee one." She bent over and laid her head on Mina's right shoulder then on her left as she made the "tsk" sound in each ear. "Ye may greet me properly when ye are up to it."

Mina closed her eyes remembering how Papa always liked to be greeted in this manner and wondered why this custom seemed be theirs alone, and she whispered. "Please, Grandma, make sure James is all right. I just need to rest for a minute."

LouElla kept silent about her intentions and left the house by the front door. Where to find someone to do the cooking and cleaning? This was a strange town to her. She had visited Mina here only once before. Right now Antoinette or Margareatha would be a great deal of help. She climbed into her rented carriage and snapped the reins. Mayhap she should try the middle of town and look for the newspaper office. Someone there should know about such things. At least Mina was sleeping. LouElla did not know how to do housework, she was a warrior. Keepers took care of domestic duties, although here they called them housekeepers, butlers, maids, or cooks.

James was waiting for her when she returned, a black and blue lump on his chin. "If you put one foot into this house, I'll have you arrested."

LouElla looked down at the short (five-foot-eight), slim form and snorted. "Ye may do so, but what twill ye do when Lorenz or my laddie arrive?"

The thought of his six-foot-nine father-in-law almost weakened his resolve. James's hand tightened on the door knob until his knuckles whitened. Then he remembered MacDonald was safely up in the forests of Washington and nowhere near them. It would take the man three months to get here and by that time, Mina would be a mother and everything like it was. If Lorenz were to come, James was certain, he would listen to the words in the Bible, and even Lorenz couldn't get here for a week or two.

"Madame, you have caused enough mischief in this house. I refuse to admit you and if you persist, I will have you arrested for trespassing and assault." He closed the door.

LouElla almost tore the door off and then stopped. The law would protect this weak being, and she did not dare risk being questioned. She climbed back in the carriage to cancel the housekeeper for a week and send telegrams to Lorenz and her Llewellyn.

Chapter 14

James Confronts the Unknown

Dusk was falling and Mina sat swaying in her chair at the supper table, too sick and too tired to think about rising to start the dishes. James was frowning, she knew, but right now she could barely lift her head. She clenched her hands when she heard him clear his throat. Dear God, all she wanted was sleep. Both of them jumped when the knock came at the door.

"I'll answer that while you clear the table." James's voice was harsh and his words were a command.

Mina pretended to rise as he walked towards the front and then she slumped back into the chair no longer caring if anyone saw her.

James walked rapidly towards the door. It was probably a parishioner coming to consult der Pastor or one of the Elders. He preferred supper earlier, but Mina was so slow and he found it necessary to keep reminding her what to do. The shame of her neglect was beginning to inconvenience him. He would need to ask whoever it was to go over to the church if they wished to talk. The smile on his face vanished when he opened the door and looked up at his brother-in-law.

"I hear y'all are mistreating my sister."

It was a not an inquiry, but the statement was mild enough. How had the man arrived so rapidly? It was but five days since he'd slammed the door on LouElla.

"I am protecting my God given rights as the head-of-the-household. If you have come here to tell us how to live, you are not welcomed."

James held his head high at this pronouncement. He was in control, but something went wrong. He saw the grey eyes turn to cold slate and Lorenz's lips tighten; and then the pain in his head started. James found himself walking backwards toward the dining room, the pain in his head guiding him. His arm reached backward and he lowered himself onto the chair, unable to do anything but sit there and stare stupidly at the wall.

"Lorenz, oh no, Grandma sent for you. Oh dear." Mina could only stare hopelessly at her brother. Lorenz, she knew, would kill James rather than obey a threat about going to jail. "Please, please, don't hurt James. I love him. I'll be all right. I just need to rest." Tears were clouding her eyes.

"Of course, y'all can rest, honey. I'll help y'all into the bedroom." His voice was gentle, just like when she was little and fell or cut herself.

James tried to protest, but the pain shot through his head again. Somehow he knew if he tried to rise the pain would be worse. He watched Lorenz help Mina to her feet and guide her to the doorway.

"I'm all right, Lorenz, really I am." Mina's voice was weak. "I can put myself to bed."

Lorenz ignored her protests and made sure she was safely on the bed. "I'll be back," he promised as he closed the door behind him, and walked back to James.

"Just what the hell do y'all think y'all are doing?"

For a moment the pain left James and he stared up at his brother-in-law. "I, I will not allow such language in my house."

"Young James, that woman is my sister and y'all have been remiss. I've talked with Grandma, and Mina needs help."

"I'm the one who decides that." James snapped back and started to rise when he slammed back into the chair again. He had to obey that command in his brain.

"Wrong." Lorenz's voice was hard. "Now, y'all just keep your butt in that chair while we work things out."

"How do you do that?" James was almost whispering. "What are you? Why can't I move?"

"Y'all will know the answer to that when Mina tells your child Mina's Story. Until then y'all are going to heed what I say or y'all will stay in that chair or a bed the rest of your life. I did not come here to talk about me. We are talking about Mina.

"This house is a mess, and she looks big enough to have twins or else there is something seriously wrong with the baby. Where are your eyes? Why didn't y'all let Grandmère take charge and bring in that housekeeper? And, James, try telling the truth."

James swallowed. The vise around his brain seemed to loosen, then tighten. "I cannot stand that woman. She's not natural. She has to be over 70, yet she looks like she's in her thirties."

A small smile twitched at the right side of Lorenz's mouth. "Well, well, y'all do have eyes, but Grandmère's looks aren't what we're talking about either. Why didn't y'all let the housekeeper come in here? One is certainly needed."

"I can't afford that on a Pastor's salary," James admitted stiffly and tried to rise, but his legs refused to move.

"Mina has money. Papa settled $10,000.00 dollars on her on her twenty-first birthday."

"But I can't touch it. You're the trustee of the account."

"That is correct, James, we don't trust y'all. All I needed was a letter or telegram from Mina and the letter of credit would have been here within two weeks."

"We need to live on my salary."

"Y'all are being an ass. Face it, James, what y'all want is control of that money. Then y'all would do something stupid with it, like build another church or give it to the seminary."

"There's nothing wrong with giving back to God."

"Agreed, but not with someone else's money. Now back to Mina. Since y'all are not treating her according to St. Paul's instructions, y'all are going to listen to her brother's instructions."

James looked bewildered. "I am the head of the household as anyone who knows God's Word would agree."

"Y'all want me to point out the passage about treating your wife like your own body?"

"The MacDonald's are known for spoiling their women."

"James, shut up and listen. The housekeeper comes in here tomorrow. Grandmère will be here and stay with Mina all day. Whether she sleeps here or not is up to her. Y'all will get your doctor in here, and then a specialist from the hospital if Grandmère doesn't like him. Have I made myself clear?"

James tried to fold his arms over his chest and found that they remained inert. His efforts at trying to move were futile and moisture was building on his forehead and upper lip from the exertion.

"Why can't I move?" His words were a cry of anguish.

"Because I won't let y'all," came the mild words. "We haven't reached an agreement yet."

James's lips went white. "Only God or the Devil can do such things."

"Wrong, Young James, I'm neither; it's simply that my parentage isn't yours. I just want y'all to realize that the same bloodlines run in Papa's family so there's the chance that the child Mina carries will be more like us than y'all."

James shuddered. He was in the middle of a nightmare and he couldn't wake up. Somehow he must have help. He started to yell, but his mouth closed and no sound came.

"Y'all want to consider for a while? We could clear the table while y'all think about it."

James squirmed trying to move, but his feet remained glued to the floor and his body still. Finally, he whispered. "What else can you do?"

"Remember Shelton after his gunnies nearly killed Papa? Shelton couldn't talk, walk, or hold a pencil. Somebody had to feed him. I did that James. Get that through your thick, German skull, but right now I'm here to make sure Mina lives to have that baby. From the looks of her, that might not happen. Hasn't that occurred to y'all?"

"All women walk through the valley of death when they have a baby."

"That is not true. Good Lord, man, what's wrong with y'all? Mama had six of us and never a problem. One died, and that had nothing to do with the birth. My wife, your sister, and your sister-in-law have had children and never looked like Mina."

James was white lipped. He didn't want to talk about such matters even though Lorenz was correct. How to get this man out of his house?

"James, I suggest y'all be reasonable. Right now y'all are dealing with me. Y'all really want to face Papa if something happens to his wee lassie? Y'all think I'm a hard ass? Papa won't even bother to reason with y'all. Now have y'all reconsidered? Remember should that child be like Papa or me, y'all will need help in the raising."

James slumped back against the chair. "Papa MacDonald can do what you're doing?"

"This and break bones with his bare hands; which I can't."

"Why didn't Mina tell me?" His voice was back to a whisper.

"I don't believe Papa ever told Mina everything. He just told her Mina's Story. Perhaps in his own way, he felt Mina would never have children. He probably

75

plans on telling her once she does have a child. Y'all will have to ask him, if Mina and the baby live. Which will it be, James? Mina having the care she needs or y'all losing everything?"

"What do you mean everything?" James was stiff-lipped.

"I reckon that's for y'all to worry about." Lorenz smiled down at his brother-in-law, the scar on right side of his face pulling the lips higher than the left.

James knew he had lost. "Do you really believe Martin will be your friend when I tell him about this?"

"Oh, I intend to tell Martin that I raised holy hell with y'all over the way y'all treated Mina." The smile became wider.

"Y'all don't really think Martin's going to believe much of what y'all say. He'll just think y'all were too scared to stand up when your tongue couldn't get things your way. Now what's it going to be. Are y'all going to let Grandmère, the housekeeper, and the doctor come in here to take care of Mina?" Lorenz's voice rose on the last sentence.

James hid his face in his hands. At least he could move them again, and he looked up at Lorenz. The man was implacable.

"Very well, but Mina still needs to take care of this table."

"Y'all are an idiot. We are going to take care of the table and the dishes once we come to an agreement. Mina is staying in bed where she belongs. Get that through your head."

James considered. He hadn't done dishes since he was a boy and Olga had moved out when she married Tom Jackson. Papa and Martin didn't care if the plate was clean or not. Tonight was the same. There was no way out if he ever wanted to stand again.

"What will my congregants think if I have a housekeeper?"

"Who cares?"

"They may never pay me again. I don't have a ranch." The bitterness lashed out. His father had followed the old ways of giving all to the older son. Other than paying for his education, James was given nothing material; only memories and memories weren't currency.

"James, if you're a good pastor, remind them that the laborer is worthy of his hire." Inside, Lorenz harbored a certain amount of sympathy for James's complaint. Pastor's salaries were low and too often consisted of unneeded garden produce. "As I said, Mina has money. Now it's time to decide. No more objections, and don't try to tell me y'all will have me excommunicated. I won't let it happen even if one of the other Elders believed y'all." His voice and eyes hardened.

James considered long enough for the vise on his head to tighten, then loosen. If he tried to explain his reasons that Lorenz possessed supernatural powers or committed them to paper, sane people would think that he, James, was insane. If Lorenz's boast about Shelton was true, how could he prove it? Shelton was dead. His mouth was dry and he desperately wanted to regain use of his legs. He expelled a burst of air from his lungs.

"All right, the housekeeper may come here, but first Mina will have to clean it."

"No, that's for the housekeeper to do, and y'all didn't say a thing about Grandmère."

James looked at the set face of his brother-in-law and knew that he must agree. Not only agree, but live with the fact that Lorenz would still tell Martin about how "he rescued his sister" in San Antonio and Martin would simply nod his head or laugh. Right now, it was difficult for James to decide which man he detested most.

"Very well, the housekeeper and your Grandmother, but neither may stay overnight. There isn't room."

"Thank y'all, James. I really think you're the one to go tell Mina, if she's awake. Don't wake her. I'll put the water on to heat, and we'll both take care of the dishes."

James stood, surprised that his legs weren't shaking. With one last glare at Lorenz he stalked into the bedroom. Mina was lying on the bed, her clothes on, sleeping soundly. He shook his head and backed out, suspecting that if he woke her, Lorenz would know. Already, he was thinking of ways to avoid Lorenz for the rest of his life.

* * *

"Toni, listen to this. It's from Grandmère."

It was the last week of May, 1887, and Lorenz was reading a letter one of the hands had brought back from Arles.

"Dear Younger Laddie and Toni, Tis the grandest news. Mina has given birth to two wee laddies. She tis fine, but a bit weak. The ritual of baptism is to be soon, although as a precaution I think the young fool of a counselor that Mina wed did so already. The babes twere a bit early by two weeks. They've named them James Wilhelm Rolfe, Jr. and Lamar Victor Rolfe. The last born tis named in honor of my own dear brither although what he would do with a second and third name tis puzzling. This world uses two or three words when one twould do.

I twill remain here till Llewellyn arrives. Then we twill do a proper presentation. Ye, Lorenz, as Laird should be here. Should Mina still remain weak after her fither arrives, I twill remain. The housekeeper shall stay as long as Mina needs her. James seems to accept this as someone he considers important (Lorenz could almost hear LouElla snorting) thought him quite prudent in money management while keeping the household together and still working long hours for the church. Mina tis delighted with the babes and proud that James has been asked to forward church news to some place in Missouri.

When twill ye be here?

Yere loving Elder Mither."

Chapter 15

Blizzard

Antoinette woke thinking the morning was quite warm. She stretched and sat up. Dawn was still with them, but light was beginning to seep into the room. Lorenz was gone, his side of the bed already cold. Randall was in the East going to school. Kendall had begged off schooling for one year to work with Lorenz on the ranch. Melissa was in her last year of schooling here on the ranch. She stretched again, knowing she should move and dress for breakfast. Conchita knocked on the door and entered.

"Breakfast is almost ready. Do you want a bath afterwards, Senora?"

"No, I do believe I'll save that for this afternoon. It's going to be a warm day." She swung her legs over the edge. "For now I'll just wear my robe and you may do my hair afterward."

Toni had reason to regret her words. The day was "warm." So warm it felt like summer. Strange, this was January: January 12, 1888. It should be cool at the very least. This was the time for sewing clothes for the coming season before the work of planting the gardens arrived. Time to write long letters to friends before the rhythm of ranch life went back to working from morning to night. Not that Toni did physical work from morning until night, but she oversaw the servants who did, saw to their needs, and ran the ranch during Lorenz's absence.

She asked for lunch on the back porch to watch the men breaking the almost two-year-old horses for ranch work. She looked up as the cook approached.

"Senora, do you still want your coffee out here?" Josephina spoke in Spanish.

Startled Toni looked up and realized she was growing cold, the wind stiff and unpleasant. She had been thinking of those long ago pleasant rides with

Daniel, his body so much a part of the horse it was pure pleasure just watching him. She stood. The wind seemed to be coming from the east and then from the north. How strange.

"No, Josephina, I'll take the coffee inside. Please take the tray with y'all."

Before following Josephina inside, Antoinette walked to the north end of the porch and gasped at the black, roiling clouds that seemed to cover the sky at a 180 degree curve. Something is wrong flashed through her mind. Where is Lorenz? Yes, he'd gone to their western section where the railroad was coming through. He had said something about checking on the crew's progress and moving the herd out of the way. Quickly she entered the house as the temperature seemed to verge on freezing. How could it drop so rapidly?

She had entered by the back French doors and hurried through the long, sweeping hall that had once been part of the dining area. The staircase swept up from the front and curved to a large landing before turning to enter the hall dividing the upper floor bedrooms. Then a narrower staircase ran towards the newly added attic.

"Conchita, my shawl, por favor. I'm going to check on whether Mr. Mac-Donald has returned."

Before she could step off the front porch, she realized the shawl was inadequate and was about to turn back when she saw Lorenz pounding into the ranch yard. He saw her and raced his horse toward her.

"Keep everybody inside! I stopped at the school and they are all coming here. Tell the people inside to stay there or to go get their children if they have any. This one is bad. I'll get men and the Rolfe boys started on bringing in wood after they put up their horses. Y'all better order several large pots of beans for tonight." He yelled his words and whirled the horse to head towards the barn.

Toni looked down the lane and saw the younger Rolfe boys, Ernest, Kasper, Fritz, and Teddy, riding in with set faces. Melissa and Arthur Plank were riding double with Ernest and Kasper. Melissa slid off at the fence and helped Arthur down. Together they ran up to the porch.

"Mama, y'all should have heard Pawpaw shouting at everybody." Melissa had started talking at nine months. Papa had come out as Pawpaw and so he remained. Her southern accent was almost as thick as her mother's. "He says we are to stay inside and do exactly as y'all say."

At fourteen, Melissa was planning to go to Saint Louis or New York for school. Antoinette had not decided which. Melissa was a replica of her mother except her eyes were as grey as her father's and she stood five-foot five; tall for a woman in 1888.

Five-year-old Arthur looked upset. "Daddy will come for me." He took off his hat as they entered the house.

Toni blanched at the idea. Dear God, I hope Gerald has enough sense to stay home if it's as bad as Lorenz says, she thought, and then there was no time for thinking.

For a moment even the wind held its breath. Then the wind slammed against any creature still outside while pounding them with tiny, tiny pellets of hard, frozen snow; not ice, but tiny, compacted snow as fine as flour filled the air so thickly that within ten minutes the landscape changed from the brown of a prairie winter to a billowing, white sea. Drifts were piling up and stretching out, adhering to the side of anything facing north or northwest. Landmarks disappeared under the onslaught; men bent over trying to move against its force lost; any child outside was soon lost and frozen. Horses had sense enough to turn their backs to the wind and many would survive. But cattle? The cattle from parts of Texas into Canada stood or lay where they were as placidly as ever while the snow covered them and froze their nostrils shut. People fortunate enough to make it inside lit their fires and pulled their blankets around them as they waited and waited.

* * *

Toni blinked her eyes against the dark and realized the snoring from the other room had awakened her. Who was in her house? Before panic could over-whelm her, she remembered the events of the last two days.

"We're bringing all the mattresses downstairs and closing the upper floors off." Lorenz had announced after they'd taken turns eating. Most had eaten at the large kitchen table. The Rolfe boys and Arthur Plank had joined them at the dining room table, and then after they'd finished two of the hands and the rest of the Mexican family members who had not fit at the kitchen table were served.

"And all of the chamber pots," Toni quickly commanded. "We can sit them outside the kitchen door on the porch."

That method proved futile as the wind threatened to throw the empty pots skyward or smash them into the wall if a person let loose of the handle. That left the living room, the secluded room for their baths, Lorenz's office, or a blanketed off section of the kitchen. All were really unacceptable alternatives in Antoinette's mind as she could feature some hand with a bad aim ruining her floors or precious carpeting.

Lorenz solved the problem by selecting his office and closing the door. The two men, boys really, who had been carrying in the firewood looked at her with smirks and happily followed their employer's orders on retrieving the mattresses while Toni tried to issue orders as to which bedding to bring down.

"Honey, the warmest, and y'all and the women can bring it down." He turned to the men. "Put your coats on. We're bringing the rest of the wood in that we can and putting it in the office too. We'll use a rope tied to the door and to each other to keep from getting lost out there."

Now she lay here in the darkness, Lorenz asleep beside her, their son and daughter, and Conchita on mattresses in their bedroom.

After two days, the smells from all those people were disturbing, and the cold cut through everything. She found herself praying for those out in the bunkhouse, for their headman and family, the teachers in their own home by the school, and the Mexican families that stayed in their cabins. It was obvious the beans and stew had not agreed with everyone's system, and Toni's prayers turned towards asking for sleep. It was cold, too cold to think of moving and, as Lorenz had warned, the wood had to last for cooking and heating when people were out from under the covers.

The sounds of people snorting, farting, moving, closing doors, and talking woke Toni. She slid out of bed, put on her dressing gown, and wrapped the top blanket around her shoulders and headed into what had been her bathroom. Conchita was there using the chamber pot.

"I'm sorry, Senora, but there is nowhere else. The woman stood, embarrassed as the sound and odor of her morning wind filled the room.

Toni looked at the chamber pot and knew it would hold her urine, but that was all. She set her lips and went looking for her husband.

"Lorenz, the chamber pots must be emptied. They are filled and I will not have people using our floors."

"Honey, how do y'all propose we do that?" Lorenz tried to keep his voice low. "Snow is blocking every window and several of us already tried the front and back doors. They won't open."

"You all can go through the French doors to the back veranda. I moved the blanket from over the doors to look out and the snow is not as deep there."

Lorenz realized that as usual, Antoinette was right for the wrong reason. Unlike most Texans, she had not objected when he had their Lutheran trained teacher include the ranch hands' children. He had to abide by the custom of sitting the Mexican and black children in the back, but Toni did not want her servants to be ignorant. If they were to be "more genteel," they needed a certain amount of education. The studies that his father and grandmother plied him with over the years stressed that sanitation was paramount. The livestock in the barn would be getting desperate and he needed to check on the men caught in the bunkhouse.

"I might have to break one of the doors if they are frozen tight."

"We can put another blanket or feather tick over it until the cold goes away and we replace it." She was standing tall and her eyes had a glint in them that Lorenz rarely saw.

"All right, I'll get my coat and take one of the men."

"And make sure you all carry them far enough away from the house." She gave the last order to his retreating back.

A grinning Kendall ran upstairs for his own gear while his father went into the bedroom to retrieve muffler, hat, and a warmer coat. He was going out. No way was he staying inside.

Chapter 16

A Frozen World

Lorenz, Kendall, and the hands caught in the main house used gloved hands and cooking utensils to hack their way up and through the drift to stand on the top. The Rearing Bear Ranch buildings were almost buried on the northern and western sides. Gone from sight were the fences, the trunks of trees, and the extra horses where before one saw fenced pasture. No matter the direction they turned, it was a land of white: pure, glistening and blinding. Smoke ascending from the heaped over, now melting domed white roofs showed there were still people alive, fighting off the cold until the snow went down.

"Start taking the pots out behind the washhouse, and I'll check on those in the bunkhouse and quarters. Kendall, y'all give them a hand."

"Y'all will need help digging them out."

"I didn't say I was going to dig them out. Pray God it warms up enough to melt this stuff." He did not want to look at his land. He knew what lie underneath and there was no one to blame, no one upon whom he could seek vengeance. Right now he wanted his son inside and safe. He turned and started to direct Kendall to return to the house when he saw the puzzlement build in the boy's blue eyes looking directly into his.

At sixteen, Kendall was as tall as his father, and had begged off going back to the Veterinarian School in San Antonio. "I've learned enough. I can go back in another year. I'd rather work the ranch with y'all, Pawpaw."

Lorenz sensed that Kendall, unlike Randall, was desperate for his approval; but damn it, Kendall's cells wouldn't regenerate like his. He drew his breath inward, the cold cutting at his lungs.

"All right. Let's go check on the hands."

They worked their way over the drifts and to the northwest, striking mostly westward to miss the barn and the water tank. Lorenz could see the roof of the washhouse, but the outhouse lie buried below the snow. During the slow struggle to reach the roof of the bunkhouse, they saw a land of white waves punctured by tree tops cloaked in whiteness. The back of the barn, like the house, had less snow and offered an entrance. Once he looked at the bunkhouse, he realized the barn was first; the men could wait, the remaining livestock, if any, could not. Smoke drifting up from the bunkhouse chimney proclaimed that the hands were alive. The desperately needed shovel was inside the barn.

The cattle inside the barn were bawling in hunger, but the north entrance was blocked by a drift as high as the roof. They made their way to the east side where the drifts were smaller. The door to the horses' stalls was a Dutch door. The bottom could remain fastened while the upper opened for air. It took a couple of blows to push the bar upward. The noise alerted the animals within. The horses began whinnying and pawing against the stalls. He and Kendall used their knives to pry the partially frozen door open to be able to climb through the upper half.

The horse closest to the door aimed a backward hoof at them, and Lorenz was thankful they'd tied them in. They skirted the horses and walked into the front portion where the cows greeted them with renewed bawling.

"Grab a pitchfork, son. It's their turn to eat. We'll figure out water somehow. Then we'll take the shovel and see about the men. We need to milk them as soon as possible or they'll be ruined. I don't want another dead cow."

Everything else that day was in slow motion; carefully wading through and across the drifts, praying they wouldn't collapse; digging the men out, and sending them over to the family area to check if those people were all right. Once done they retreated to the house for Kendall's face was becoming white from the cold.

"Fool kid," Lorenz muttered to Toni that night. "He wouldn't keep his face covered."

"Don't fret, darling, we wrapped his face in cool, then warm towels. He's young. He'll be fine. I'm so glad y'all got the bunkhouse open. Do y'all think the rest can go back to their places tomorrow?"

"It depends on the temperature, honey. If the snow drops enough I'd like to get our godsons back to Martin before Brigetta comes tromping through the snow after them."

"The same goes for Artie. Gerald and Emily must be absolutely sick with worry."

Lorenz was sure that Gerald wasn't sick, but the man had to be worried. To the relief of everyone the rising temperature the next morning was settling the snow downward. They bundled the two younger boys up as well as they could and once again Kendall accompanied Lorenz. Ernest, Fritz, and Kasper were on their own horses. Teddy rode behind Kendall and Lorenz had five-year-old Artie on his horse in front of him. Normally the ride to Rolfe's took less than an hour. Today it took over two. Martin and August, clad in coats and mufflers, met them halfway.

"By God, glad to see you all are still alive." He smiled broadly and took Teddy on his horse, settling the boy in front of him.

"Same here, Martin. How's Brigetta and the rest? Did everyone make it back to the ranch?"

Martin grimaced. "A couple of the hands didn't. Marty and two others are out looking. They found the one just a few feet from the bunkhouse. We don't know what happened to the other one." He glanced around the white landscape. The high hills to the East were covered with snow, some of the trees just barely showing trunks to create an alien world. "What about the cattle, Lorenz?"

Lorenz looked at him blankly. "They're dead, Martin."

Martin turned his face away. "We're busted," he muttered.

"We're alive, Martin. Y'all haven't spent nearly the money on house and furniture that we did, and we have enough to replenish our stock. Sure, it'll be a smaller herd. We'll have to upgrade the beef and build fences, but by God we're not busted and I don't think y'all are either."

Martin stared at him and he had no words. Lorenz realized that Martin's eyes were as cold blue as Uncle Herman's when Martin's father faced a dangerous situation. No wonder Martin refused to invest his money when Lorenz, MacDonald, Grandmère, Margareatha, and Red formed the MacDonald Corporation complete with a bank in Schmidt's Corner. Martin was a hoarder of money. They turned their mounts towards the Rolfe ranch.

No words passed between them until the Rolfe's turned into the lane leading up to the main house. "No need for y'all to come in. It's still a long, cold ride into Schmidt's Corner. Any word for Brigetta from Antoinette?"

"Yes, Toni says she will pay a visit as soon as the snow melts enough unless Brigetta drives over first." They smiled at each other at the thought of Brigetta driving a team. It wasn't likely. She hated horses, and Lorenz assumed she hated the cows too.

He and Kendall nodded their farewells and turned their horses towards Schmidt's Corner. They topped the second rise when they saw a man riding towards them. "Want to bet it's your Papa, Artie?"

Arthur straightened and waved. The approaching rider returned the wave. They kept riding towards each other, and as they met, Gerald gratefully reached for his son.

"I told Emily that you all would keep him safe and sound." He hugged the boy and set him in front. "It seems I owe y'all twice over for my life."

Lorenz shook his head. "The first time around was Chalky's doing. If he hadn't been so persistent, y'all would have still been in Arles."

Gerald gave a half-smile as he thought of his straw-haired, scrawny, and incapable of learning, cow trail dead brother. Chalky had died doing the one thing he could do. He was working the remuda when a stampede caught him. Gerald hugged his son again. If he worked hard enough, his son would never face those hardships.

"Emily gives her thanks also."

Chapter 17

Der Pastor Becomes The Shepherd

Pastor James Rolfe was returning to St. Louis, Missouri by train and his thoughts were on composing a sermon and controlling the jolting paper and pencil. He was in the last passenger car, the caboose swaying behind them. This car was reserved for the less affluent traveler and comforts were slim. The seats were hard and stiff, and filled with farmers, immigrant families, vagabonds who went from job to job, the less prosperous drummers, and clerks returning from family visits. There was a small, round, potbelly stove with a day's supply of wood at each end and a lavatory next to each stove. Since they were less than two hours out of St. Louis, the lavatories were in deplorable condition and most tried to avoid them. As usual, there were a few men less than sober, but they were gathered around the stove near the door leading to the rest of the train.

Most had shed their overcoats and were in their suit coats as the day was pleasant for January. The cold starting to seep through the windows shook many of them out of their apathy; all except Pastor Rolfe. He didn't hear the murmuring or see the mothers pointing at the sky. Men looked worriedly at their pocket watches—if they had one. The conductor entered from the caboose behind their car and the opened door spewed cold throughout the compartment.

"Sorry, folks, but I need to go forward and check on weather conditions. I should be back within fifteen minutes." He hurried through, blasted everyone again with the opening of the second door and vanished.

James looked up, frowning slightly. He did not like being interrupted while composing. Before he looked down again he saw the black sky closing around them and started to stand when another blast of air from the opening door and two of the drunks around the stove rushed out.

"Rats deserting the ship." One man with a bulbous nose announced.

And the snow began to fall. Fascinated, the people watched and then grew worried, excited murmurs grew in volume as the landscape disappeared and the drifts piled higher and higher. The train slowed and ground to a halt. Women began to whisper to their husbands to go find out what was going on or how long would they be here. Men were milling in the aisle, putting on their heavier coats, starting for the door, and then returning when the other door to the rest of the train was locked.

"We ain't wanted."

"Let's organize and ram the door down."

"With what?"

"We can beat the windows open."

A chorus of assents went up and men began to look for the heaviest pieces of wood.

James felt his stomach tightened. They were fools. If they went out there, they would freeze or get lost. Where was the strong man to stop this foolishness? He searched the faces of each one, looking for a man like his father or Uncle Mac; and there was no one.

One man grabbed at another's food basket. The other objected. Fists began flying and then the two men were rolling on the floor while women screamed and children yelled. Men gathered around to cheer them on and they jostled and shoved to get closer. Others began yelling and threatening the others with their fists.

James sat white faced and realized he was the pastor; the man who was suppose to guide them. *Dear Father in heaven I am inadequate, help me. These people do not know me. What if they don't listen?* Fear knotted his stomach. His place was the pulpit where respect for his position was automatic. He took a deep breath and wanted to hold his hands over his ears when a man began screaming curses.

Instead, James boosted himself up on the seat and stood, proclaiming in his authoritative pastor's voice, "In the name of the Father, Son, and Holy Ghost, amen."

His strong preaching voice overrode the hubbub around him. "Let us first ask our Father in heaven for his blessing before we decide what is best for our survival."

Men hooted at the white faced man with the clerical collar.

"How would a pastor know?"

"First we turn to God in prayer." James's voice was firm, far firmer than his knees.

"Be you a Methodist? We don't pray without a Methodist leading us."

James ignored him and clasped his hands. He almost started in German and realized that these people might not understand. He began in English.

"Our Father which art in heaven..."

By the end of the prayer all had joined in, even the toughs by the door. The Catholics in the car hadn't intoned the conclusion, but James had chosen wisely. Everyone knew that prayer.

He looked at his impromptu congregation and began.

"My father was a fur trapper in the old days. When he became a rancher, he showed us how to survive when a blue northern blizzard suddenly hit when out on the prairie branding cattle." That James hadn't been present that day didn't matter. He'd heard the tale over and over again.

"We have wood and we are only a couple hours out of St. Louis. We'll be one of the first trains they hunt for, but we still need to make the wood last as long as possible. We can only put one log in at a time. If it gets colder, you'll have to put on every piece of clothing you have with you.

"There will be wood in the caboose. Before the doors freeze shut, we can make a human chain and bring that wood in here. We'll also need to see if the conductor left any food. If there is a pail or a pot in there, we'll need it too. People can survive without food, but we will need water." He pointed at the snow half-way up the windows and still rising.

"There's plenty of water out there. It's just in the solid form. If we fill up any pot that might be around, we can melt the snow by placing the pot beside the stove. The heat from the stoves should keep the doors from freezing. We'll take turns sipping the water."

"Yeah, and who's going to be in charge of the water?" One beefy man was still trying to understand why this slender, scholarly man was up there telling people what to do. "What if we are here for days?"

"As I said, we aren't that far from St. Louis. They'll have to come this way once things start to clear. This track will need to be cleared for the other trains coming to or out of St. Louis." Pastor Rolfe pulled in his breath and continued.

"Before we go to the caboose, I suggest we sing a song in praise of God who will take care of us. Does anyone have a favorite?" He couldn't believe he was asking, but it was doubtful if these people knew his hymns.

"Rock of Ages," someone called out.

Inwardly, James heaved a sigh of relief. It was one of the few songs in English he had memorized. He gave a "hmm" for the correct note and began singing, the people again joining in.

Once the song was over, James put on his coat and gloves. Somehow he knew he could not sit there and let the other men do the work. They joined hands to keep from slipping and went into the caboose, quickly passing the firewood forward. Like the wood in their compartment, it was enough for one day. The day had been warm and no one had kept the fire going. There was a large, blue enameled coffee pot, a smaller, dirtied pot with the remnants of the man's stew, and a half-eaten loaf of bread.

One man grabbed the spoon and started to eat the stew.

"No," James stepped in front of the man. "There may be someone who needs it more. There are women and children in there. Divide that between the children or the expectant mother. We are the ones responsible for them."

The man looked around and saw the others nodding in agreement and a sheepish look came over his face.

"I was jest cleaning it out sos we could melt snow."

"We can put snow in it once the children are fed." The image of his nearly one-year-old twins rose in his mind and he prayed they were all safely at home. He could not think about them now. His work was here.

A quick check of the caboose produced two blankets, another lard bucket used as a lunch pail, a thin pillow, and a mattress and blanket from the daybed. All were transferred into their passenger car. The blowing snow was filling the space between the caboose and their car. It was a relief to be back in the semi-warm compartment and close the door.

The meager remains of the stew were given to the two skinniest children and the too-thin expectant mother. Her eyes were fearful and her skin an unhealthy pallor.

There was no way to clean the pot out, but the door was opened one more time to fill it with snow and then slammed shut. Pastor Rolfe saw two more lard buckets (probably used for someone's lunch) filled with snow set by each stove.

Good, thought James, someone had the sense to fill them. Snowdrifts were blocking the windows and the light became dim and dimmer, making it difficult to see inside or out. James wet his lips before making his suggestion.

"We can pass the time by singing hymns."

Once again the impromptu congregation sang. Finally, someone suggested Oh, Suzanna and a round of popular songs followed.

By consensus people quit singing and gradually grew quiet.

"Okay, Reverend," one man snarled, "who gets them blankets?"

James stood. "One of the things my father taught me was that when trapped in the cold, people must sleep together. Your body heat will stay higher when next to another body. For families that is easy. You can spread your overcoats over each other. I suggest for the single people, two men in each seat, for the single women, two women together. That way you share each other's body heat." He did not add the part about sleeping nude together wrapped up in blankets. It was a solution that would not sit well with these people.

James looked at the expectant mother and she was shivering in her thin coat.

"Why don't we let her have one of the blankets? She is trying to create warmth for another. Whoever is selected to tend the stoves will have the other and the mattress."

Somehow everyone got squared away and covered. Pastor Rolfe helped with the children and then offered to tend the fires during the night when no one volunteered. No one wanted to lose their seat closest to the stove, any blanket, or heavy overcoat. Pastor Rolfe found a spot on the floor and put the mattress close to the stove. He burned his hand twice while opening the stove doors and putting in the one log. His sleep was fitful and in the morning the cold woke him.

It was another day in the dim lit area; people complaining of hunger and thirst; people complaining about the stench coming from the lavatories. The lavatories were simply seats with holes cut in them and the earth absorbed the droppings as the trains rushed onward. Here it just piled up and froze.

By the middle of the day the wood was gone and the men began breaking up the seats, and the bitter cold left them with little energy to sing. A few joined

Pastor Rolfe in evening prayers and the rest joined in when the entreaty went out to the Lord for their rescue.

Pastor Rolfe was shivering badly when dawn broke, but he realized the snow was melting. Like the others, his lips were cracked and bleeding. Two of the men tried pushing the doors open to see what the temperature was outside and if there was any chance of finding wood. It was futile and everyone seemed to withdraw into their own little band to keep warm. Young children whimpered at times from the cold. Others ran like crazy to the lavatories and then ran back to crawl under the coats. The expectant mother kept her eyes closed and continued to shiver.

James tried again to lead them in song, but the effort was too much for the exhausted group.

"Look!" One boy who had pressed his nose against the upper corner of the window was pointing outside and yelling. "It's horses and wagons."

The men heaved against the door and it opened enough to allow one person at a time to squeeze through. Two of the men walked forward and returned in a few minutes.

"They're unloading the high-muckety-mucks first. We gotta wait inside our car, or we can't get on. Sure hope there's enough room."

Pastor Rolfe straightened. The expectant mother was gray-faced, her lips almost white. Occasionally, she would moan. This was not right. She should be among the first transported to warmth and safety. James went striding forward. He did not notice the snow sifting into his shoes, melting, and then freezing to the sock. Like everyone one else he was cold, so cold he didn't notice—at first. When he did notice, his determination to find a ride for the suffering woman was undeterred. He approached the man obviously in charge of overseeing the removal and seating of the passengers.

"There is a lady in the last car that is with child, suffering from the cold and is apt to have the baby before long. She is on her way to St. Louis for better care. I beg you in the name of our gracious and merciful Triune God to take her now. If it means the loss of a seat, I'll gladly stay here."

The comfortably clad, well-fed man looked with amazement at the shivering man of the cloth, with his not too new clothes and clerical collar.

"I'm sorry, Reverend, but I have my orders. We take from the front cars first."

"If the woman and her child die, how do you intend to explain that at the throne on judgment day?"

The man's face was already red from the cold and he was about to raise his fist when another man stepped forward.

"I can take the next sleigh. Put the woman into my place."

"Sir, I cannot. You would have to take her place in the last car. Let me warn you. That car will be bitterly cold. There was no coal distributed from the stoker's bin that far back. Gentlemen like you are too important for the likes of..."

"Enough! Since this car is empty, we shall take the coal from this car back to the other car with us. Is that suitable, Reverend, er, I don't know your name, sir."

"I'm Pastor James Rolfe and your solution is admirable. There are children there too."

"Mr. Matthew Anheuser." Their gloved hands shook.

"Follow me, Reverend Rolfe."

Pastor Rolfe was too cold to chide the man for using the English term showing respect for a Lutheran pastor. The thought of how much good the coal would accomplish until his group of passengers was rescued drove him on. Everyone in that car was cold, miserable, and hungry. They had shared what little food they had and tried to provide the water as necessary, but once the wood ran out the snow would not melt.

The well-fed man was still directing the loading when they reappeared carrying the heaped up coal bucket and another lard bucket put into service as an improvised basket.

"Mr. Anheuser, sir, I cannot leave you for the last wagon."

"Very well, I'll take the next wagon or sleigh. I expect to see your men back there for the lady in distress." He and James continued on.

"We are the closest train to St. Louis. That is why the wagons reached us so rapidly. It seems the entire mid-section of the country has been hit by this horrendous storm."

Pastor James shook, but it was hard to tell if it was from the cold or the news.

The people in the car stared with disbelief when they arrived with the coal. The expectant mother was wrapped as warmly as possible. Mr. Anheuser felt that carrying the coal was charity enough and he returned to the next wagon being loaded when the men arrived to transport the woman forward.

"Everyone will have to walk forward to the wagons. It will take too long to clear a path back here. We'll let you know when we are ready." One of the drivers yelled in at them.

Thirty minutes later a different man appeared and led the passengers forward through the snow and bitter cold. Someone offered James a drink of water. James noted they offered the other men whiskey, but they probably assumed a Reverend wouldn't touch the stuff. It didn't matter; he had ensured the safety of Mrs. Jensen, the expectant mother.

The trip back to town was almost as cold as the cabin, even with the wool blankets. People were numb and most of the women and children had to be helped into the station. The ladies of a Methodist church were there to greet them with hot coffee and soup. Pastor James's hands were still shaking when a young man tapped him on the shoulder.

"Sir, Pastor Rolfe, I have a cart outside."

Pastor Rolfe eyes were blank as he looked at the young man. His feet felt strange; almost detached.

"Your wife asked me to come here and look for you today. I'm your neighbor, Luke Wagner."

"Oh, yes, sorry, I didn't get much sleep the last two evenings." For some reason he was surprisingly grateful and vowed to tell Mina what a miserable excuse of a Christian he had been during her pregnancy. It was then the pains began; horrible knifing, needle sharp pains in his feet. He needed help climbing in and out of the cart and walking into his house.

* * *

Two months later Pastor Rolfe woke, unaware of where he was, his head and body were bathed with sweat, and Mina was sitting on his bed washing his face and offering him water.

"Where am I?"

"It's all right, James. Lorenz sent some medicine with Grandma. It just didn't come in time to stop the amputation. Grandma is with the boys now. You're in the hospital. The doctor says you are a miracle. He doesn't understand how the gangrene stopped. Don't be mad. I had to do something. Lorenz sent a letter for you to read when you feel better."

"What did they amputate? When? Let me up." Frantically, James felt at his arms, then reached for his thighs. He tried to push upward, but found he was too weak and he lay back panting, the pain starting in his feet and spreading upward. He seemed to remember days and nights of pain and fever. "They just took part of your right foot and the toes from your left foot." Mina was hiccupping sobs between her words.

"I couldn't get a telegram to Lorenz or Grandma any faster. Everyone was hit by that horrible storm. You read the papers when you came home."

She gave James another drink of water. "I had to put the liquid they sent in your water to get it into you. The salve I put on when everybody wasn't looking. Oh, please, James, say you are not angry because I used what Lorenz sent. I love you. I couldn't let you die."

James found the strength to reach for her hand. "It's all right," he was able to whisper. "I-I'm surprised Lorenz sent anything."

"Here, I'll read Lorenz's letter." She brought out the paper.

"Dear James, We are all praying this reaches you and Mina in time. You did an incredibly brave thing. I'm only sorry Uncle Herman isn't here to know what a brave man you are. Once again, our prayers are for your quick recovery. I hope you accept this in better grace than I did when you told me so many years ago that you all had been praying for my safe return.

Respectfully, your brother-in-Christ and your brother-by-marriage, Lorenz.

Chapter 18

The Bargain

Three days after returning the stranded children, Lorenz and Kendall rode towards the spring where the homesteaders had filed. Lorenz's and Kendall's saddlebags were filled with flour, beans, and rice. From Lorenz's saddle hung an axe, and from Kendall's a miner's shovel. Kendall had almost stayed at home, and then decided he wanted to watch and listen. He would have lots to report to Marty.

"Why are y'all taking that food to the homesteaders, Pawpaw? That'll just help them stay."

"Maybe, maybe not, but it doesn't matter. I won't have people starving to death on my land."

Kendall almost reminded his father that the government considered it the homesteaders' land, but held his tongue. Neither he nor Randall had ever won an argument with his father. Only Melissa could win and she never had to argue. It was like she never even spoke. But then it was the same in the Rolfe family. Chrissie always got her way with her father while the boys worked all hours on the ranch whenever they weren't in school.

He thought about Chrissie while they were riding. She always seemed more like a sister than Melissa. After all, her middle name was the same as his grandmother's, and he had spent as much time teasing Chrissie as his own sister. Melissa wasn't any fun to tease. She didn't cry or scream. She would just look at him with those cold, grey eyes like their father's and say, "I'll get even."

Strange. A little more than a year younger than he, Melissa would prove an annoying antagonist as she would get even. "Even" meant anything from ants in his clothes to extra salt on his food and he couldn't tell on a girl.

Chrissie ran, screamed, or cried when she was little. Lately though, Chrissie would giggle and say things like, "Oh, you!" Then she would giggle some more. Plus, he noticed it really wasn't safe to be around her. She wanted to hug, and he would find himself more than willing to hug. Once, when his father caught them inside the barn, Lorenz cautioned him about being alone with Chrissie.

"Y'all might want to back off until y'all are a bit older. I'd hate to see y'all married and raising children before the age of eighteen."

Kendall had protested his innocence while he father just looked at him, those grey eyes filled with amusement and not really believing him. But it had been sobering. He realized he would have everybody mad at him if he did do something stupid and there were times when he definitely had wanted to do what men do. Why hadn't his father taken him into Arles to the sporting house? Tom Jackson had taken Thomas once. 'Course Aunt Olga didn't know anything about it. And Marty had been there too without Uncle Martin knowing about it. Marty had to use his own money though 'cause Uncle sure wouldn't let loose of any.

They rode steadily, picking their way through snow covered ground, going ever higher. Three times they had to dig through the drifts rather than let the horses ruin their legs by going through or being cut on the sharp edged branches hidden underneath.

It was close to noon when they rode into the yard. The two Gavin men were taking what remained of the corral and carrying it into the house. They both stood stiffly at the door looking at them with hate-filled eyes. Frank Gavin moved in front of his son before he spoke.

"Come to gloat?"

Lorenz felt his shoulders straighten. "No, we came to bring food and to see if you all were still alive. We've flour, beans, and rice in these saddle bags if you all need it. The way into town is still snow filled. I don't think a wagon could make it."

For a moment need argued with pride and need won. "We thank you, but I'll have to ride into town anyway. Our young 'un caught something in this cold and he..." Gavin swallowed. "He's dead." The voice was harsh. "I am obliged for the food."

"Mr. Gavin, I, we ask the Lord to bless your family and ease your sorrow. We'll be glad to give you all a hand with the wood."

"Much obliged."

The house was little more than one room with a rope for a blanket to divide the space. The blanket was missing, probably put to use during the cold thought Lorenz. Mrs. Gavin was sitting in the rocker, holding the dead two-year-old Bernard in her arms. She had wrapped him in a shawl and her eyes had a flat quality. Her hair was uncombed. A blanket was wrapped around her hunched shoulders and the dead child. She looked straight ahead at the door as they entered and did not see them.

"Mrs. Gavin, these nice folks have come to pay their respects and give us a hand." Frank Gavin tried to rouse his wife, but she continued to look straight ahead, her eyes blinking every so often as she rocked back and forth.

Elias, the seventeen-year-old, hurriedly put some wood in the cast iron cooker that served as the kitchen range and the stove for heat.

Lorenz took off his hat and quickly looked at his son before he spoke. Kendall promptly removed his hat.

"Ma'am, I know y'all must be suffering with a grief I cannot understand. My son and I offer y'all our deepest sympathy and our prayers."

The woman's eyes did not widen, nor did she speak.

"She ain't said much since little Bernie died." Mr. Gavin's voice was thick as he continued.

"I do thank you for the food. You know you've won. We'll be leaving as soon as we can earn enough for a horse to pull us down the hill."

"That doesn't mean I win. The county agent in Arles will just send some other hopeful soul or family up here with a bunch of lies about how good the land is for farming. The next one might not be an honest man and try rustling my cattle for his income. I'd rather stake you until you proof up your claim. Then I'll buy all six hundred and forty acres and your buildings. Y'all would come out of it with about three hundred dollars. That's enough to take your family where there's farming land and y'all can buy your place."

"That's tempting, but it's not legal."

Lorenz's smile was tight. "It is if folks think y'all can't repay the loan the bank has given y'all to keep farming. I'll cover the loss at the bank too and make it five hundred dollars. That means if y'all give up farming, y'all could buy a real house in a town."

"Yes."

They all stared at Mrs. Gavin. She was looking at Lorenz, her face and lips white, her eyes almost feverish. "And my baby gets buried in your graveyard among good folk."

Lorenz nodded his head towards her. "Yes, ma'am, y'all are welcomed to a grave plot. I'll even have Mr. Jackson build the coffin for him. I just can't let y'all believe that only "good" folk are buried there. It's a town graveyard and some of them are there because they tried to kill someone in town."

"Isn't your mother buried there?"

"Yes, ma'am, so are my brother, cousin, and uncle. It's where Tante Gerde, Mrs. Schmidt, will be buried too."

"Then that's settled. We'll bring him down as soon as the road is clear." She closed her eyes and rocked backward; then opened her eyes as she rocked forward. The empty look returned to her eyes and she continued her swaying back and forth.

The men walked outside, glad to pull clean, cold air into their lungs.

"She's been like that since last night. I'm sorry. Elias and I will bury Bernard here tonight when she's asleep."

"Mr. Gavin, the ground is still frozen solid. I'll get word into town and we'll get a wagon as close as possible. I'm praying she'll be all right as soon as she knows the baby's properly buried. Tell her a Baptist minister rides through here every three months or so. We'll let you all know when he's there if you all would like a Baptist service."

Lorenz stuck out his hand. "I'd like to shake on our agreement."

"How do you know I'll keep my part of the bargain?"

Lorenz's smile was wider. "Because, sir, y'all are an honest man, and we've made a gentlemen's agreement." He nodded at Kendall after the two men shook, and they mounted their horses.

Gavin's voice was bitter. "You know I've lost all my livestock. Had you counted that in?"

Lorenz settled into the saddle. "Yes, sir, I did. Most of my livestock died too."

Kendall waited until they were out of earshot and asked, "Why did y'all do that, Pawpaw?"

"That family just lost a child, and the woman has almost lost her mind. This way they have hope and they'll let me buy the land. It's the Christian thing to do."

"Yeah, but is breaking the law when y'all stake them and then buy the land Christian?"

Lorenz turned toward him. "The damn government is putting too many laws on the books. It used to be men were free out here, and no one questioned whether that spring and range were part of the MacDonald's range."

Chapter 19

Christina in Love

"Christina Anna, where are you?"

Brigetta was shouting in German. She'd already checked every hiding place in the house and in the washhouse. The spring day was growing warmer. The billowing clouds chasing each other across the blue Texas sky were lost on Brigetta. She was too busy searching for her daughter to look skyward. It was ironing and housecleaning day, and the morning half gone. Sixteen-year-old Christina would ride in the morning, but she always returned to help with the cleaning and food preparation.

She trudged upstairs one more time to check Christina's room, knowing what she would find or wouldn't find. Brigetta made a hasty survey through the armoire and the small closet. She already knew which dress was in the ironing, which dress was in the wash, which dress Christina was wearing, and the spare clean dress was gone. Gone too were the extra pair of clean, cotton stockings, and other linens. Brigetta gritted her teeth. Did she now make a spectacle of herself running down to the one, old hand who doubled as a bunkhouse cook and general flunky and asking whether Christina was back? Or did she just send him after Martin and the boys to go after Christina? But where had Christina gone? Why? Christina had been moody and then suddenly full of song, singing in that horrible, chirpy soprano until one wanted to box her ears. Or else Christina would sit quietly sewing while deep, deep sighs filled the room.

Brigetta sat down and rapidly wrote a note to Martin in German. What did it matter who was with Christina? That was Martin's little girl and he would be furious. He had to know now. She walked briskly to the front of the bunkhouse where she knew John would be making futile attempts to appear busy.

"Du are to take this to Mr. Rolfe immediately. Vait it cannot. Be as fast as can be."

Brigetta marched back to the house and started the weekly ironing. As she grew older she had begun to appreciate all the help Toni had over the years and quietly had enlisted the help of one of the ranch hand's woman. She watched to make sure John left with some appearance of haste. She knew around Martin the man never appeared to dawdle.

Martin looked up as John approached. What was wrong? John did not ride that mule of his unless forced into it. He dropped the posthole digger and accepted the note.

John was swaying back and forth on his heels and watched his boss's face and lips tighten. He'd figured something was wrong, but hadn't gotten to the solution.

"Y'all want me to take a message back?"

Instead of an answer, he had Martin's blue eyes locked on his own.

"Who rode as a guard with my daughter this morning?"

John cleared his throat. "Well, I do believe it was that Ortega fellow y'all had doing the wood cutting fer next winter."

Marty was beside his father, hurriedly buttoning his shirt. Like his grandfather Rolfe, he sensed when something was not right. "What's wrong, Papa?"

Martin replied in German. "Christina has run off with Ortega."

Marty whirled on John. "Which way did my sister ride?"

John found himself confronted by another pair of cold, blue eyes. He stomach started upward. This man was dangerous and John had spent his life not having to confront danger.

"Uh, ain't quite certain sure about that, Mr. Rolfe. They could have gone towards Schmidt's Corner or maybe towards them dinky mountains where y'all get yore wood for winter. Y'all want me to take a look when I get back."

"No, I don't want anyone near where they might have ridden." Marty turned back to his father. "Papa, we're going to have to trail them and Grandpa died too soon to teach me much. We need Uncle.

"Kendall told Auggie that Uncle was finishing the deal concerning the depot today. I'm riding to the Rearing Bear and if Uncle's not back, I'll go into

Schmidt's Corner. Y'all get everything ready, horses, food, gear, and for God's sake don't go near their tracks."

He ran for his horse. Martin stood speechless; stunned by the vehemence in Marty's voice. It was like listening to his father. If possible, his lips tightened even more. He was a Texan. He would find those tracks and be on the trail by the time Marty returned with Lorenz. Let them find him.

Chapter 20

A Hanging

Lorenz was on his haunches, slowly moving back and forth across the ground leading off the Rolfe ranch. Marty was a few feet behind him and leading Lorenz's gelding and his own horse. The rest of the men were mounted, but well behind them waiting for a signal to move forward. Finally Lorenz raised his arm and Marty approached and handed him the reins.

Lorenz took the reins, grateful to stand upright. He'd been on his haunches for an hour or more this morning, and a night of sleeping on Martin's sofa hadn't improved his disposition. When he, Marty, and Kendall arrived at Rolfe's headquarters, night was already falling and Martin and his men had managed to foul up the ground for yards around.

"Sorry it took so long, Martin. I'm not as good as Uncle Herman."

Martin simply nodded. Neither Lorenz nor Marty had reproached him for mucking up the tracks, but he knew they were a day behind and now his little girl would be damaged goods in the eyes of the world. Listening to Brigetta cry all night had not helped.

Lorenz and Marty mounted their horses and the rest followed behind them as they led out. The group included Lorenz, Kendall, Martin and his three oldest sons, Marty, August, and Ernest. Jake Halen, a trusted, off and on Rolfe hand, rode with them.

The going was slow as Lorenz led them southward. Martin was certain that the two couldn't possibly be planning on going through Arles. Christina might not have wit enough to know that as Yankees, the Rolfe's and MacDonald's were a hated bunch, and a white woman with a Mexican would cause bloodshed, but Ortega should realize the latter. It was, mused Martin, one of the few times he had admitted that Christina might not be as bright as his boys or her mother. He wasn't even sure he should have blamed Brigetta for not keeping a better eye on her. He hadn't noticed anything and neither had his boys. They would have been the first to tease or accuse Christina if they had seen or guessed anything.

As evening approached Lorenz chose a camp nearly a day's ride from where he had nearly gut-shot his father almost twenty-three years ago. It was one of the few unfenced open stretches of river left and the river here wasn't much; enough to water your mount and wet your throat, but far better than a dry camp.

"Shouldn't we have pushed on? They can't be going on to Arles."

"Martin, I don't think they'll both go into Arles, but Ortega probably will to buy supplies. That'll take part of their day or longer. I'll be up by first day's light and the rest of you all can follow behind again. I have a hunch they'll be slower in finding water as they won't want to be seen until they are well past Arles. We'll catch up with them in less than three days." And that, thought Lorenz, is strictly a wild guess.

The next two days were almost as frustrating. Marty dogged Lorenz trying to absorb as much as he could about reading sign. Late in the fourth afternoon they found where they had camped. Lorenz motioned everyone to ride up.

"They camped here for longer than one night. Someone, I'm guessing Ortega, rode into Arles for supplies. They didn't move on until two days later We're closer, and I say let's keep going. Those clouds are starting to build in the south. If they bring in rain tomorrow, I could lose their trail for good if they decide to hit the main roads. My tracking was never as good as Uncle Herman's, but I'm betting they won't try the main roads until they're farther away from Arles."

"Let's hope to God you are right," Martin snapped in German.

The air and ground were still warm and rain was looking closer and closer. He ignored Martin's crossness, knowing that if this were his daughter he'd be just as relentless. They moved out in single file, the rest following him.

The next day at midmorning, Lorenz found what he'd been searching for: a mind connection. He no longer needed to trail, but couldn't disclose this fact by suddenly motioning them onward. Martin might not realize something was different, but Marty would. He could pick up the pace and did; he knew where the two were going.

They were headed for Mexico. Fool girl, thought Lorenz. Christina knew nothing about how to live in poverty. He dismounted less and less. At least the two had stayed off the road after trying to confuse anyone following them by riding on the road and then cutting off of it when they found a rocky stretch of ground. Ortega, like most men, didn't realize it took more than that to throw off a determined tracker. The wind grew brisker and he sent the thought command to find shelter early from the coming storm into Ortega's mind. He motioned Martin to catch up.

"Martin, I'm thinking they'll look for a place to camp early to keep out of the wind and rain. This country's been tame a long time. They might try to find a riverbank with an over hang, but that's not too safe in a downpour, plus, it would be on someone's land. It's more likely that they'll head for a rancher's line shack. Did Ortega say whether he's worked for other ranchers in this area?"

"Ja, he worked for Edwards' Triple E."

"Ask your hand, Jake, if he knows where the line shacks are located. I know he's worked for Edwards. If their prints swing in that direction, we'll ride hard."

For the first time in five days, Lorenz saw hope in Martin's eyes. Martin motioned Jake forward and the situation hurriedly explained.

"I can scratch you all out a map."

"Do so."

All three men dismounted and Jake took a stick and hurriedly scratched an outline in the dirt. "That's Edwards' land and his home. He put cabins here, here, and here. This one up towards the hills is actually the closest 'cause the other two are on the other side of the road."

Lorenz studied it briefly and nodded. "Thanks, that's probably where they're headed.

"Martin, do y'all trust my hunches?"

Martin looked at him dumbfounded, his face reddening. "Y'all ain't trusting to being like your mother, are y'all?"

"Not entirely, but these tracks have been moving towards the southwest. I think he's headed for shelter tonight and then riding hard for the border for the next two to four days before stopping for supplies again."

Martin's lips tightened and he nodded his assent.

"Let's ride."

"Jake, y'all lead the way until we're about a mile within range. Then I'll make sure that they are there. We don't want to scare them off."

Martin's eyes may have looked doubtful, but his chin was set, and he nodded. The men spurred their horses into a run. At nightfall, they stopped for a quick supper of jerky heated in water.

"I say we keep going if Jake can lead us in the dark." Lorenz glanced up at the cloud covered sky. "There's not going to be much light from the moon, but maybe it'll be enough since we'll have to go slow."

"We keep going." Martin's voice was hard.

Around midnight, Jake held up his right arm and Martin and Lorenz moved up beside him.

"It's about a mile or so from here. This ain't much of a place for us to bed down."

"It'll do. Martin, you all get some rest. I'll scout on ahead and see if they're there. I'll be back in a couple of hours for some sleep. Post someone as a lookout. I don't want one of Edward's men to start shooting, and we don't want to shoot any of them."

To his satisfaction, Lorenz saw smoke coming from the line cabin when he was near enough to see its outline and two horses hobbled nearby. He turned his gelding around and headed back to camp. Marty was the lookout and recognized Lorenz's whistle. He added his horse to the remuda and gratefully wrapped the blanket around himself before falling asleep. Lorenz had been asleep less than two hours when Martin shook his shoulder.

"Y'all are living dangerously waking a man like that."

"Ja, but Marty says it will soon start to break light." Desperation edged his voice.

A desperation Lorenz understood. Martin had but one thought: get Christina to safety. He couldn't disagree with him. Ortega had no intention of marrying Christina. He'd gleaned that much from Ortega's mind.

No one bothered with breakfast. They simply saddled the hobbled horses.

"Are we riding in or walking in?"

"Martin, I'd rather take Marty and sneak down there and wait for them to walk out. No one gets hurt that way. If Christina walks out first, he's yours."

"We'll follow slow like. If someone walks out fine, otherwise I kick the door in."

"Why not just open it? There's no lock on a line shack." Lorenz reminded him.

"It would make me feel better."

Lorenz pulled on his boots and rolled up his blanket. He joined the rest and saddled his horse. The younger boys were too skittery; too ready to fire.

"Put that revolver away, Kendall. I don't want it going off accidentally."

"It wouldn't, Pawpaw."

Lorenz looked at his son. The answer was too confident, too cocksure. Martin's son August was holding a rifle.

"Nobody rides with their guns out. We're not expected, and I don't want Christina accidentally shot. Now put them away."

He ignored the sick look that crossed his son's face. Kendall's practice with guns proved his natural abilities. His aim was deadly, but when a group of men started shooting at a building, anyone could be hit. Fool kid crossed his mind.

"I suggest we ride in as close as possible without being seen. We can put Kendall and Ernest in charge of the horses and we'll sneak up close. With luck, we can grab the first one that comes out. If not, we'll take Ortega when they come out ready to ride."

Martin swallowed. "I can't think of anything better." He looked at Marty who was swinging into the saddle. Marty looked back at the group.

"Uncle's right. We don't want Christina hurt any worse than she already is."

The land was rolling prairie with only an occasional oak or juniper. There were no high hills, gullies, or natural lines of shrubbery to hide a man. They stopped about a quarter of a mile away and handed the horses over to the two youngest. Kendall protested.

"Ernest can handle the horses by himself. I'm sixteen now."

"He's right." Martin looked at Lorenz. "We want as many people around that cabin as possible."

Lorenz gave a curt nod. Why was it, he wondered, a man may have been deeply involved in violence at a young age, but then did not want his children to have the same experience. Was the drive to protect the young that strong?

"Hunker down and move quiet." Lorenz gave the advice to all but Marty. "Nobody draws a gun or jacks in a shell unless we're fired at. When we're close, try to find a spot that hides your body."

Light was breaking through the thick clouds as they moved through the new prairie grass, not yet really tall enough to hide them. All of them understood that dawn's grey light could play tricks with the eyesight and not reveal as much as daylight. Lorenz wondered if they'd ride today or wait out a rain. Probably ride as they would not want to be caught on Triple E land.

The line shack was several slabs of grey wood with a door and no windows. Metal roofing provided shelter from rain. This one had a stovepipe sticking up through the roof, but no smoke billowed upward this morning.

The door opened and Christina walked out and looked around for a place of concealment while taking care of nature's demands. Her blond hair hanging loose around her shoulders and down to her waist was a shock to Marty and his anger emptied bile into his mouth. He hadn't seen her without braids in years. No decent woman let anyone but her husband see her with her hair down.

Christina's light blue eyes looked for a tree or a bush in any direction. She finally decided upon the higher grass where Lorenz lay prone in a depression between the swells and ebb of the land. She walked rapidly as she hugged her shawl around her shoulders.

Ortega stepped out of the door and walked a couple steps, unbuttoned his fly, and brought out his penis to relieve himself. As he began the morning ritual, Lorenz rose and pulled Christina down. Marty, positioned on the east side of the shack, stood with his rifle pointed at Ortega.

The man had enough presence of mind to start to move backward, still spraying out his liquid when Marty shot at Ortega's hands. Blood spurted as Ortega screamed, and Marty moved closer, a tight lipped smile of satisfaction on his face. He hadn't emasculated the man, but Ortega would feel pain from the organ that violated his sister until he swung. And Marty fully intended a hanging would be next.

Christina was flailing her arms and screaming, trying to get to Ortega. She ignored Lorenz's attempts to quiet her when suddenly Martin was in front of them.

"What have you done?" Martin shouted in German.

Christina's blue eyes where filled with tears and she stopped screaming Ortega's name long enough to scream, "Please, Papa, I love him."

Lorenz was still trying to keep Christina from running to Ortega and had her arms pinioned when Martin's hand cracked against Christina's face.

"What is the matter with y'all? He's a Mex."

Lorenz dropped his arms and Christina started stumbling towards Ortega.

Martin grabbed her and shook her. "Y'all are going home."

"Lorenz, get her out of here." He spun and walked back to where the others stood around Ortega shouting while he walked.

"Marty, get the rope."

Christina was holding her face, rocking back and forth, unable to accept the fact that her father had actually struck her.

Lorenz was almost as dumbfounded, but found his voice and shouted at Martin. "Y'all can't hang him here. That shot will bring Edwards men. We don't want a witness. Not with our boys here, and y'all need to grab anything they might have left in the shack. Kendall, y'all saddle Christina's horse for me."

Marty ran into the cabin and picked up the canvas bag the couple had used to carry their goods. He rapidly stuck anything of theirs into it. He picked up a petticoat belonging to Christina and realized it was stained with blood. The son-of-bitch, he thought. Hanging's too damn good. He set his mouth and shoved it into the bag to hide away his sister's shame. As he stepped outside he saw someone had tied Ortega's hands with a belt, the two-fingered hand was dripping blood downward to leave stains on the grass.

Lorenz and Christina were on her horse. "I'll send Ernest back with the horses. With luck we're out of here before anyone from the Triple E shows up. We need to head further north to where there's a bend in the river." He used his knees to start the horse.

He had no particular desire to watch a hanging, and wanted to prevent Kendall and Ernest from seeing it, but knew it was futile. Trying to stop the hanging was more futile. Martin was angry and Marty had that same dangerous, cold look of his grandfather. Even if he could convince Martin to hand Ortega over to the law for kidnapping, Ortega would still hang on the general premise that he was a Mexican with a white woman.

By the time Ernest brought up the horses, Ortega was being supported by Jake and Marty. The man continued to bleed and was sobbing. Between breaths he was pleading with his captors.

"Please, seniors, patron, please."

"Better stick him on his horse."

Once they were mounted, Martin turned to Jake.

"We thank y'all for the help. I want y'all to ride back to my ranch and tell Mrs. Rolfe that Christina is safe and we'll be riding in right behind y'all."

Jake nodded and hit the trail back. He was disappointed. A man stuck out on a ranch miles from the county seat didn't get to see many hangings. Of course, this way he couldn't testify against them either. He considered following, but gave it up. This country was too open and MacDonald had a reputation he didn't want to test.

They rode cross-country, fast and hard to avoid any travelers. Christina sobbing against Lorenz's chest calling on him and God to save Ortega.

Marty lashed his horse on ahead to make sure no one would be at the old campsite Lorenz had designated. It was spring and there were men out on the range stringing the hated barbwire, knowing it was the only way to contain the upgraded beef stock, cursing the man that invented it and the times that made it necessary. Some of the hands carried their own branding iron. Who cared what happened to a few strays? Maybe, with luck, they could acquire enough for a drive south to Mexico or north to Montana or Wyoming. Martin wanted to avoid them.

Marty reappeared and waved his hat as an all clear.

"Let's go." Martin's face was set, the words barking through equally set lips.

"Let me stay back here with Christina."

Martin swung in the saddle to face Lorenz. "Why? She needs to see what happens."

"She doesn't need to hate y'all to the end of her life. She already knows what happens."

Christina's sobs and hiccups were audible. Some inkling of the fact that her papa would not be dissuaded from his actions must have penetrated. Her blue eyes were tear filled, and she seemed unable to focus them on anyone.

"Uncle's right, Papa." Ernest rode between them. "It isn't any place for a woman. Mama wouldn't like it." Ernest wasn't sure he wanted to see this through, but knew his older brothers would never let him live it down if he backed away from avenging his sister. He'd seen Marty's face at the line shack and something was wrong: awfully wrong.

Martin nodded at Lorenz and led the rest to the riverbank and down among the willows and cottonwood trees. Ortega slumped across the horse's neck, his body was wracked from pain and weary from blood loss.

"Papa, that one has a good sturdy limb. I'll climb up and secure the rope." Marty pointed at the cottonwood tree branch that shaded part of the bank.

Martin loosened the lariat he used for roping and tossed it to Marty. In his mind, it was regrettable to lose such a fine rope, but the task needed a rope that was supple and strong. He'd have another one made.

They watched as Marty rode his horse over to the tree and swung his own rope up and over. Then he dismounted, slipped the rolled up lariat his father had tossed him over his shoulder, tied one end his rope to the tree trunk, and used the dangling portion to pull himself up. Once seated on the branch, he proceeded to tie off his father's prized rope.

"Let me know when the length is right. Bring Ortega over so I can adjust it."

Ortega looked desperately around and found the men were hard faced, the MacDonald boy wide-eyed, and Ernest unable to meet his eyes. He knew appeal would be useless and closed his eyes as though by not seeing, nothing would happen.

Martin led Ortega's horse beneath the branch and dropped the noose around Ortega's neck, making sure the knot rested under the right ear. "A little tighter make it," he yelled up at his son.

Marty finished tying off the rope and slid down the tree using his own rope as a guideline. Once on the ground he pulled his rope down, untied it before re-coiling it, and mounted. He moved his horse over to the group.

Martin backed his horse several steps, used his hat to slap the Mexican's horse on the rump, and yelled, "Hi ya yi," the ya yi ending in a sharp, almost yodeling yell.

The startled horse broke into a run. Ortega tried using his knees to retain a grip on the horse, but the pain in his testicles was too much and he slid off the back. He ended up dangling vertically from the rope, his body revolving in circles, while body fluids cascaded down through his trousers to hit the ground in a rush.

They stayed just long enough for Martin to make sure the man was dead. They left him hanging there with his pants split open.

"Let 'em see what happens to a Mexican when he messes with a white girl."

Chapter 21

The Telegram

Martin's last words as they parted to ride for their individual ranches haunted Lorenz.

"Who's going to want her now that a Mexican's had his way? What do I do if there's a baby? What did we do wrong in bringing her up?" He had expected no answer and had almost ridden off before Lorenz answered him.

"Y'all and Brigetta didn't do anything wrong. I'm sure our wives will know what do to if Christina does have a child."

The more he thought about it, the less he thought his answer to Martin was right. What if there was a baby? The world would consider it a half-breed and scorn them both. He knew he had to tell Antoinette the details and hoped she could provide some sort of solution. Right now he wanted coffee, food, cleaned up, and his wife. It was as though somehow she could pull him into her and cleanse him of all that was wrong in this world that didn't recognize him as a half-breed. To his biological father's people he would be classified as a mutant, an equivalent to half-breed or mulatto in their rarified world. Here in this world, his parentage didn't show in his skin color and no one could see his two hearts or realize what he could and did do with his mind.

Toni met them at the door with a tumbler of whiskey in her hand. "I've ordered your bath and your favorite dinner. Y'all can tell me all about it when y'all are bathing."

"Honey, I don't think I need that."

"Yes, y'all do. Kendall, y'all need to bathe before dinner too. They're heating water in the washhouse for y'all and your clean clothes are out there." She stood on her tiptoes for her son to kiss her cheek. "Now scoot."

She led Lorenz into the bedroom. "Y'all look rode-hard, darling." She closed the door before continuing. "Was Christina violated?"

Lorenz looked down at her. "I reckon it depends on what y'all mean by violated. Of course, she was. Damn it, woman, y'all know she went with him on purpose."

"We won't talk about that just now. Did you all hang him?"

Lorenz set his gear on the floor and his butt on the bed. "Yes, he's dead."

"Good! I was afraid y'all would try to convince Martin to take him to the sheriff." It never occurred to Toni's that Christina would not have been found.

"Poor Brigetta would never have lived down the shame of that."

Lorenz looked up at her in disbelief. "Poor Brigetta?" he repeated stupidly. After almost twenty years of marriage she could still baffle him.

"What about Christina, or the whole family for that matter? And what about the man that died because Christina chose to ignore every one of the social taboos of where she lived?"

"Well, what good would it have done to turn him over to the law? They would have just hung him after airing everything in public."

Both of them heard the women approaching with the warm water to pour in the tub in the adjoining room. Talking ceased and Toni smiled at him. Then she went to the wardrobe to pull out his clean clothes.

"While they fill the tub, I'll bring the telegram to read to y'all. We can discuss what y'all are going to do. I've already packed your bag."

"What telegram?" He was talking to a closing door. What the hell had happened while he'd been gone for a few days? Telegrams were for emergencies, for deaths, or for some other dire event. Rarely did they contain good news. He stripped off his boots and socks and then the rest of his clothes. Toni, holding the telegram, came back into the room as the maid on the other side knocked on the door.

"We're through, senor." They heard the other bathroom door close as the maid exited.

"Really, darling, y'all do need a bath first."

Lorenz didn't care. He pulled her close and hugged. She was his refuge, his safety, and she held him securely in her arms.

After a minute, Toni pushed him away. "Now y'all take your bath and I'll read this."

"Read it now."

"I will not. Y'all need that bath and y'all are not going to rush out of here until tomorrow."

"I could just take it."

"Of course, y'all could, but then it spoils everything."

Which he admitted to himself was true. He strode into the bathroom and settled into the tub. "Once we remake what we lost this winter, I'm putting running water in here and make it a real bathroom."

"And we would still have to heat the water in the kitchen."

He grimaced and used the soap to work up a lather in his hair, and then Toni poured water over his head from a pitcher to rinse it out. Years of training his hair to lie in waves couldn't stop the wet hair from going into short curls all over his head. Toni claimed it gave the sardonic expression on his face a cherubic quality.

"I still don't see why y'all won't let me do the same when y'all wash your hair, Toni."

"Because Conchita does it ever so much better, and y'all never get out all of the soap."

"Maybe I should have Conchita do mine."

"Hmph!" She dumped a second, much cooler pitcher of water over him.

"Hey!"

"Serves y'all right." She turned away and opened the cabinet to withdraw a bottle to freshen his drink for him. Then she drew up a chair. "Now y'all can finish bathing while I read this from a Mr. Jethro Collins."

Her words stopped his hand. "What? Why is he writing?"

"Well, if y'all will be silent, I'll read it." She peered over the telegram before reading. "This is to inform you that your sister, Margareatha Buckley, has lost her husband and children to smallpox. She was trapped by the snow for months and unable to bury them. The events have deranged her. She is now a danger to the town and herself. Cannot stop the authorities from committing her. Come as soon as possible. Jethro Collins."

Lorenz was standing in the tub ready to step out.

"Darling, do finish your bath. Y'all cannot do anything until y'all get to the train station and a telegraph office, and y'all are having dinner here with your family tonight."

"She saved my life twice over and didn't hesitate one minute."

"Y'all are not hesitating. Y'all are being sensible; besides, I don't really believe she'll let them commit her. Didn't y'all say she could use her mind to stop people?"

Lorenz had grabbed the towel and was drying himself. "Yes, but only one at a time. She can't stop a whole town or two or three deputies. She'll kill someone in the melee if she's truly deranged. I'll take the Scout and figure out someway to hide it once I'm there."

Toni looked at him as though he were the deranged one. "And how are y'all going to hide that thing? Someone might find it. And do y'all just intend to walk into town like a bum?"

"I'll sneak in at night if I have to." He was pulling on his fresh clothes while Antoinette looked at him helplessly. Usually he succumbed to her every whim, but this time she knew it was futile.

"What if someone discovers that, that flying thing, whatever y'all call it?"

"I'll take their memory." He walked into the bedroom and pulled on his boots.

"Well, are y'all at least going to take the trunk I've packed for y'all?"

"No, a small bag will suffice. Also some jerky and biscuits, if there are any."

Chapter 22

Mad Maggie

Margareatha woke to a mountain spring day spewing sunlight through the cracks in the shack's dingy, crowded interior. She focused sleep-bleary eyes on the opposite wall six feet away and sat up thinking about how much she wanted to sleep and how little she was able to sleep. When had she gone to bed? Dawn was starting to break when she stumbled in here. Jethro Collins didn't really want her sleeping in the storage shack, but screw Collins. He owed her for all the time she once spent on his inept attempt at keeping records for Red. Then she remembered why she couldn't sleep and doubled over clutching at her middle and groaning, "Why, God? Why them?"

The hurt inside was like it had been for months: a red hot iron claw raking up and down with a burning that never subsided.

With effort she threw her legs over the side of the cot, stared at the floor, and tried to pray. It did no good. All she could see was the cold, dead eyes of her little twin boys. Gone was the mischief in those blue eyes; gone, gone like the spark of adoration in Brent's blue eyes whenever he looked at her. Then she remembered the three of them laid out on her marriage bed staring upward at the ceiling.

She closed her eyes and pulled on her shoes, not bothering to tie them, and knocked away the crate she'd set in front of the door before opening it. For a moment she opened her eyes and rapidly snapped them shut against the brilliance of the afternoon sun. She didn't want to see beauty. She wanted...Dear God, she wanted her boys, her man, and they were dead.

Margareatha choked back a sob and marched towards the outhouse. She hated her body. Nature continually demanded she do the most mundane functions: eat and shit. She couldn't stop the process. She had considered suicide alone in that cabin with no way to bury her husband and her children; no way to walk or ride through the snow for help, but the instilled abhorrence of disobeying God's law and her own wicked desire to live thwarted any action. She opened the privy door and the stench was almost overwhelming. In a way, shitting was a punishment for her neglect. It was her fault. She knew it. She admitted it. Her arrogance in believing her children would have her immunity killed them. She should have had them vaccinated against small pox. Why had she been so blind? Dear God, forgive me. I cannot forgive myself.

Once she finished, her hunger drove her outward, but today she would not let herself eat. Today she would walk and walk and collapse. Then maybe she could die without the outright act of killing herself, the nuances of such an argument eluding her.

The fine dust of Carson City's early years mingled with the smell of sawdust hanging in the air was gone, but the stamp mills slamming down on ore to crush the rocks could still be heard day and night. None of these buildings were new. She practically ran through the town, through the poor quarters where women either jeered at her or made the sign of the cross for protection.

Margareatha did not know how far she walked. She could not have told anyone what the scenery was like except from memory. She avoided the roads and any place a rider, wagon, or lone prospector might be. She nearly stumbled over the pebbles by a small creek and realized she was thirsty, but this was not drinkable. The water was fouled with debris from a miner's sluice farther upstream.

She sank down on the red-orange ground and considered. Right now her body screamed for water. Margareatha could recognize the fact that her cells were trying to renew and repair the damage she inflicted on her body by her erratic eating, too little sleep, and too much brandy. She struggled back to her feet and for a moment reality hit her. She was too close to town. She had started too late. Here someone would find her, force water down her throat, and take her to the doctor. Then the secret of her two hearts would be out. Would they burn her at the stake or try to make an exhibit out of her? Either was a possibility. It would be best to return to town and prepare to walk or ride far enough away to hide from any passerby tomorrow. Right now she needed food and water. She swung back towards the town where the sounds from the stamp, stamp, stamp of the iron blows hitting the ore matched the pounding in her head.

She kept to the back streets as the quickest way to Red's saloon. Jethro Collins still ran it, but not the brothels. It wasn't that Red didn't trust Jethro. He felt Jethro was too soft hearted where the women were concerned. The back street also meant she avoided the stares or shouts from drivers of wagons for her to get out of the way, or the stray, truant child from running after her and chanting.

"Mad Maggie, Mad Maggie, feeds on maggots, mad, Mad Maggie."

Margareatha slammed the backdoor as she entered the back of the building, effectively waking the supposed guard Jethro had hired. What an incredible waste of money. Her mind held his as she stalked through the hall and walked to the bar.

"Where are the peanuts or the hard boiled eggs?" She snarled the question at the bulky bartender while ignoring every man and woman in the place. She also ignored the man wrinkling his nose at the smell of her.

"Sorry, Missus, but it's too early in the day." It was a lie. This was her regular time and he'd taken the edibles to the back. His boss was hoping she'd go elsewhere to eat.

"Bring me a brandy and send someone after a plate from Harvey's." She blazed the command at him with her voice and her mind, and she continued to use her mind to command him as she returned stare for stare.

"Uh, that takes money, Missus." The man was trying to edge away, his brown eyes darting from side-to-side as he realized he couldn't move his legs, and still her mind locked his with her command.

"Charge it to Mr. Collins. He keeps a running tab here, and hand me that brandy." She watched him pour the brandy. Smithers redirected the beer bucket carrying kid (hired for outside solicitation) to the restaurant for a plate of hash and gravy. He then handed over the filled brandy glass and the bottle.

Brandy in hand, Margareatha marched to the table nearest the door she just came in. It was an ill lit little table with two chairs, but it was quiet and later when crowded, people would ignore her. She could always slip out the back if things became too rough. She fished in her pocket before sitting down and pulled out a deck of playing cards. Once she was seated, she dealt out a hand of solitaire. This was her ritual during waking hours, one hand after the other; a mindless activity to while away the time while her mind dwelt back in the cabin, reliving every painful moment. She picked at the food when it was delivered, but the brandy she drank and drank.

Smithers sent a hurried note to Jethro, but Jethro ignored the plea to come in early until his regular time at the saloon. He was nearing sixty and the years of running this place, sometimes the sporting houses, acting as a rider-messenger across state lines when the written word was too dangerous, a gunny, and whatever other job O'Neal would assign had taken its toll. His hair was gray, his once slim body had developed a paunch, and he slept far later than when he was younger. A fight with Margareatha would mean a fight with Red or possibly the end of his employment; situations Jethro preferred not to happen. Where were her brothers? Damn it! He'd sent for them. Daniel was the closest, but at least one of them could have sent an answering telegram. Jethro pushed aside the swinging doors and went in, a smile plastered across his face as he greeted the regulars.

His eyes swung around the place, men were drinking, chatting, wandering in and out, and the night barkeep, Magnusson, was coming downstairs carrying a tray of empty glasses. That meant card games were in progress upstairs. The mine managers and owners preferred a quiet room, and he knew how to please. His smile faded as he saw Margareatha playing away, her bottle nearly empty and the cigarillo smoke curling up around her face. Damn. The woman must be well into her forties now, but her face didn't show it. Too bad she never washed it. Still, the slovenly dress and tangled hair gave the appearance of age and lost youth. Smithers and Magnusson were being swamped at the bar and he went behind the bar to handle the overflow. When Magnusson departed with another tray, he finally had a chance to talk with Smithers.

"What did she order for her meal?"

"Nothing. I just had the kid bring her some hash and gravy."

"Fine, we'll just let her be. If something happens, I'll be upstairs in my office."

He escaped from the smoke and the noise. Not that the smoke and noise didn't drift upward, but in comparison, it was relatively quiet; as quiet as it could be with the stamp mills running. He pulled out a cigar and started sorting the invoices, receipts, paid markers, and deposit slips. These would go to the bookkeeper tomorrow. With Margareatha incapable of doing the books, he had to hire someone. Certain bills of lading he would forward on to Red. It was an annoyance, but, Jethro reflected, O'Neal paid well, and there was always The Sporting Palace when he needed a female. Somehow those times seemed to come less and less. He began clipping the piles together when the sudden quiet below alerted him. He quickly headed for the door as he shrugged into his jacket. He hoped his bouncer was on top of things. Things weren't like the old days when it took two toughs to keep the peace at night. As he started down the stairs, he could see the crowd of miners gathered around Margareatha's table. Most were young men or new men in town who hadn't known her in the days when she dealt the cards and regularly cleaned out the best of players. Neither did they know that she would open her house to the sick. All they saw was a crazy woman who didn't belong in a saloon.

Chapter 23

Rescue

Two miners were standing next to the table where Margareatha played her endless game of solitaire. Dirt from the floating dust of the mines was ground into any exposed pore and under their fingernails. Their clothes were sweat stained and dust covered. The younger one was grinning and smirking, occasionally winking at those on the side. The older one's beard was streaked with grey and he bent over the table, raising his voice as Margareatha had ignored his first invitation.

"I said you're wasting your time with them cards. You need to come with me and enjoy the evening. Hell, I'll even buy you another glass of brandy seeing as how that one's almost empty."

Margareatha raised her copper eyes enough to flick a glance at the man. "Go away." She resumed her game.

He reached forward and grasped her left wrist. "Now, now, pretty lady, you've got something better to spend your time on: me."

Loud guffaws and cheers greeted that speech. The younger miner patted the older man's back.

"You son of a bitch!" Margareatha's right fist slammed upward into the man's Adam's apple as she screamed at him.

The man went to his knees, his eyes wild. In the now quiet room it was possible to hear his struggle to get his breath.

"Get him out of here." Rita glared at the others and resumed her game. "Smithers, I need another bottle."

The younger miner leaned forward. "You can't treat Caleb like that, you bitch. You need a lesson."

Margareatha glared at him, trying to use her mind to cause him pain when she realized she had drunk too much. This couldn't be one of those that could block her mind. He'd been drinking too. She almost giggled over that fact when she realized more than one young man was coming at her. What right did these snickering, pimpled-faced youths have to live when her own boys were dead? She grabbed the brandy bottle, stood, shoved the table at the closest youth, and slammed the bottle down on his head. She tried to break the bottle on the table, but the table had been caught by four hands and shoved back at her, and someone from the other side grabbed at her hair. She turned to meet that assailant when others grabbed her arms.

No one had noticed the cowman stepping inside the door and making his way towards the back. His progress was impeded by the men trying to get a closer look at the action and the nearer ones shoving back at the others. Their attention was further distracted by some of them reacting to the shoves with blows. The cowman found himself trapped between two combatants and swung his fist into the gut of one, whirled, and slugged the jaw at the next one. The crowd pushed him up against the bar. Instinct made him duck. A bottle slammed down on the bar behind him spraying him and the person in front with glass and liquid.

Lorenz pushed upward and withdrew his handgun. The person directly in front of him backed away, hands in the air and was promptly elbowed in the back. Lorenz used the opportunity to step away from the bar and used the barrel of the gun to whack at any head in his way. Finally the group of miners was too thick to dislodge.

He shrugged and fired a bullet into the ceiling at the same time Smithers let loose with a blast from the shotgun. Quiet descended over the groups of milling men. Some dropped to the floor ready to crawl behind a table or a chair, and others milled around uncertainly.

"Gentlemen, that is no way to behave." Lorenz held the gun at hip level to indicate he wasn't threatening them unless they moved toward him.

Bewildered Margareatha looked around, not recognizing his voice.

"Now, I want you all to step aside. Then Mrs. Buckley and I will go upstairs and visit with Mr. Collins."

"I prefer not to go upstairs. I wish to be left alone." Margareatha was seething.

"Mr. MacDonald, it's a pleasure to see you." Jethro hurried down the stairs. It had been years since he had seen Lorenz, but this wasn't Daniel. There was no mustache, and this man had a scar.

"Smithers, find one of my special bottles for my friend here and bring it upstairs. Men, why don't you give the lady and gentlemen some room before the night deputy gets here."

Jethro kept control and authority in his voice. He would have preferred inviting the two of them out of his place, but right now he had to get Margareatha away from the miners. He was smiling pleasantly at everyone as though the disturbance was too minor to bother with.

"This way, please." Jethro stood to the side for them to pass upward.

Margareatha was still dazed from the sudden violence, but the fumes in her head were dissipating and she doubled her fist to swing at Lorenz.

"Damn you, your three are still alive!"

Lorenz hastily dropped the gun into his holster and enfolded her with his arms. He couldn't believe the stench coming off her, but this was no time for remonstrations, and he pulled her close.

"It's all right, Rity."

"No," her scream was muffled. "It's not all right. My babies, my Brent, they're dead. That's not right, and I want my brandy."

"Shh, we'll order more. Come on, Rity. Mr. Collins is waiting for us." He used his mind and kept one arm securely around her to lead her to the stairs.

It was hell inside of her mind: dark, twisted, filled with sobs echoing back into his head and soul. He gritted his teeth, taking it one step at a time. Time seemed endless but finally they were at the top of the stairs, and he supported her down the narrow hall.

Jethro brought up the rear, thankful that Lorenz was here, but he wondered how the man could arrive from Texas faster than Daniel from Arizona. He did not ask the question, but said, "It's the first door on the left."

Step after step Lorenz led Margareatha into a decent sized room and Collins was closing the door behind them. Lorenz withdrew from Margareatha's mind and helped her into one of the armchairs in front of the desk.

"I want brandy, and I want my cards." Rita glared at him and Jethro.

"I've ordered my special reserve sent up. Smithers will be here shortly." Jethro went to the cabinet and took down three glasses.

"None for me, but thanks for the offer."

Jethro, a puzzled look on his face, turned. Lorenz was standing beside his sister, making sure she was settled. What kind of Texas cattleman refused a drink? Then the smell off Rita reminded him that maybe it was a good thing the man wasn't drinking. He wanted the two of them out of here. He smiled at Lorenz.

"Won't you be seated?" Jethro indicated the chair beside Lorenz and went to answer the knock at his door. Smithers stuck his head and the bottle inside.

"Here you go, boss man. Anything else?"

"Yes, keep everyone away from here. That means Melville if he comes by to check about the shooting. Tell him it was strictly for control and no one was hurt. Then offer him a drink."

He started to close the door when Lorenz interrupted.

"Have him send up a plate of food from somewhere. I didn't stop to eat." He withdrew a silver dollar and handed it over. "If I need something else, I'll square up payment before we leave."

Jethro looked at Smithers. "See if Sally is still serving and order something from there." He closed the door and threw the bolt home. "Now, if you don't mind, I'll join Mrs. Buckley in a drink."

Lorenz shook his head. "No, I don't mind. Right now I need to know if there is a hotel around here that will take us in."

"You, yes, her, I'm not sure." Jethro quickly splashed the brandy into a glass and handed it to Margareatha along with a new deck of cards. He didn't want her to start screaming. "You could try the Miner's Roost at the end of town, but I don't recommend that place." He had visions of this man or his father coming after him if things went wrong. He remembered too well the size of MacDonald. Of course, the man would be older now, maybe dead.

"She's been sleeping outside in the shed. I took her some bedding, but I haven't been able to convince her to clean up and change into something else. Why don't you take her back to the spread she and Buckley had? It's only three days…" Jethro's voice trailed away at the hard look crawling over Lorenz's face and the lip on the scarred side of his face curling upward.

"The hell with that! Y'all are going to order some food for Margareatha if she wants some, and then y'all are going to find a room for us in a decent hotel or we spend the night here. Y'all will be providing the bedding. Now which do y'all want?"

Jethro swallowed. "I'm not sure Mr. O'Neal…"

"O'Neal doesn't own this place. The MacDonald Corporation does. A fact y'all should be familiar with, and Mister, I am a MacDonald and part of the board. O'Neal just runs this segment of the corporation. Now y'all make those arrangements or someone else will be occupying your chair, guaranteed!"

Margareatha snickered.

Lorenz turned to her. "Rity, I've ordered dinner. Do y'all want something?"

She looked up at him and shook her head no, her hands continuing to slap the cards on the table. For a moment Lorenz saw the pain in her eyes and looked away.

"Do y'all have any idea when she last ate?"

"Smithers ordered her a plate about five. I don't think she's had anything since."

"Then get your man back up here. She's too thin."

Jethro rose. He disliked the man, but the job was easy and he was too old to ride for long miles and hire out as a gunny. "Beef stew and biscuits okay with you?" He kept his voice even.

"That'll be fine."

Lorenz watch the man leave. He didn't care whether he was liked or disliked. Right now he was hungry and worried about getting Margareatha to a hotel. He needed food before he went into her mind again if she refused to go to the hotel with him. That still left the problem of getting her back to the Scout.

Chapter 24

Anna's Boys

Sheriff Dougherty sat his cup on the desk when the man wearing a star entered. Years of watching men had trained his eyes to note this tall man wore a dust covered suit, good hat, expensive boots, and two very expensive pieces of hardware on his hips. The man politely removed his hat and nodded at him.

"Sheriff, my name is Daniel Hunter. I'm a town marshal for a small city over in Arizona and thought it best to check in with you before searching for my sister." He smiled briefly.

Dougherty also noted the wide shoulders, well built frame, and grey somber eyes that met his directly.

"Her name is Margareatha Buckley. Could you tell me where I might find her?"

Dougherty stood and continued looking at the man as he offered his hand.

"I thank you for coming here first. Your sister, I'm sorry to say, has created quite a problem. I'm preparing a deposition for the court right now. The community believes it is safer to have her committed and that will be done as soon as I get the doctor's notarized opinion. What was a straightforward case is now complicated. It seems another brother arrived last night and refused to even consider the town's solution. It was late, and I believe, we should have waited until this morning to present our findings to him. It's always best to have a family member sign the papers. We can, of course proceed without that."

Daniel stared at the man. Rita committed? Another brother? Which one beat him here, Lorenz or O'Neal? He felt his stomach muscles tighten. It didn't matter whether it was Lorenz or O'Neal. He didn't want to see either of them. Even more puzzling, how did either one of them get here before he did? Another subject he preferred not to dwell on.

"Perhaps it might help if you tell me why you believe Mrs. Buckley is insane."

"You may not be aware that she lost her children and her husband to smallpox during the winter. We've never had a snow like that. There was no way anyone could get in or out of where their ranch is located. When someone finally made it, they found her living outside the house in the barn with the horses and one cow, and the dead inside on one of the beds. The cold had preserved their bodies, and the ground was still too frozen to bury them. It took several men to subdue her and bring her and the bodies back to town for the undertaker to embalm them for burial. The doctor felt that sleep and food would cure her shock. It really was too much for a woman to bear, even one as big and strong as Mrs. Buckley. Mr. Collins offered her a place to recuperate, but things haven't improved."

Dougherty knew there was a great deal lacking in his recital and those steady, grey eyes burning into his weren't showing whether he was believed or not.

"I think it's wise if I were to talk with Collins or with whoever is here first before I commit to signing anything. Where would I find a decent place to eat and where would I find either Collins or the other brother?"

Inwardly Dougherty heaved a sigh. At least he hadn't been told no. This man looked like a hired gunny that wore a badge to keep the worst of the elements in a bad town subdued. He'd be able to deal with the other man. There was not a doubt in Dougherty's mind that the woman had gone mad through her experience.

"Any of the places along the two main blocks serve a respectable meal at a respectable price. According to the note I have here from the town committee, your brother and sister are in the St. Charles-Muller Hotel. Mr. Collins won't be at the Full Shot until about five or later. I can have someone direct you to his home if you like."

"No, thank you. I'll go grab some breakfast and then go see Mrs. Buckley."

Daniel was in a sour mood during breakfast. No one recognized him from years ago, but he'd been a kid then, not a man grown. If it was Lorenz, no one was startled by their resemblance. He'd have to check with the hotel clerk.

The hotel clerk tried to deny that Mrs. Buckley or anyone related to her was on the premises. Daniel leaned forward, his six-foot three body towering over the middle aged clerk, his grey eyes slate.

"Sheriff Dougherty told me they were here. Now which room?"

The clerk capitulated and Daniel walked up three flights of stairs. He preferred to have done with the whole business. He had little desire to see any of his white family and had responded to Collins's telegram out of a sense of obligation to Collins for all he had taught him so many years ago, and the fact that Rita had saved his butt from Red's assault.

He had tried to challenge O'Neal in Wichita the summer after the beating Red had inflicted, but MacDonald had interfered: MacDonald and Lorenz. The remembrance still brought bitterness to his mind. He had sent a newspaper hawking kid to deliver the challenge to Red and where he, Daniel, would be waiting for him. When he saw Red approaching, he stepped out. MacDonald and Lorenz stepped out from the sidewalk a few paces in front of him. MacDonald faced O'Neal and Lorenz had swung around to face him. He still saw the dust rising in the street. He could not forget the sight of that pulled up, crooked mouth of Lorenz's and the grey eyes looking at him so intently. MacDonald's rumbling words still rang in his ears.

"Mr. O'Neal, ye brutalized a young member of my House. My challenge tis before Daniel's as ye had been warned. Tis to a fight with fists that I challenge ye for that tis the weapons ye used against a laddie. Ye may fight me or apologize to Daniel."

He had tried to barge by Lorenz, but Lorenz was there in front of him, his voice flat and low.

"Don't try it, Daniel."

"Why?"

"For Mama's sake."

Lorenz's eyes never left his, and Daniel's hand started for his gun and then he froze. He could not move. He could see, he could hear, he could breathe, but he could not move or speak, and MacDonald's wide shoulders were blocking his view of Red. He could only wonder at how Red's face looked or the thoughts racing through his mind. Lorenz was in his mind again, controlling his movements, just as Lorenz always did whether in a physical fight or (Daniel was certain) to force Antoinette into marrying Lorenz. Daniel knew that to fight MacDonald would be folly; a conclusion that Red must have reached for he had heard the words.

"My apologies, Daniel. I was in the wrong. You had not been plotting against me or my sister. It was Lorenz. Perhaps it is him I should challenge."

Lorenz stepped back and started to turn towards Red, his hands moving down toward his gun butts.

"Mayhap ye had better thank yere God that I twill nay allow that. Ye twould die.

"Daniel, do ye accept Mr. O'Neal's apology?"

MacDonald had stepped aside, and Daniel remembered looking at Red. The man's face was flushed red and the copper eyes were half shrouded by the lids. He was swallowing and his lips were white. It wasn't the satisfaction he had sought, but this was something Red would live with the rest of his life.

"I will for now." He had swung on his heel and walked stiffly to his horse, mounted, and rode away vowing never to have contact with his white family again.

The letters started arriving three years later. News of his white uncle's death and then his white mother's death within months of each other; news of his inheritance from his uncle and mother; news of the corporation and bank that MacDonald, Lorenz, Margareatha, LouElla, and O'Neal had set up; news of his stock in the corporation; and news of his bank account where they kept putting money from dividends and interest. He had assumed that no answer and his vagabond life would stop the letters or they would lose track of him, but his assumption proved wrong. Now he stood at the hotel door and knocked.

"Who is it?"

"Daniel Hunter."

The door swung open and Lorenz's grey eyes stared at him, the right side of his mouth higher than usual.

"Daniel, thank God. Y'all don't know what a welcome sight y'all are." He put out his hand as though to shake.

Daniel stepped backward. "I am not particularly glad to see you."

Lorenz straightened and his shoulders bunched.

"Then why are y'all here? I need help, not a fight."

"Rita needs the help. May I step inside? It's better that we're not overheard."

Lorenz stepped back and Daniel walked into the small room. He wondered where Lorenz had slept as Margareatha was still snoring on the bed. It was then that the stench hit him.

"What the hell is that smell?"

"Mostly her. She hasn't had a bath since before they brought everyone down from Buckley's and her spread. I have no idea when she last changed her clothes or washed her hair. I didn't dare step outside for fear she'd wake up so I had to use the damn chamber pot."

Daniel's gaze shifted from the bed back to Lorenz. Daniel was three inches taller, no broader in the shoulders, his hair straighter, and his upper lip sported a mustache, but the resemblance between the two made the world wonder if they were twins. It was hard to believe the woman he knew as his white sister would ever appear in public looking like the creature in those dirty, ragged clothes.

"Is she mad then?"

Lorenz ran his hand through the uncombed waves and curls. "I don't know." He sighed. "I'm hoping it's just bad booze, not enough sleep, and not enough food. She's skinny as a rail. She's sleeping now because I had the doctor give her a shot last night after Collins arranged for us to be here. All she wanted was more brandy and her cards."

"She let him give her a shot?" Daniel found the concept preposterous.

"No, I had to go into her mind and physically hold her." Lorenz turned towards the window. "I don't want to do that again. It was brutal."

Daniel almost snorted. "I don't believe you. You've never minded going into a mind and controlling others."

Lorenz turned back to him. "Daniel, that's not true. What happened when we were boys happened before I knew I could do it and before I learned how to control it."

"I'd say you learned the control part well."

"Daniel, I'm not going to argue. I need breakfast for both of us and clothes for her. I don't dare step outside or she might wake up and leave. I also need a wagon and team to get out us of here. If y'all don't want to help, just say so and go wake Collins." His voice began to take on an edge.

"You don't have time for breakfast or clothes. The sheriff and the powers that be are planning to commit her to an insane asylum as soon as the paperwork is done. I figure that will take less than two hours."

"I can't let that happen. She'll kill someone if they try it or succeed in getting her there." He pulled up his shirt and revealed a money belt and began to peel out some bills. "Can y'all rent that wagon and horses for us? Maybe pick up some men's clothes in your size for her. They sure won't have women's clothes in her size. She can change when we're out of town."

"Why not just a horse for her? Saddleback is faster."

"I don't have a horse here. I used the scouting craft from the *Golden One* and walked into town. My muscles are still screaming. What's more, I don't think Rity is going to go willingly. I may have to hold her again."

Daniel looked at his brother in amazement. His mind had rejected the idea of flying machines and people from other planets as ridiculous. He had refused to go with MacDonald to its hiding place. Yet, how else could Lorenz have arrived here? That MacDonald and his white father were from somewhere else was probable, but not from different planets.

"How far did you walk?"

"Four, maybe five miles. I had to keep off the main road until it became dark. I didn't want to explain a cattleman walking."

Daniel smiled inwardly with satisfaction at the thought of Lorenz hiking into town in his boots. He almost started to refuse, but remembered it wasn't Lorenz that faced going to the madhouse.

"All right, I'll get the wagon. If it looks like there's time, I'll pick up the clothes. I suggest we meet out back. If you take her through the front, there might be trouble. Give me at least thirty to forty-five minutes before you come down."

Lorenz paced the room, smoking one rolled cigarette after the other until the place smelled worse than before. The open window did nothing but let in very little air and flies.

"And every other flying insect," he muttered to himself as he swatted at the wasp that flew in looking for water. He tried fanning the flies away from Margareatha, but that proved futile. He checked his pocket watch again. Thirty-five minutes since Daniel had left. It was time to wake Rita make it down the stairs and out the back. He prayed she'd be reasonable.

"Come on, Rity. It's time to wake up."

He gently shook her shoulder, and she rolled away.

"Leave me alone." Her voice was sleep-laced and thick.

I hope the hell Daniel gets some water Lorenz thought. "Come on, Rity. I'll help y'all. We have stairs to go down."

He put his arm under her shoulders, helped her to sit up, and used his other arm to swing her legs over the side of the bed. "We have to go see Daniel. Then we'll go home."

"Home? Is Mama there?"

"No, Rity, it's my home were going to."

"Lemme be." She started to push at him. "I want to sleep. I hurt inside. You don't understand. Go away." Her last words were a wail.

Lorenz pulled her up, swallowing at the smell of her. "Rity, Daniel is downstairs waiting for us. Y'all don't want to disappoint him, do y'all? Mama wouldn't like it if he left without us saying goodbye."

"Mama's dead," she reminded him. "Just like my Brent and my babies. Now go away and let me be. Your children are still living, aren't they?"

Her eyes widened. "I'm sorry, Lorenz, I didn't mean it like it sounded. I don't want your children to die."

"Of course, you don't Rity. Come on now, let's get out of here."

Margareatha straightened and looked around the room. "How did I get here? This isn't where I sleep." She tried to push away again.

"Now I remember. You tricked me. You were in my mind last night." Her voice grew louder.

"Don't be angry, Rity. Y'all were sick and needed sleep. I'd like to buy y'all some breakfast, but the town doesn't like y'all anymore. They want to put y'all away in an insane asylum. We have to get out of here."

"The bastards! Let's fight them. My babies and Brent are buried here. I'd rather be buried here than leave."

"Rity, we can't do that. We'd kill someone before we would let them take us. Daniel's here too. Y'all don't want three of Mama's living children to die. Mama would haunt y'all."

"Daniel's here? Why would Daniel be here?"

"He found out y'all needed help. He felt obliged to come. He's our brother."

Margareatha frowned. "He's never acknowledged that before."

"Well, maybe he figured we were all doing just fine without him. At least he came when y'all needed help."

"I do not need help." She started to protest again and realized that nature's wake up call could not wait. "Now go away I need to use the chamber pot."

"Y'all will have to go outside. I've filled it up."

She threw him a disgusted glance, stood, and flounced out the door. Margareatha started toward the front stairs with Lorenz following.

"Let's go down the back way, Rity. It's quicker."

Lorenz heaved a sigh of relief as they walked out the back and he saw Daniel driving the buckboard toward them, his horse tied onto the back. It didn't matter whether Daniel came with them or not. It meant he and Margareatha did not have to walk back to the Scout. Margareatha dashed for the outhouse.

Daniel pulled up while she was still inside. "I bought some men's clothes. The pants may be too short, but they're clean. They're in the bundle in the back."

"How much do I owe y'all?"

"Put it in that so-called bank account that you say has my name on it."

"It is yours. It's in your name."

"You set it up. You can do with it what you wish."

"I didn't set it up. We had the lawyer do that when Uncle Kasper passed away. We just kept adding to it when Mama died. When we set up the corporation, we used your share of the ranch and general store as the value for the stock. It's been a good investment. Y'all have to come back or send a notarized letter before we can disperse anything."

"That would be the same as acknowledging that the money is mine."

"It is yours. So is the stock we're holding in your name. The stock can only go to family members." Lorenz eyed the outhouse. "How much time do we have?"

"Not much. I saw the sheriff heading for the courthouse. Can't you hurry her up?"

Lorenz approached the reeking public building. It had been given a fresh coat of whitewash for spring, but nothing helped the odors. He could see a man in a brown serge suit and derby hurrying towards them. "Come on Rity, we've got to go."

"I'll come out when you go away."

"Y'all come out now, or I'll drag y'all out."

"I'll scream."

"That's exactly what the town expects of a stark, raving mad woman. Come on, there's someone coming."

A reluctant Margareatha emerged. She knew Lorenz too well to know that he wasn't joking.

"I'm hungry."

"So am I, but we'll get something later." He helped her up onto the front seat as she fought her skirts.

"Daniel, are y'all leaving us now?"

"Just how would you return this rig and the horses if I didn't accompany you?"

"I wouldn't."

"Right, and then they would be looking for me as a horse thief. You may have the reins. I'll ride my horse. You know where you're going. I suggest the back way. It might be slower, but fewer will see us. It's too bad she didn't have time to change."

Lorenz snapped the reins and headed the team away from the street that led back to the higher priced saloons and turned east for a couple of streets before turning to the south. When they were out of the alleyway he heard shouting back at the hotel.

"It seems they've discovered you're not there."

Margareatha's face hardened and she folded her arms around her torso as though reassuring herself that she was physically there. "They once called me an angel for nursing the sick."

"People have notoriously short memories when it suits them," Lorenz muttered.

Silence reigned as they quickly went through the gradually thinning residences. A few dogs barked at their passing, but no one seemed particularly interested except a loiterer at the stables located at the edge of town.

Daniel suppressed his lips. He'd probably have some explaining to do when he returned, and where was Lorenz headed?

Lorenz had landed the Justine Scout just after daybreak. Toni had been right. There was no need for him to leave before dinner. He had used the Scout's scanners to ascertain no humans were in the vicinity and the landscape a jumbled mass of rock and earth from the played out mines. He used energy pulses to hollow out a depression deep enough for the craft. Once on the ground, it took hours to find weathered timber from the abandoned mines to use with downed limbs, and brush to cover the scout before the hike into town. He hadn't worried about what questions his sudden appearance would cause. Now he was thankful for the precautions.

His musings were interrupted by Margareatha preparing to step down. He slapped the reins to speed up their progress and yelled at her.

"What the hell are y'all trying to do? Kill yourself?"

"I want to go back. My babies are there."

"Why, Rity? Y'all can't bring them back. Right now y'all need food and rest. We'll come back when y'all feel better."

Margareatha glared at him. "And who decides I'm better? You?"

"No, when y'all show me y'all are strong enough to ensure your land is safe and y'all are acting like my sister again."

She lapsed into silence, her mind a jumble of hurt and smells; the feelings of warm arms wrapped around her, small hands pulling at her skirt or touching her face, the smells of cooking from her oven, the smells of new days and warm evenings. All of it replaced with cold: cold, cold white covered earth and cold white faces. And she wanted to scream at him, at the world, and at God, and screaming would accomplish nothing for Brent and the boys were dead.

"I'm hungry. We should go back," she announced.

"We've been hungry before."

"We should have stood up to them. They wouldn't have been able to touch us."

"It was too risky. Someone might have died, and there is no way we could have controlled a mob, let alone explain to the next lawman or judge how we manage to evade the law. They would equate it with the supernatural."

"You are so concerned with the outward trappings of living like a normal human being that you are almost Justine in your one-minded pursuit of fooling the world while you do as you please. Well, I tried it, and my babies are dead." Her voice had risen to a wail.

"I know, Rity, I know." Inwardly he winced as Margareatha had described him perfectly.

"And don't give me any of the platitudes about being with the Lord. It doesn't help or make the hurt go away. It doesn't change anything. My babies are dead and cold."

"Rity, don't torture yourself. Go ahead and cry if it makes y'all feel better. Martha cried when Lazarus died even though she knew he would live again. So did Christ who brought him back to life."

Margareatha's voice was vicious. "I always thought Jesus cried for the sins of man bringing death."

"I've always ascribed it to something more human. To me, the good Lord cried because his friend suffered and died and would suffer the same fate again."

Once again Margareatha crossed her arms and ignored the jolting of the buckboard until Lorenz turned off the road onto a faint trail leading up into the higher areas.

"Where are we going? Do you mean you left horses back in here? Why?"

"I didn't use horses, Rity."

"Let me out. I'll walk back."

"Rity, if y'all get out, I'll just have to knock y'all down and tie y'all up. Mama would be mad at both of us. Ye Gods, Rity, y'all are Mama's daughter. Think of what she went through when the Comanche raided our cabin. We never found Augustav, remember."

"And she was skin and bones when Mac found her…"

"The Comanche withheld food when she tried to talk with Daniel, her own child."

Daniel started to deny the accusation and thought the better of it. They would both turn on him if he were to say it was because she wouldn't act like a human being. Lorenz arguing with Margareatha was a preferable situation.

"And I've never been completely sure she wasn't a bit mad when Mac took her out of there."

"Does that justify what y'all are doing?"

Once more Margareatha subsided into silence, her mind churning. Why, why, why, was all she could think, and why were both Lorenz and Daniel here? Was this some sort of joke God was playing on her? Was she supposed to heal the breach between her two brothers? She couldn't heal herself.

Finally Lorenz drove behind a hillock of earth and stone and pulled the reins back.

"We're here."

"There is nothing here." Scorn stressed Margareatha's words.

"Look again. I pulled the brush and rocks over the opening. I just prayed I wasn't gone too long. Someone might think I was hiding pay dirt diggings."

Daniel rode up to collect the reins and to tie his horse onto the back.

"Are you intending to hoof it all the way back to Texas, little brother? I thought you had a way to leave this country."

Lorenz's face lit with eagerness. "We're not walking. Watch this." He strode over to the brush and began pulling it away. Daniel fought with the horses that started taking offense at the noise and sudden movement.

"You could give me a chance to turn this rig around."

"And y'all could give a hand here if y'all are in such a hurry to see me gone."

Margareatha stood watching the two of them her arms crossed below her bosom. She knew them too well. Lorenz had the Justine ability to mindspeak and possessed two hearts, while Daniel was entirely Earth. Physically they resembled each other, except Daniel's extra three inches, but Lorenz had adopted some of Mac's body training and his arms and legs were bulkier.

Within minutes the golden gleam of a metal dome was seen. Then what looked like tinted glass followed by more golden metal. Sleek and streamlined, no doors showing, but a craft large enough for four people. Daniel whistled.

"What is that?"

"It's a scouting craft from the *Golden One*. Papa taught me to fly it years ago. We'll be home in less than an hour once we've lifted." Lorenz's grey eyes gleamed. He felt at home in this vehicle where he could soar above the clouds and go beyond anything that man had contrived or yet dreamed. It was power he could use unlike his mind which must lie hidden from the world.

Daniel's face had gone grey and he turned his back. He refused to look at anything that shouted of his biological father's world.

"How did you explain all of that to Antoinette, or did you even bother?"

The hate in his voice was a living force that slammed into Lorenz's sensibilities.

"It took most of one night and then a visit to the *Golden One*. Just like Mama, she went where y'all wouldn't go, big brother."

Daniel whirled on him, his hands balled into fists.

Her mother's admonishments rang in Margareatha's mind. "Du must not let the boys fight vhen I am not there." The thought jarred her into action.

"You two stop it right now. Mama will be mad."

They stared at her, then at each other, a sick look coming over their faces. Up until now, neither had really acknowledged the fact that Margareatha had lost touch with reality. Lorenz drew a deep, ragged breath. He could feel the light breeze tugging at his hat. For some reason Daniel's hat showed no signs of moving. By pausing, he had time to consider. Rity was right. They were behaving like boys. Were they little, Mama would be mad and lambaste the two of them. He turned back to Daniel.

"Rity is right, Daniel. We're behaving like kids. I had no right to imply you were or are a coward. My apologies, if y'all will accept them."

Daniel looked at him, his grey eyes like slate. "We end this now if you promise to see that she is cared for."

"It's why I'm here."

"I do not need to be cared for, and I know full well Mama is dead; dead and cold in the ground like my babies." Margareatha turned her back on them and stalked toward the buckboard.

Lorenz caught her by the arm. "Rity, we're going in the Scout. Daniel will take the buckboard back to town."

"I'm hungry."

Her lips were beginning to crack, and the heat made the stench from her clothes worse.

"Sure y'all are, but we'll be where there's food faster if we take the Scout."

Her eyes lost the hardness for a moment as though puzzling over what he said. "Will there be brandy there?"

"No, but it's only a couple of hours away. Come on, Rity, y'all ride with me and as soon as I can, I promise I'll pour y'all a glass of brandy." He caught the bundle of clothes Daniel tossed in their direction.

Daniel looked at them with disgust written on his face and climbed into the buckboard. As he picked up the reins, he saw a cloud of dust in the direction of the town they had left. He looked back at his siblings walking towards the machine in the depression.

"I think the town has sent someone after us. I suggest you leave immediately."

He snapped the reins and headed out. At the top of the draw he looked back. Lorenz had managed to put Margareatha into one side and was hurrying back around to enter from the other side. He waved at Daniel.

"Thanks, Daniel. If that posse sees a golden streak, tell them it must have been ball lightning. I'll let y'all know how she is."

"Don't bother," Daniel muttered. That Margareatha would eventually return to normal was possible. All he wanted was to get back to his town, his job, and never see either of them again.

Chapter 25

Christina in Exile

Mrs. Brewster smiled at the two Texan matrons and their respective daughters as they entered her office. The taller woman had black, curled hair perfectly arranged. Her clothes, a muted summer violet suit trimmed with darker velvet, were elegantly cut, draped, and accessorized with matching hat, gloves, and (she judged from the bulge on the woman's fingers) jewels. The girl behind her was slightly taller, moved without the awkwardness of most young ladies, and was equally outfitted in blue. The very type Mrs. Brewster had often tried to attract to her school for young ladies but failed. She envied them and therefore hated them.

The other woman was clad in a tight fitting two piece suit of gray and trimmed with black rickrack. She was perspiring freely and the wet was creeping downward and outward. Her hat was of some grey material trimmed with black netting that looked ill-at-ease on top of the straight blond hair, braided and pulled into a bun at the back. If she wore any jewels, they were well hidden. The girl behind her sported the same hair-do, the same type of dress, and walked with a clumping gait. Her face was tanned from far too much sun for a lady, and the blue eyes lacked the intelligence that the other girl and woman possessed. These two, Mrs. Brewster perceived as dull, uncouth, creatures with far more money than she would ever possess and she despised them.

"Mrs. Rolfe and Mrs. MacDonald, welcome to St. Louis and to our school. I hope your young ladies will be very happy here and acquire the necessary arts to function as skilled housewives. Won't you be seated while we go over the contracts?"

"There's seems to be a misperception here, Mrs. Brewster. As my letter stated, it is Miss Christina Rolfe who will be attending, not my daughter. Miss Mac-Donald will be attending a boarding school in the East preparing for college." Antoinette's drawl came through as sweetly as ever. She smiled and seated herself as the rest did the same. "As ah explained in my letter, ah simply handled the correspondence for Mr. and Mrs. Rolfe."

Mrs. Brewster's smile remained fixed. "I'm sure we could accomplish the same thing."

Toni smiled gently at such an absurdity. "Why, no, ah don't believe so. Miss MacDonald needs some advanced coaching in math, French, and Latin before college. Your school's specialties are sewing and culinary arts."

"Such studying can often harm a woman's nervous disposition. We've found it far better to stress the social graces. If perhaps you change your mind during the year, I'm sure we could accommodate her." She turned to Brigetta.

"Did you find everything satisfactory during your tour of our school?"

Brigetta's face reddened. The tour had consisted of seeing the dining room, kitchen, brief glances into one of the schoolrooms, and one of the bedrooms that four students would share. All of it looked rather sparse to her, but she nodded yes as Antoinette spoke again.

"In your letter, y'all mentioned riding classes. Ah'm afraid we didn't see anything resembling a stable or horses on your property.

Mrs. Brewster's smile was becoming forced. "We have one quarter devoted to teaching young ladies to ride properly. We utilize a stable not far from here. Too many of our Western students are unfamiliar with the sidesaddle."

"A very sensible solution ah'm sure. Ah do have one more question as the issue wasn't raised, but ah'm sure y'all will understand. Miss Rolfe's father was very reluctant to let his daughter travel so far from home and he does worry about security in such a large city area. Y'all know we hear about such dreadful crimes."

Mrs. Brewster smiled. "I can assure you that our staff locks all the doors in the evenings and I check them personally since Mr. Brewster passed away. One can't be too careful. Now there is a small matter of payment."

Brigetta opened her purse and slowly counted out the money. She did not dare look at Christina or she would burst out crying. Both she and Martin had given thanks when there was no sign of an impending birth, but the strain of keeping Christina home and safe was becoming too much. Perhaps being with young people her own age that weren't as smart as the MacDonald children or her own siblings was the answer, and people at home would have other things to talk about with Christina away. Christina could be happy here.

"Study hard and pray your Papa will let you stay home next year," Brigetta told Christina in German when they hugged farewell. "I think you will be happy here."

Instead, Christina was miserable. She hated the school, the lessons, and the other students. At first they tried to be friendly, but Christina's bad handwriting, her inability to figure any kind of sum, or her slow, halting reading soon produced giggles. The girls vied to be among those that managed to draw, write with a fine hand, or produce an exquisite piece of hand embroidery. To Christina, the place was sheer drudgery.

Early in the morning, Christina would slip into the kitchen and beg the staff to let her help. At least here she could be comfortable and listen to the women chat away without making fun of her. She even took to helping them bring in the vegetables from the garden, and later the produce, grain, or poultry from the back of the farmer's wagons. It was the only time she felt less than forsaken. Her pleas to come home in the two letters she wrote to her parents were ignored. Her mother's letters to her were in German, and she could not read them. Brigetta never believed that Christina wasn't able to learn German. Christina began spending every moment she could in the kitchen.

Mrs. Brewster's reports to the Rolfe's were short and to the point. There was an improvement in Miss Rolfe's deportment. She had been able to teach the young lady how to walk properly. She left out the part about banging the heavy stick on the toes if the young lady did not comply. Mrs. Brewster also wrote that she had decided that a stint in the kitchen would help Christina understand the "running" of the household and would include learning menu planning and horticulture. She did not state that Christina was too dense to learn anything else.

Christina was delighted to spend the hours in the kitchen and the garden. It was away from the hated classes where letters and numbers were jumbled, and most of all, away from the snickering girls. One of the farmers that came every morning was pleasant to her and smiled at her. His build was stocky and he looked about the same height as her father. His clothes made him look like what Papa would call a dirt farmer, but he had nice teeth and brown eyes that lit up when he saw her. He refused to let her carry anything heavy, but would talk about how many chickens he had. That Bill Price was almost as old as her father never occurred to her. Something in his shy nature appealed to her and she loved to talk with him. Christina missed her father and her brothers more than her mother, and here was a man she could talk with, who listened to her and made her feel wanted.

"Don't y'all have horses to ride?"

"No, miss, I don't. My horses are working horses."

His answer puzzled Christina. People rode horses in Texas, but they were used for ranch work.

Price felt he had insulted her. "I'm sorry, miss, but I'm not rich like your folks."

"Oh, la, who cares about money? Papa keeps it all. And please, call me Christina. Nobody else will."

They were nearing the door and she opened it for him as he was carrying a wooden cradle of eggs and a pail of milk. He set them inside the delivery porch, picked up the empty egg cradle and empty pail, and went back to the wagon for the box of live chickens. These would be put in the pen and appear on the dinner table throughout the week. As they walked away from the door, their conversation resumed.

"I can't use your first name. It wouldn't be proper."

Christina pouted. "I don't know why not. I like you, and everyone here calls me Miss Rolfe. Y'all aren't help here. Y'all own your own farm, and I'm so sick of this place. Everybody laughs at me."

He hefted the crate of chickens and walked toward the pen. "I can't imagine why, Miss Rolfe. If it gets too bad, you let me know. You promise?"

Christina's eyes filled with tears. "Oh, yes, oh, yes, oh, thank you."

Chapter 26

Escape

Mrs. Brewster allowed Christina to spend more and more time in the kitchen. The girl could not learn, but she could cook and bake, sparing her the expense of another salary. Her December letter to the Rolfe's extolled Christina's home-making skills. This arrangement was proving quite profitable.

Christina didn't mind. The kitchen was warm and Mrs. Reilly, the cook, let her make biscuits and cookies. Mrs. Reilly would even compliment the results. Christina hated the cold schoolrooms and everyone in them. Her two letters to her parents pleading to come home had not worked. Fall slipped into winter, mild and rainy. Then came the first of December and the ground froze solid. Bill Price came less and less often, only once a week now. She found herself standing on the back stoop waiting to catch sight of his team pulling into the back yard and then running to greet him.

Christina was faced with the fact that she would be here until spring when her mother would arrive to take her home again. It would mean that Christmas would be cold and miserable. There would be no gingerbread, no Nurnberg cookies with almonds, and no spicy zimsternes. In her mind she saw the little star cookies glistening from their tops being brushed with frothy egg whites and her mouth watered. She wouldn't be at home for the Christmas songs and bible readings around Aunt Olga's organ. There was no mother or father to wish her well on Christ's birthday. She did not know if these people would even have a tree. Gradually the idea formed in her mind that Bill Price would be her escape from here. Her father and Uncle Lorenz were too far away. They couldn't catch her this time.

Price thought of her as something untouchable. She was a daughter a wealthy Texan rancher, but he was often lonely; a man that did not drink and tried to live by the principles of his Baptist religion. He had married once when he returned from the War at age 17. His Eleanor and their child had died from scarlet fever and his nights and days had been long and cheerless for fifteen years. The other women in his church were either married or too clever for him and he desperately needed a helpmeet (as God's word called woman). Christina's blue eyes and welcoming smile warmed him. He banished the thought of ever having a strong, young wife like her. She would never accept him.

Two weeks before Christmas, he pulled into the school yard bearing his eggs, milk, and chickens. He had hoped for an order for geese or ducks, but none had been proffered. Christina came running to greet him, her plain, grey muffler flapping on both sides.

"Oh, Mr. Price, this place is just terrible. I won't be allowed to eat Christmas dinner with even the staff. I'll be the only one here. Everyone else has a relative living here or their homes are close by. I'll be all alone with that horrible, snooty Miss Winthrop, and she only wants soup and bread. Mrs. Brewster is mad at me because I can't learn to spell right and my writing is always wrong. She claims I can't even have soup if I don't turn in three neatly written pages. Can't I just sneak in your wagon and hide?"

"Where would you go? They'll arrest me for kidnapping." The thought of breaking the law was beyond him.

"Not if we get married. I can cook, and sew, and keep house."

The man was stunned and stood there in his dirty overalls, heavy Macklin coat, green plaid winter cap pulled over his ears, and high buckled overshoes splashed with farm mud and barnyard muck. His mouth opened and closed a few times.

"Miss Rolfe, I ain't rich like your folks."

"I don't care. Papa never gives me any money anyway. Oh, please, please…"

She threw her arms around him and kissed his cheek and began to sob. "I can't bear it here. I'm so lonely."

"Miss Rolfe, I must put the eggs up now. You must never talk of this again." He gave her a quick hug and hurried to the back entrance and stepped inside.

His voice had been gruff, but his face had blushed red. She ran behind the outhouse to watch for him when he returned for the chickens. Price lifted the crate with the chickens, walked to the henhouse, and stepped inside. Christina ran to the back of the wagon, climbed in, and crawled up against the headboard under the wagon seat. This was always his last stop. She knew he never looked in the wagon when he returned. He just set the crate over the sideboards and climbed up into the seat.

Price returned to the wagon, dumped the crate inside, and climbed up into the seat. "Up now, Buster, Molly, gee-up." The wagon jolted off onto the rutted roads. Christina remained very quiet and very still. She smiled to herself. What a nice surprise she had in store for Bill Price.

Chapter 27

Panic

Soon to be nineteen-years-old Kendall had dropped deep into thought reliving the quarrel he had heard between his father and mother. He and the older Rolfe brothers were in a gully guarded by an oak tree. They'd been waiting at least thirty minutes for Marty, and the five young men had pretty well exhausted the subject of what they would do should they ever acquire visiting rights to a woman. So far Marty was the only one to have found a willing female, but then Marty was one likeable cuss. When he'd bragged to them about going to a whorehouse in Arles, the older ones had approached their respective sires. Martin was outraged.

"I never wasted money on a whore and I'll be damned if I give my boys money for that. Go find yourselves a gut wife when old enough du are." His lapsing into German words and syntax told his sons just how angry he was.

Kendall hadn't fared any better when he finally found the courage to approach his father. Lorenz's eyes glinted with amusement as he mulled the possibility.

"I don't think it's a good idea. If y'all don't marry as young as I did, y'all are apt to give your woman a disease. Why do y'all think I didn't go?"

"Because Grandma wouldn't allow it."

"So, y'all have talked with your grandfather when he was here."

"Uh, well, sorta."

"That wasn't the only reason, son. I was already in love with your mother. I knew it would be a betrayal and a sin against the good Lord. I won't take y'all there and I won't give y'all money for it. If y'all do go, stop by the drugstore first and buy some of those rubbers."

The discussion, Kendall knew, was closed. Right now he couldn't say how he felt. At first resentful, but part of that was because everything was changing. Both Melissa and Randall were away at schools. He had returned home after two months of higher mathematics and Latin. He chaffed at the confinement, the discipline, and to him, the tediousness of prolonged study, but it was the quarrel he'd overheard between his parents that held him deep in thought tonight, and he slipped deeper into his reverie.

He had retired to his room after talking with his father about visiting a cathouse. It didn't take long to realize he was sulking like a ten-year-old. No wonder his paw had discouraged him. Hell, it must look like he couldn't accomplish anything: not school, not his work, not being able to go to a woman with money of his own. He should be outside right now working on something. Pawpaw had already chided him for working so much over at the Rolfe's ranch. If he was ever going to run the Rearing Bear, he needed to prove he was man enough; prove that he could work without someone pointing out what needed done. There were horses to break and a barn that needed cleaning and he should be outside, not in his bedroom.

He wasn't sure if his mother was napping or in her sewing room. Since he didn't hear the whirr of the sewing machine, he was fairly certain she was napping. He had picked up his boots and carried them downstairs with the intention of putting them on in the kitchen.

As he came down the stairs and passed his parent's bedroom door, he had heard his father. "I have to tell him."

"No, he's too young."

"He wants to go to a woman in Arles."

"That's just wild oats."

"Antoinette, he's almost nineteen. I should have told him years ago."

"No, he's mine. Randall and Melissa are yours and they needed to know."

"I was under the impression that we both are responsible for all three."

"Oh, for heaven's sake, Lorenz, y'all didn't tell me until I was twenty-three. Y'all can at least wait until he's an adult."

"I'll wait until his birthday and that's it. Y'all can be there when I do."

Kendall had fled for the kitchen on the chance his father was leaving the room. He drew out a chair and pulled his boots on thankful that the kitchen help was all outside. His mind was racing. Randall and Melissa knew something he didn't. What? Why was he his mother's and the other two his father's? Did that mean there was some credence to Randall's charge that Mama let him do things she wouldn't allow Randall to do? Somewhere in the back of his mind was the inkling that his siblings were different. He'd put it down to Randall being a bookworm and Melissa a girl. Still he knew instinctively there was something else. Something that meant he didn't measure up to the other two. He wasn't waiting for his birthday. He'd ask Pawpaw tomorrow and he would have his answer. That was what made a man. A man had the ability to stand his ground and demand to know. The decision brought him out of his dream world and he looked around. It seemed for a moment the night grew silent and he heard the sound of a horse walking slowly.

"Did y'all hear something?" Kendall glanced around the group sitting in front of their horses. As usual it was him and the four middle Rolfe boys, August, Ernest, Kasper, and Frank. Fritz Rolfe had insisted everyone call him Frank when he was confirmed at fourteen.

"Naw," said August for his brothers. He knew Ernst was too wrapped up dreaming about doing the accounts at the bank. For some reason, Aunt Margareatha had taught Ernest the ins and outs of accounting when she recovered. Ernest didn't really listen to any sounds carried by the evening breeze, and the younger ones deferred to him if Marty wasn't present. "But it's time Marty's through with that Mex. I'm not waiting all night for him to screw somebody. Let's go pull him out of there and then go to Olivia's and have a drink. Half-an hour's long enough." He really wanted a drink and Olivia would serve them when the new tavern at Schmidt's Corner wouldn't.

Kendall couldn't help thinking that it was okay for Marty to be with a Mexican, but not Christina. Of course, for men it was different—or was it? He knew his father and Uncle Martin wouldn't, but they were old-fashioned. Randall? Naw, Randall would not consider anyone so beneath his intellectual standards. Melissa? Kendall figured Melissa, like Randall, would go her own way. Kendall held onto his stirrup for a moment, stunned at this revelation. That was what his father expected of him: someone choosing his own way and not relying on friends or parents to point out the proper direction.

They mounted their horses and returned to the back of the shack where Julia lived with her maybe husband Miguel. Marty went to her whenever she was alone during the time Miguel worked at the Tillman ranch. Kendall marveled at Marty's ease of explaining how to be with a woman and a bottle of whiskey. He couldn't imagine drinking that much whiskey in such a short time.

"It helps relax her and gives me a buzz." And Marty would smile broadly at the thought.

They were almost in position to swing down when the back door opened and a tooth-gleaming Marty came out accompanied by Julia. He slipped his arm around her waist, pulled her close, and kissed her soundly. Then he turned her around and slapped her on the buttocks. He grinned at them again and swaggered to his horse. At twenty-two Marty was a blocky, rock-hard, blue-eyed replica of his Grandfather Rolfe and equally adept with a knife or living off the land. He slipped his reins off the sagging porch rail and flung himself into the saddle. "Get impatient, did you all? Hell, these things take time. Let's go get a beer."

As one they turned their horses, each knowing full well their parents would give them holy hell for this escapade if ever discovered, but right now no one cared. Everyone looked up to Marty and followed his lead. Each secretly wished to be that type of man. Kendall sensed somehow his father's abilities were unattainable, but Marty, hell, he'd known him all his life. He knew that in two areas, he beat them all. Not one of the other young men could ride a horse or handle a gun like he did. He started to slow his mount for Marty to catch up.

A rifle blast roared into the night. "Everybody hightail it," Marty yelled. "We'll meet in town."

Another shot splintered the evening sounds and everyone bent lower and urged speed to their mounts with Kendall's horse surging to the lead. Miguel's horse was nothing but a rangy roan. He couldn't catch them. Within seconds they rounded the bend towards Schmidt's Corner. Kendall pulled up and looked around, his mouth dropping almost as far as his stomach. Where was Marty?

Without thinking he swung his horse around and rode back towards the Mex's cabin. A woman's screams mixed with the sound of another shot filling the night air, blotting out the sounds of katydids and night creatures. The others followed him.

Kendall pulled up his horse when he realized what the words were that Julia was screaming in Spanish.

"He's dead. They'll hang you. Run, run, run."

Marty lay face down on the ground, his right arm outstretched. Blood covered the wound in the back and slopped out of a blown away skull. Julia continued to scream, "Run, run."

Miguel raised his rifle and began shooting at the approaching young men, the bullets whizzing past their own heads and their horses' heads. This time the horses bolted.

Kendall didn't know if a lucky shot had felled his friend or if Miguel had been waiting. Right now the bullets were too damn close and he kept his reins working. Marty had said to hightail it. Maybe that's what he ought to do. There was no way he could explain this to Pawpaw or Uncle Martin. He was a coward that ran at the first shot. He knew his father would have done something. Just what Pawpaw would have done, he didn't know, and that was the worst part.

Kendall felt shame as he rode away, the knowledge deep inside his gut that he would never know what made a man like Pawpaw. The thing that his father was going to tell him would remain unknown. Home was forever closed to him.

Chapter 28

1892: The Rolfe's Anniversary

Brigetta looked with satisfaction at the band playing on the stage built behind their house. She had recovered from her earlier shock when Martin had readily agreed to spend the money for building the stage, a dance floor, and paying real musicians. The band was playing a waltz with a recognizable tempo. The food tables were loaded and even people from Arles were here to celebrate her and Martin's twenty-fifth anniversary. She had directed August to place the specially tooled saddle she'd bought Martin in the pantry. She ran a hand over her aqua taffeta gown and smiled out at the dancers as Toni and Lorenz swirled by her.

Antoinette was clad in a low cut, violet taffeta ball gown, a heavy, deep purple, amethyst pendant nestled against her skin and the low cut gown. Her figure was slightly heavier than a few years ago and her head was tilted upward at Lorenz as he gracefully whirled her in a circle. Lorenz was in a black, western cut suit with shiny new, black boots. Brigetta saw him smile down at Toni, his right hand confidently placed on the small of her back, his dark hair curling around his handsome face as he executed another twirl. It left Brigetta almost in a rage. How could Toni have that kind of love and devotion from such a handsome man?

What did she have? The response leapt into her mind: a lonesome life in a wild society that had claimed her favorite son; a loveless life with a man that valued her a little less than his cows. She became dreamy eyed at the thought of what life would be like with her handsome neighbor. Why had she never realized before how handsome Lorenz was? She thought for a moment about how wonderful life would be if she were in his arms, whirling to the music instead of Toni. Her eyes blinked open, a red flush enveloped her cheeks.

What am I thinking? Why is it suddenly so hot out here? Dear God, the man was incredibly graceful and handsome, and suddenly her lower region felt unlike it had ever felt in twenty-five years of marriage. She wanted to lie in bed with Lorenz and the hardness of him would take away all her sorrow and hurt over Marty while he cradled her....

Brigetta turned and fled to the front of the house, gasping in air. She could not, would not think such horrible, sinful thoughts again. She had never done so in her life. What was wrong with her? Right now she wanted to tear open the tight, stuffy bodice and let the cooling, early evening air soothe the flames raging inside. Her fan moved back and forth with the rapidity of a humming bird hovering in midair. She clung to one of the posts of her front porch. Her body was enflamed and she wanted to die. She barely heard the quick steps behind her, but the voice was unmistakable.

"Brigetta, are y'all all right? I saw y'all run out here, and it looked like y'all didn't feel well. Would y'all like a chair?"

Brigetta slowly turned. Surely Toni must know what caused her to run. How could she face her friend? Brigetta's chest was heaving and she tried to apologize to Antoinette, but all she could say was, "I'm sorry, but I so varm got."

"Oh, dear, that's right. Y'all are at that age. Let me bring some water. I'll have someone get y'all a chair." She disappeared, her skirts rustling in time with the music.

Brigetta was left trying to keep her sobs to herself. Everything had turned topsy-turvy these last few years. Their Christina running away from the boarding school in Missouri to marry a dirt farmer; their Marty lying dead in some Mexican woman's yard; Kendall running away and not heard from by anyone; and Melissa, a teacher in another state engaged to some deputy. Most of her sons were out on the range for days and weeks with no chance of marrying. Ernest lived in town and spent more time at the bank than with human company. It was confusing. Who was her family? Toni was the only friend she'd made in all her years in this country, and Toni was so thoroughly Texan.

Toni had always been the strong, beautiful one; the hard, cold one who ran from her family's home to marry Lorenz; who fought and killed Indians to save them and their children; the one who ran a beautiful house; the one with a son becoming a lawyer; the one who was unafraid when their husbands were gone for long months on a drive; the one who coolly gut shot a man with her derringer hidden under her embroidery when he threatened to take over the ranch while Lorenz and Martin were on a drive to Sedalia. Toni the perfect hostess who knew how to throw perfect parties and always, always made her feel so inadequate. Why had she ever left Germany for this agony?

One of Toni's kitchen workers who had been hired to help with the party appeared with a chair as Toni returned carrying a glass of water.

"Here, y'all are. It's not chilled, but it's cool. Now y'all sit down and drink every bit of it."

Brigetta was still blinking her eyes and incapable of talking. She obediently sat and gulped the water.

"I, I don't know vhat happened. I just became so hot. I've spoiled things for everyvon." Inadequate words seem to come out of her mouth.

"Oh, nonsense, Brigetta, y'all haven't spoiled anything. Now then, we know what the matter is. Y'all will need to grit your teeth against that and hold your head high because Martin is about to give a speech, and he wants y'all there."

Brigetta closed her eyes and stood. She did not see Toni motion to someone to stay back. She let Toni guide her to where Martin and all the people waited. As they entered the back yard, Martin's voice boomed out.

"There she is folks, my lovely bride of twenty-five years. Come on up here, Brigetta. I've got something to say."

Somehow one foot went in front of the other as she walked down between the clapping ranchers, their families, and the ranch hands. She knew her face was red and she prayed everyone thought it was from embarrassment and not from guilt. She fought an impulse to find Lorenz's face in the crowd. It seemed forever but finally she was on the stage with Martin. He was beaming at her, his blue eyes as guileless as the day she met him. He reached out, took her hand, and turned to face everyone.

"Folks, y'all know the Lord has blessed us, and it got me to thinking." He paused as some of the men hooted. "Not everyone gets a good wife like I got: a nice, good looking woman who gave me lots of sons."

The crowd laughed and clapped. All of them knew how hard Martin worked his sons on the ranch in lieu of hiring more hands.

"We got the boys and one girl. Our girl's married now and she's given us a grandchild in Missouri. All this time Brigetta has kept the house, cooked the meals, and run the ranch when I was gone in the early days on the drives. Not once did she complain about never seeing Germany again. She never asked for anything, but gave a lot. So I tried to think of something I gave her other than that fancy pin she's wearing and lots of lonesome years. You all know what? It didn't seem fair. I asked myself, what would someone from another country want the most out here in God's country?"

Whistles and jeers greeted his statement. Some were drunk, but they were Texans in Texas. Who could want anything else?

"Well I decided it was time to say thank y'all by surprising her with something she hasn't had since she left the old world: roses." He paused. "Bring them up here."

Brigetta's head was clearing. She couldn't be hearing correctly. She turned to look towards the front and a Mexican man was carrying a huge bouquet of white roses towards them. Martin leaned over, scooped them up, and held them out to her.

"Thank y'all, Brigetta, for all the years of not complaining."

Somehow her arms came up around the roses, the scent, the glorious scent filling her nostrils, and tears were rolling down her cheeks.

"There's more, folks. Tomorrow, Jorge here," he pointed down to the man standing awkwardly to the side, "is going to plant a bed of roses and then stay here to take care of them until they're doing fine. Brigetta will finally have her flowers that she had as a little girl."

The people in front were clapping, the women coming closer to catch the scent and to "ooh" and "ahh," over the mass of flowers Brigetta was supporting.

"Thank du," she finally managed. She forced herself to take a deep breath. "Boys, go bring the present for your father."

August must have known what Martin had planned, for he appeared carrying the saddle. Since Marty's death he had taken on Marty's responsibilities. Like Marty, he resembled Martin. Perhaps it was fashion, perhaps it was vanity, but he cultivated a large, walrus mustache to show there was something about August that differed from Marty.

"Hey, people, look at that. See what a wife she is." Martin reached down and pulled the saddle up. "It's a fine, fine piece of workmanship." He smiled at Brigetta and hefted the saddle upward for all to admire. "Okay, everyone, there's still plenty of food and drinks, and the boys here will be playing until everyone's too tired to move."

The crowd clapped, and Martin took her arm and helped her down the steps. He handed the saddle back to August. "Here, put it up. I wouldn't want it to get ruined."

He turned to Brigetta. "Uh, well, I guess that's it. Did y'all want to say more?"

Brigetta's eyes were still streaming, her heart overflowing. How could she have been so blind? It was Martin who loved her and she loved him, and for the second time that evening Brigetta knew what it was to feel desire.

Later that night Martin would mutter to himself, "I should have given her flowers years ago."

Chapter 29

Love and Marriage

"Melissa, consider what will happen if you have children."

"Y'all mean they might be like me or father?" Melissa's lips smiled, but her eyes never wavered.

"That's exactly what I mean. You can't marry Edward until you've told tell him."

"Why is that, Uncle Daniel? Pawpaw didn't tell Mama until after I was born."

Daniel and Melissa were in his office. His mustache had grayed over the years and blended into his lips that were tightened in a white line. He fought with his emotions to marshal his thoughts for an answer. Melissa's grey eyes were steady and her face bland. He'd known there would be trouble when Mrs. Montgomery had insisted the school board hire her friend from some woman's college back east and he heard the name Melissa MacDonald. Being right was bitter fruit right now. Melissa was intent on marrying his deputy, Edward Carson. Ed had taken one look at the slim, tall, elegantly clad young woman alighting from the railroad car and fallen in love.

The town fathers, school board members, ministers, and genteel ladies of the town had been shocked when Melissa refused to board with the selected family. Ignoring proprieties, Melissa had purchased a small home.

"Unmarried ladies do not live in their own house. It's scandalous!" Whispers spread, passions were heated, but it was too late to hire another teacher for the wilds of Wyoming and Mrs. Montgomery was adamant that Melissa MacDonald remain. Clive Montgomery was thirty years older than his wife and the biggest land owner around. Whatever Mrs. Montgomery wanted, Mr. Montgomery wanted. None defied him. White men and their woman were still a bafflement to Daniel.

That Ed should love Melissa, Daniel could understand. She was a taller version of Antoinette except for those damned grey eyes: grey eyes like his and Lorenz's. It was Melissa falling in love with Ed that surprised him. Ed wasn't rich or educated beyond the eighth grade, if that.

Before Daniel could answer, Melissa stood. "Uncle Daniel, I did not come here to argue with you. Pawpaw and Mama are arriving on the next train and you are invited to dine with us. I know that you oppose our wedding, but I do hope you will serve as Edward's best man. He thinks the world of you." Daniel noticed she dropped her y'alls whenever she wished. "You will not need to speak with Pawpaw, but I do request that you remain civil."

"Have you warned Ed how rich your parents are?"

"La, Uncle Daniel, he certainly knows by now."

She was, thought Daniel, worse than Lorenz. In a way, Ed was the son he never dared to have. What if his children were like Lorenz? The wedding was in two days time, the rehearsal tomorrow afternoon. He had begged off dining with everyone at the Montgomery ranch afterward as someone needed to be here.

The whole town was talking about the amount money being spent. Expensive fabrics had been shipped in months ago for the wedding dress and trousseau, and a seamstress hired. A hotel room had been reserved for the Lutheran pastor coming with the MacDonald's, and several more for other guests. Daniel figured one would be for Margareatha and another for MacDonald. How would he disguise his age? Daniel did not wish to see either.

"Have you warned him about your Grandfather?"

"Why, of course. I've told him he was younger than grandmother, and the biggest man in size and heart he will ever meet." She smiled sweetly at Daniel and whirled out the door as the train whistled the approach of the two o'clock arrival.

The town would think it strange that he did not greet his own brother, but Daniel refused to move. Edward would have the carriage there to take them to Melissa's house and transport any other passenger of the wedding party. He began to clean his revolver.

An hour later the tedium was broken as boot heels clicked over the opening and a shadow filled the room. Daniel looked up expecting to see Edward or one of the townspeople. Instead the man removing his hat was his mirror image without a mustache. He was clad in a suit rather than work denims and the sideburns were grey. He relaxed when he realized Lorenz was without his revolvers.

"I'm glad we won't need to argue about you removing your guns."

Lorenz smiled, his whole face changing from grimness to one of genuine likeability. It was as though an aura appeared around his face, a warm glow that drew people to him. Daniel could remember MacDonald telling them how magnificent their mother looked whenever she smiled.

"Hello, big brother. Melissa said she had invited y'all for dinner tonight, and I wanted to make sure y'all knew we will be disappointed if y'all don't show up."

"I'm sorry, but I've given Edward the evening off to be with you." Daniel found his voice stiff and his eyes and lips unable to smile.

The smile disappeared from Lorenz's face and he shrugged. "Tomorrow then." And the doorway was empty.

Daniel made it through the night and part of the morning before heading to Melissa's house. He knew Lorenz, MacDonald, and the pastor were out riding with Edward to see the country. The seamstress was at Melissa's house for the last of the fittings before the whole party left for the Montgomery ranch for the rehearsal, the wedding, and the celebration. He needed to ask Antoinette one question.

A Mexican woman clad in a grey dress opened the front door at his knock and then stood there open-mouthed looking at his mustache. Finally she blinked her eyes and remembered to say, "Si, senor?"

"Is Mrs. MacDonald in? Tell her it's Daniel Hunter."

The door opened directly into the parlor, and he heard Antoinette's voice. "Conchita, let Mr. Hunter in and bring us some coffee, por favor."

The maid opened the door wider. Daniel was desperate to talk with Antoinette and the idea of a servant annoyed him. He stepped inside to find Antoinette sitting on the sofa, a writing desk on her lap while she wrote.

"Daniel, what a pleasant surprise this is. Won't y'all have a seat? Y'all know, of course, that Lorenz and Father MacDonald are riding with Edward, or target practicing, or something similar to become better acquainted." She was smiling, but not a "you are really welcome here" type of smile.

"Yes, but it's you I wish to speak with. I was hoping for something more private. Perhaps somewhere outside would be better as I have a question that needs answering."

"No, Daniel, it wouldn't." She smiled again. "I believe Conchita will be back soon with the coffee. She'll retire to the back where the last of the fittings are going on, and then we can talk." Her head indicated the delicate chair by the fancy little table adorned with a floral blue and gold lamp.

How, Daniel wondered, was a man supposed to live in a house like this? Why hadn't Edward insisted they move into something smaller, or have Melissa share his room at the boarding house? He removed his hat and sat on the indicated chair. The cherry arms and legs were rounded and a blue floral crewel was on the upholstered seat. It was almost as fancy as chairs at the better bordellos. His hat he hung on his knee.

"I'm so glad you've decided to participate in the wedding ceremony. Edward seems to think of y'all as the father he doesn't have."

Daniel scowled. He hadn't decided to participate. Antoinette's answer would decide that issue. Before he could respond, Conchita returned carrying a tray with two cups of coffee. First she offered one to him and then the other to Antoinette.

"That will be all, Conchita. Please, see if Miss MacDonald needs some extra help. Y'all have such a lovely way with clothes and hair."

She turned back to Daniel. "Now, I believe y'all said y'all had a question."

Daniel took a deep breath. "I need to know why you chose Lorenz."

Antoinette stared at him and he plunged on. "Did he force you by going into your mind and you've been afraid to tell anyone all of these years."

"Oh for heaven's sake, Daniel, where did y'all every come up with such a silly idea? Lorenz was hundreds of miles away and could not have been in my mind. His abilities aren't that far reaching."

Daniel rose from the chair, his coffee untouched. The taste in his mouth was bitter enough.

"Then why, Antoinette? Why did you choose him? I was older, better able to protect you and earn a decent wage."

Antoinette leaned back slightly, disbelief on her face. "Daniel, Lorenz was going to inherit the ranch."

"You chose him instead of me because of a ranch?"

"Father MacDonald offered you the same terms. Y'all told me y'all turned it down. Y'all believed more in that pagan Comanche mumbo-jumbo than you ever did in Christ. What's more y'all rejected your own mother for Indians. As for your wages, y'all were a hired gunny. That meant I'd have to follow y'all from town to town. That certainly is not what I wanted: living like some poor, white trash." The last words were practically spit out.

It was like a blow to his stomach. "Then all of those rides, those picnics, they were a farce?"

"Daniel, I was a wicked flirt. I do admit that, but we were young, and I was the same way with all the other young men."

"You didn't go riding with them." Daniel's voice sounded strangled even to his own ears.

"Well, of course not. Red would never have permitted it. Y'all were being paid to protect me, and y'all were certainly a lot more fun than those old men with bad breath and big stomachs. Red told me what his plans were for me and how he would ship me to a convent if I didn't marry one of them."

Daniel began to breathe again. "I could have taken you out of there."

"Where would we have gone that Red couldn't have found us and taken me back?"

"I was still on good terms with the Comanche. Not even Red..."

The horrified look on her face stopped his words. "I would never, never have considered going to an Indian village and living like some sort of squaw. I told both you and Lorenz that when I was sixteen. If you must know, I had accepted Lorenz while I was back East the year before we were wed." The drawl was gone from her voice.

He took two steps toward her and stopped. "Why, Antoinette? Why Lorenz? I can't believe you didn't love me."

Antoinette stood. "Daniel, y'all are being unreasonable. Y'all and Lorenz are still two of the most handsome men I have ever seen, but Lorenz offered me a future."

"I don't see you objecting to Melissa marrying Ed because of their future."

"Do y'all think we could really stop Melissa? I'm sure Edward will find another occupation or a higher office one day that will be more rewarding." Her voice was cool, her eyes distant.

Daniel finally noticed the jeweled pendant, the rings on her fingers, and the elaborate watch pinned to her work dress. Her clothes, her hair, everything said money. For years he held the belief that Antoinette was a woman who followed the lead and desires of the man she loved. Instead, she was a woman who wanted all the trappings of the white man's world.

"Your worldly possessions mean more to you than being honest." He turned on his heel and walked out of the door. All these years he'd been a fool dreaming of rescuing the woman he loved. Antoinette did not love either of them. Did Lorenz know? Then it hit him. Lorenz didn't care. Lorenz had what he wanted: Antoinette. Outside Daniel mounted and rode away.

Chapter 30

Death in a Frontier Town

Melissa waved to Eddie who was standing by the Constable's office before she entered Farren's Grocery Market. This was the town's newest store built across the street and kitty-cornered from the bank. "Plain dealing for plain folks," Farren boasted.

Farren had left Kansas and headed north for the new cow country. He missed the trail crews and followers. The trail towns had withered without them, and farmers were a sober lot. Montana was still cow country and he felt a certain kinship for the rawness of the area. It was almost like Kansas once was. Farren, however, was a realist.

Like many people who lived through the drover era, Farren believed any town based on cattle economy would suffer violence. He kept two rifles, loaded and ready, one over the door entering from the street and another close to hand under the counter by the cash register.

Eddie had been unable to convince the man that in 1896, these precautions were no longer necessary. The fact that he was running for the newly created office of county sheriff when Constable Hunter moved on at the end of this year should have given weight to his argument. Farren would have none of it.

"I ain't but five-foot five and nearing 60. How else am I going to stop some drunken cowboy from taking all my hard-earned cash to squander on some fallen dove? Beg your pardon, ma'am." He lowered his voice to avoid disturbing his customers.

"This conversation is over, Deputy. Now you can have Constable Hunter come talk to me, but that ain't going to work either. I've got customers that need my assistance." He grabbed the hook and marched over to a lady looking up at the soap powders on a fourth level shelf.

Melissa smiled to herself as she remembered that conversation and nodded to Farren. He was busy helping some matron with her grocery list, neatly snagging the items off the shelf or sending the boy to the back to fetch the larger items.

She wandered over to the bolts of material and back. Mama always ordered the latest fashionable materials and shipped them to her. Eddie never knew the cost. He accepted the fact that her parents were rich Texas ranchers without realizing that the MacDonald family had settled ten thousand dollars on her in 1895; the year she turned twenty-one. Melissa instructed the family lawyer to purchase five thousand dollars worth of General Electric stock. A company that supplied lighting like that in the *Golden One* couldn't fail. She knew she had a knack for picking just the right investment. It was hard to keep track of things here though. If she were in New York, she'd have to hire a man to work at the exchange. Women weren't allowed on the floor. Melissa sighed. For now she would have to let things ride. Perhaps she and Eddie could go to New York after he'd served as County Sheriff. There was no doubt in her mind that Eddie would win the upcoming election. After he had served in that capacity for a few years, Eddie could run for the state congress and then the federal.

Farren was busy adding up the woman's purchases when Melissa heard yelling outside. Something was wrong. She felt her stomach tighten and she glanced up and down the street. Eddie was running towards the bank carrying his Winchester. Clyde Munson, the newspaperman, was following behind him, his pad and pencil in hand.

She was so intent on watching her husband, Melissa didn't see the three men run out of the bank, but she heard the gunshots. Eddie fell downward into the dust, blindly firing his rifle in the direction of the three men mounting their horses.

Melissa reached up and yanked the rifle down. Her Eddie was down and those men were still shooting at him and at anyone on the street. Rage filled her and her mind cleared of all other thoughts.

She set the rifle into her shoulder and stepped through the opened door unmindful of the bullets. The men had ridden past her and she shot: once, twice, thrice.

Two of the men tumbled from their saddles and the third clutched at his shoulder, unable to fire another shot. Melissa turned slightly to keep the horse and rider in her sights and fired again at the fleeing man. She knew he would die as he slumped completely over the front of the blindly running horse.

Melissa ran to her Eddie, knelt in the dust rutted street, and started to turn him over. Suddenly, Uncle Daniel was there beside her, trying to move her away and attend to Eddie. She glared at him.

"He's dead. He died doing your job."

She could not bear to look at Eddie's opened eyes; nor would she permit herself to cry in front of these people. She was still so angry she wanted to kill and she had killed them all.

"Melissa, he was my friend."

Daniel gave up trying to move her and stood. He motioned to one of the bystanders. "Fielding, go fetch the undertaker."

He turned to the men gathered around. "I'm going after the one that rode off. He won't go far. I'll need at least one or two men. The pay is $1.00 a day. We'll probably be back by nightfall."

Two of the younger men stepped forward. They were line riders from one of the ranches who were either laid off or between jobs. The dollar each would pay for a bed, a meal, and drinks.

Mrs. Gatson from the newspaper appeared. "What about your poor niece? I'll gladly see her home and sit with her."

"Fine, if you can get her to move." Daniel could barely contain his fury. Edward had been his friend, the son he never had, and somehow, someway, Lorenz in a direct line through Melissa stole his revenge. For the first time in years he wanted to kill.

Someone brought his horse and they rode out of town. They were back before twilight. The rider had clung to the horse with a dead man's grip and the horse was in no mood to stop with the smell of blood coming from its back.

Daniel did not wish to call on his niece, but knew he must if this town was going to give him a recommendation when he left. He was surprised when Melissa opened the door and no one was with her. Melissa's eyes were not red and she showed no signs of crying.

"Uncle Daniel, I'm so glad you came by. I said a cruel thing to you today. I'm sorry." Her voice broke just a bit.

"Please, come in. Did you find that man?"

"Yes, he was dead." Daniel's throat was tight and the words barely intelligible.

"Did y'all want some water or coffee? There's some kind of food sitting on the kitchen table that the neighbors brought. I can't eat anything."

"No, thank you. Isn't someone staying with you? Didn't the doctor give you something?"

Melissa's gray eyes regarded him as though he were a stranger. "Y'all forget I'm a Texan and a MacDonald. Hysterics are for other women. I'll arrange the funeral tomorrow. Once it's over I am going east. Perhaps Aunt Margareatha will go with me. Grandpa and Grandmère LouElla already spend a better portion of the year there.

"I need for y'all to arrange for the pallbearers, Uncle Daniel. I'm sure if I did it, they would all have the same look of horror on their faces as yours." She smiled.

"Now would you care for something to eat?"

Daniel turned and walked away.

Chapter 31

The Fugitive

Wind lashed the October rain against the windows and roof while the prairie wind screamed for attention. Each bolt of lightning was followed by window rattling thunder. Toni lowered her book and looked over her glasses at Lorenz reading. Really, it was quite annoying the man didn't need glasses. She halfway sighed. At least his hair was graying faster than hers. That surprised her. They'd been married for thirty years and both were forty-nine. Lorenz hadn't really aged that much except for weather roughened skin, but the graying hair kept people from suspecting there was anything different in his heritage. Antoinette's figure was now quite matronly, but that was expected from a woman in her position. She was about to suggest they retire when he looked up and around as though searching for someone.

"What is it, dear?"

"Kendall, he's out there. He needs us. I heard him in my mind. He can't be far." Lorenz stood and laid the book down. "Y'all had best stir up that fire in the stove and heat something to eat. We'll need blankets when we get back."

He grabbed his slicker from the kitchen porch and came back through the kitchen; a wide room spread with brown and white checked linoleum. They'd sent the help to bed and were in the kitchen as the coffee was handy and the black and silver iron cook stove kept the room warm.

Antoinette looked up at him. "Are y'all sure? Kendall? What else could y'all discern?"

"Nothing, except he's exhausted and worried about somebody needing warm, dry clothes, and a blanket for some reason."

Antoinette wrinkled her nose. "Well, maybe he's lost his."

Lorenz continued walking towards the front door where his hat hung on a burnished brass tree stand. "No, it was someone needing it." He slammed the hat on his head. "I'll be back as quick as I can. Whatever y'all have to eat, make sure there's plenty of broth." He pulled the door shut against the storm.

"Dear, God, how is he going to see anything in this weather?" Toni spoke half aloud. Should she wake Conchita for help in preparing the bedroom? If Kendall wasn't out there, how could she possibly explain to a lady's maid that she had been roused for nothing? Tears filled her eyes. Her Kendall was coming home after all these years. Her baby boy. Only he wasn't a baby. He would be twenty-eight now. Her mood swung from ecstasy to bitterness. Her baby was coming home after all these years of not knowing where he was or what happened to him. But what if Lorenz was wrong and he wasn't out there? Her disappointment would be doubled.

It took Lorenz but minutes to saddle his horse and one more. He tied a tarp to the back of his saddles and rode out into the wind, rain, and muck. It was slow going. His hold on Kendall's mind was tenuous at best as Kendall wasn't capable of mindspeak. It was only when Kendall's mind wandered in desperation for the need of home and shelter that he could be sure of his bearings. The wind sliced through any exposed area and drove the rain into the horses' coats, into his neck, under his tied-down hat, and it was dark, dark, dark. A lantern in this wind would be futile.

It seemed like hours to Lorenz when he finally spotted looming shapes a few feet away. Kendall was on the ground leading two horses. One horse had an empty saddle and the other held a bulky rider swaying in the saddle. Both horses could barely move. As he pulled up alongside, Kendall fumbled at his slicker as though to pull his gun.

"Son, it's me, your father."

Kendall's head was bare and his hair flattened against his skull. In the darkness his skin was grey.

"Pawpaw?"

Lorenz swung down to stand beside his son.

"Pawpaw, how did you know? My wife, our child, you've got to get them to the ranch. They're exhausted. We can't go on, but I've got to go back."

"Why?"

"I shot a man back there. He might die. I've never killed a man, Pawpaw. I just shot to slow him down or stop him." Kendall was practically sobbing.

"Why did y'all shoot him?"

"He was trying to take our little girl back."

"Is she your daughter?"

"Yes." Kendall shouted over the wind and thunder.

"He can rot. Right now we get everyone home."

There was a viciousness in Lorenz's tone that woke Kendall. His father hadn't changed over the years. If a man tried to murder or harm someone in his family, that person could back away or die. It was a coldness of purpose that Kendall knew he did not, would not possess, but he was too tired to articulate it.

"Y'all can ride the other horse and I'll carry your wife and baby on mine."

"She won't let you. She's frightened, and she's blind. I'll have to carry her."

Lorenz leaned closer. "Are y'all able to lift her unto your horse?"

"I don't know." The words caught in his throat.

"Then convince her to let me carry her or lift her onto your horse." He turned away and mounted.

Kendall dragged himself up into the saddle, the horse shying at his heavy movements. Once mounted, he edged closer to his wife and reached out for her and their daughter. Then he realized he needed to undo the rope he'd used to lash them to the saddle. His fingers fumbled at wet rope knots that wouldn't budge. Somehow Alice was alert, but she needed to hang onto Sarah and she was unable to help him.

"It's my father," Kendall was yelling at her. "We'll all be safe in a little while." And his anger rose at his futile attempts at the rope. This horse was wearied and gaunt. It wouldn't make it carrying Alice and the baby.

Lorenz appeared on the other side and he slashed through the rope with his knife.

"Tell her, I'm going to lift her off and onto my horse. That lightning isn't letting up. We have to get home."

"Did you hear him, Alice? He'll lift and carry you both. I'm not sure I can lift you both right now."

Lorenz reached over while Kendal lifted Alice's leg from the other stirrup. The horse she rode was too exhausted to move in the muck without urging and stood with hung head and legs splayed.

Kendall saw the empty saddle and the bulk on his father's horse. He gathered the reins of the horse, rode to the one he'd been riding, and took its reins. He kicked at the flanks of his horse to move after his father. Both ranch horses were eager to return to the barn and they moved steadily homeward, both men praying the horses would keep their footing.

All the animals were wet with rain and sweat when they reined up at the front steps of the house. As if on signal the front door opened and yellow lamp light spewed out onto the porch, giving them enough light to see. Kendall dismounted, tied the horses to the rail, and then supported his wife and baby as Lorenz lowered them to the ground.

Lorenz dismounted and took Alice's other arm to help them up the steps and into the house. Once they were inside, Antoinette swung the door against the wind and closed it. She did not mention their soggy condition. She set the lamp down and was about to throw her arms around Kendall when she saw the waif-like head of a blond child emerge from under the wet blanket.

"Oh, my goodness! Kendall is that child yours and y'all didn't write?"

"Antoinette, forget the recriminations. They need dry clothes, blankets, and hot food. I'll be back as soon as I've tended to the horses."

Kendall started to follow his father and Lorenz stopped him.

"No, y'all are needed here to help your mother."

"I can't stay, Pawpaw. I've got to check on that man."

"Kendall, your responsibility is to your woman and child, and your mother needs help. Take them into the kitchen where's it warm and then carry that rocker in there."

He turned to Antoinette who was staring at all of them. "Toni, did y'all heat up some food while I was gone?"

She nodded. "I've set extra blankets on our bed just in case."

He smiled at her and left the house. The horses were too important and needed to be stabled and wiped down. Tomorrow, he'd have one of the men check on them and walk them around the corrals. He could hear Toni snapping orders as he stepped through the door.

"Kendall, I do wonder about y'all. Now take those two into the kitchen and bring that rocker in there. I'll pull out the chair. Here, let me take the little darling. What is her name? After we're in the kitchen, y'all go after those blankets I mentioned."

Kendall was practically dragging Alice along. "It's Sarah, Mama, but right now I don't think Alice can let loose of her."

He stepped into the warmth of the kitchen where heat radiated from huge, ornate wood stove and guided Alice to one of the strait-backed chairs at the table. "Alice, this is my mother. She won't hurt you or little Sarah. She has some food and blankets ready. Please let her help you while I go after the rocker."

Puzzlement was spreading across Toni's face. Was there something wrong with her daughter-in-law? The woman was looking at Kendall, but she looked nowhere else. She realized that their faces were all too thin. Not good, and then Alice's eyes closed and she seemed to hold the child closer.

"For heaven's sake, Kendall, what is the matter?"

"We've had a terrible trip, Mama. I'll hold her in the chair, if you'll bring the blankets. Sarah's teeth are chattering."

Antoinette went after the blankets, piled them in the rocker, and then lifted the rocker and carried all into the kitchen, banging a couple of her fine dining chairs as she walked pass them. The child was the priority. Why hadn't she wakened Conchita? She'd have to use one of the dish towels for make-shift britches. Her children's clothes were given away long ago, and why, why hadn't Kendall written to her? She set the rocker down with a thump.

"Y'all pull those nasty wet things off of them. I'll put one of these blankets in the rocker and then y'all set them in there. I'll give y'all a hand."

"It's all right, Mama. I'll do it. Alice is blind and she hasn't had a chance to see your face."

Antoinette stood in stunned silence, for once totally speechless. This was not what she expected, and how in the world did a blind person see? I do hope they don't start talking in some strange language. German is bad enough, she thought to herself.

"They're both dead beat, Mama. If you could heat some milk for little Sarah, please. We ran out of canned milk two days ago." He was pulling at the wet wraps and clothes, and then he guided his wife and little girl to the rocker and wrapped the blanket around them. Next he laid the other blanket over Alice and the child, extending it up and over their shoulders. He could hear his mother putting a pot on the stove and going to the back porch. It seemed that hadn't changed. This time of year, the milk would be in a covered jar in a cabinet in the back porch.

The back kitchen door closed and Antoinette returned with the covered pitcher.

"Alice, Mama's going to heat Sarah some milk. I've got to help Pawpaw with the horses. We're safe here."

He stood and looked at his mother. "That's all right, isn't it Mama? She can't fall out of the rocker and Pawpaw's got four wet horses out there."

Antoinette poured the milk in the pot and for an answer walked across the kitchen. "Not without my hug, Kendall."

She hugged and kissed him as though he would disappear again. "Now go help your father. Everything will be fine here."

Kendall hurried to the front and out the door. It took him a moment to orientate himself as he stepped onto the porch. He knew where the barn should be, but it had been almost ten years since he rode off. A jagged bolt lit up the landscape and he saw the barn. He struggled through the heavy mud as rapidly as possible before another bolt split the sky. It was then it struck his sleep deprived mind that he and has father had tracked mud through the huge entry way and dining room without his mother screaming in protest. And how, how had Pawpaw known to come after him?

The wind had died down, but the rain was steady. He entered the stable portion of the huge barn and found his father working on the second horse. The lantern cast a yellow light over the scene; enough light to drive away most of the shadows. He grabbed an old saddle blanket and began rubbing on the third horse. Kendall wasn't sure the oldest of the spent horses was going to make it and he had no idea how he would pay for another unless he could hole up here for awhile. His father nodded at him as he entered and the two worked in silence, the horses jerking their heads to pull in a mouthful of hay, then munching the hay and occasionally stomping their feet before taking another mouthful.

Kendall began reviving as they threw a blanket over the last of the dried horses.

"I'm glad your back, son." Lorenz threw his arms around the startled Kendall and pulled him close.

When had his father last hugged him? He couldn't remember.

"Where the hell have y'all been? Not many a man could give me the slip like that. We searched all over the West for y'all." Lorenz had him by the shoulders and was smiling straight into his eyes.

Kendall tried to sort that one out. Wasn't his father ashamed of him? Was he proud because he, Kendall, had managed to elude those that came after him?

"I worked in a Wild West show for awhile as Tex the Gun Slinging Man and did tricks with drawing and shooting. Not many could beat me."

"And everybody and their brother takes the nickname Tex whether they're from Texas or not. Why the lost accent if y'all were Tex?"

"I met Alice up in Keokuk, Iowa when we were doing a show. She was from the Dakotas, but was attending school there. We fell in love and I moved back there with her. People would snicker at her for marrying a real moron that couldn't talk right, so I started to speak like them."

Lorenz extinguished the lantern, carefully hung it on the hook near the door-jamb, secured the door, and they headed for the house.

Up on the porch, Lorenz led the way around to the back. "We've already tromped through the front once with mud on our boots," he said by way of explanation. The lightning and thunder had rolled on towards the north.

"Pawpaw, no matter what you say I've got to ride out in the morning and check on that man, but right now I'd like some of that food Mama had heating."

Chapter 32

Justice Texas Style

Lorenz and Kendall rode out as daylight was breaking. Kendall was praying that Alice would sleep until he returned. Antoinette had directed them to his old room. Except for the bedding, it looked like he had just left; even his clothes were in the closet, chest, and armoire. He mulled over his last conversation with his mother. She had Lawrence bring in the mattress from Melissa's old room and placed it on the floor for Sarah's bed. Tomorrow the crib could be brought down from the attic.

"Put it right beside Alice," he'd instructed her.

"She can't see. Won't there be a danger in that?"

"No, mama, she'll reach down with her hand and know whether something is there. If Sarah cries, Alice can locate her by the sound, honest."

Antoinette had looked dubious, but complied. "I've put an old dressing gown of mine on the chair and some stockings. They'll just have to do until we have sewn something different tomorrow. I'll send one of the Mexican women up here to keep an eye on the baby in the morning…"

"She's almost three, Mama."

"…so that if Sarah wakes up first, we'll take care of her." Antoinette finished her sentence. This was her household and she ran it. He wasn't sure just how Alice would respond to his mother's ideas of a properly run household.

He and his father had met as he came down the stairs and both headed for the kitchen. They each filled a bowl with the cold stew and stood while eating. They put the bowls and spoons into the dishpan and walked through the back door. Lorenz grabbed his hat from the rack in the enclosed back porch, and handed Kendall an old one.

The ground remained muddy. A light breeze blew in from the south, but the air had warmed considerably. Overhead the stars retreated behind the thinning grey clouds.

"I'll have to borrow a horse from one in your remuda, Pawpaw."

"We'll take two from the stable. It's too muddy to bother the ones outside, plus I don't keep as many as we once did. Everything has changed."

"How?"

"The whole ranch is fenced. Most of the hands spend their time riding the fence lines until roundup. At least that's the same. We cut and brand twice a year now. Then we cull the ones for market and bring them in closer to increase their feed before taking them to Schmidt's Corner to ship out."

Lorenz smiled at his son. "The railroad has made Schmidt's Corner a far more important town and we've eliminated the fights with the unreconstructed rebels in Arles when we had to take a herd in there."

Once they were in the saddle the going was slow until they reached higher, rockier ground. Kendall was frowning.

"I think it's over by Buster's Roost. It was dark when we got there, and we were all exhausted. With the storm coming in, we needed shelter. I didn't realize until almost too late that the man trailing us was that close."

"If you're sure enough, we'll ride that way. The rain will have washed out most of the tracks, but I want to check first."

Upon reaching the trail descending from Buster's Roost, Lorenz dismounted and went down into a squat, his right hand almost on the ground, as he duck walked around part of the old trail. Finally he stood. "Yes, horses came down this way last night. I don't see new tracks going up or coming down."

He swung back into the saddle and they rode on.

"Why was that man after you all?"

Kendall let out his breath. "It's a long story, Pawpaw."

"Well, try telling it." The words were a command.

"People had a hard time accepting the fact that a blind woman could care for a baby, but she could. That's why when the war with Spain broke out; I thought I could go ahead and join up. My country needed men like me, and Teddy Roosevelt is a good man, maybe he'll be a great one. If one of my friends from the lumberyard (that's where I was working), hadn't got a telegram to me before I signed up, I'd be in Cuba.

"The president of the largest bank in town and his wife had petitioned the state for our little girl. The judge, he's a friend of the banker, gave Sarah away. Alice screamed and carried on so that they put her in an insane asylum."

"I got back as fast as I could and broke Alice out of there. They weren't expecting that. Then we went back to Harlan, and I hid Alice along a creek with willows as a cover. I did have to tie a rope around her waist so she wouldn't go too far and fall in the water at night while I went after Sarah. I managed to sneak into the banker's house (I'd helped deliver the lumber and build the house), and I knew where the nursery was located. We'd all laughed about it when building it because we knew she was too old to be having any children. I didn't know they were planning to steal my daughter." His voice was bitter.

"How the hell did y'all see in there in the dark of night?"

"There was moonlight that night, moonlight so bright it gave enough light to read by. The stairs were a little tricky, but I made it. Nobody was in Sarah's room and I just scooped her up and headed out. She didn't start crying until I mounted the horse. Alice was so glad to see us she didn't chew me out until the next day for not getting some clothes and blankets."

They'd reached the area called Buster's Roost in honor of some long ago miner who had vainly searched for nonexistent silver or gold he was sure that the original land grant Mexican must have mined or hid to live this far from civilization. The pull of real silver in Mexico had eventually lured him away.

"There, he should be over there."

Both men dismounted at the empty space. The ground here was dryer, sandier and the walking was easy. The outcrop of rock ended abruptly as though it was surprised at being in a portion of Texas that was more prairie than high, rocky ground, but there was the stain of blood on the rocks.

Lorenz swung back into the saddle. "It's a ride into town, son. Either y'all just winged him or someone found him and took him there."

Kendall nodded glumly. "Pawpaw, I'm wanted up in South Dakota. I can't go into town."

"Why are y'all wanted? Did y'all rob somebody after taking off with your wife and child?"

"No, Pawpaw, the charge is for kidnapping my our own little girl. I had enough money to keep us going until we got down into Colorado. I went to work for a ranch when this bounty hunter came into town about three months ago and started asking questions. We've been working our way here since."

"Why the hell didn't y'all just write or telegraph?"

"I didn't think I'd be welcomed, but figured I could talk Mama out of some money. I know I ran like a coward when Marty was killed. I couldn't face you, Uncle Martin, or Aunt Brigetta."

Lorenz stared at his son like a stranger and then exploded. "For God's sake, Kendall, you are my son! I'd let myself die before I'd let anyone hurt you or yours. And why you think Martin and Brigetta would blame you is beyond my comprehension. They've been as worried about you as we have."

Kendall stared at his father. For the first time in his hearing, Lorenz had not said y'all. What did he mean, "let myself die," or was that a slip of the tongue too?

Lorenz's eyes were blazing. "We're going into town. This is Texas. Thomas Jackson is Justice of the Peace. Do you believe he's going to toss you into jail because you took your own child?"

Kendall shook his head. "Why would Thomas be Justice of the Peace instead of his pa?" He closed his eyes against the bright, glaring sun. *Hell, Thomas would be thirty or more now.* He opened his eyes to find his father staring down at him.

"Forget what I just said, Pawpaw, this is Texas and you and Uncle Martin run this section." He remounted his horse.

They rode single file until they were on the rolling prairie again. Once they were down, Lorenz turned and asked, "Do y'all see that rider coming?"

"Yes."

"It's our hired deputy sheriff. The county didn't want to pay for a deputy sheriff out here, so Schmidt's Corner hired one and the sheriff in Arles swore him in. The surrounding ranchers throw in a few bucks every year to help keep the peace during the time we're taking our beeves to market. He looks like a man on a mission."

Inwardly Kendall cursed. He knew he'd be arrested, possibly for murder, but running was out of the question. Why wasn't his father more concerned?

"Is this man one you and Uncle Martin picked?"

Lorenz shot his son a quizzical look. "Of course we didn't. The committee was Gerald, Thomas Jackson, and Ernest. Ernest has a house in town and runs the bank. Remember, when Margareatha stayed with us after losing her husband and children, she taught him accounting. Ernest never liked chasing after cattle."

Kendall sat back in the saddle. Things had changed, but he couldn't see that this provided a way out.

"Uh, Pawpaw, I can't afford a lawyer."

"I don't know why not. You've got close to eleven thousand dollars in your account at the bank in town."

"I what?"

"Shouting isn't necessary, son. We, that is Antoinette, Papa, and Grandmère made sure there was ten thousand dollars in cash and stock in an account for each of our children at the age of twenty-one. The stock has paid enough dividends that the account has grown. Y'all can afford any lawyer y'all want."

Kendall felt his stomach knot. Alice and Sarah were provided for no matter what happened. He knew the stock would be from the MacDonald Corporation, but he hadn't paid much attention to his father's involvement in business. He had followed Marty, and to Marty ranching and hunting were the only two fit occupations for a man.

The man on the roan pulled to a stop. A tan Stetson was set on graying hair. He was wide shouldered and stocky for a cowman. A grey mustache coved the lip area, and to Kendall the man appeared to be about forty-five.

"Howdy, Mr. MacDonald, have you seen..." and the man stopped in mid-sentence.

"Hello, Wade, y'all don't need to be so formal. This is my son, Kendall Mac-Donald; Kendall, Wade Gilliam."

Gilliam nodded at Kendall. "How do." He turned back to Lorenz.

"I'm on official business. A man was shot last night up around Buster's Roost. He's a bounty hunter out of South Dakota looking for a kidnapper. The kidnapper has a child and a mad woman with him. He's about thirty, dark haired, blue eyes, slim build, about six..." Gilliam suddenly looked back at Kendall as he realized the general description would fit.

"That would be me, except my wife isn't mad and I don't believe a man can kidnap his own child. I am guilty of shooting back at a man that shot at me first, and right now, I'm regretting that I didn't do more damage."

Gilliam swung his gaze back to Lorenz. He was a Westerner and he knew this could be dangerous. MacDonald, however, was sitting easy in the saddle.

"Kendall has explained most of what happened, and we were coming in to straighten things out. I take it the man is not only well, but will live to make a nuisance of himself."

"If y'all call someone with a valid extradition warrant from the state of South Dakota a nuisance, I reckon y'all are correct. I have to take him in."

He turned back to Kendall. "Y'all are under arrest. The Justice of the Peace will conduct a hearing on the extradition warrant. If that man wants to press charges, I'll have to add attempted murder."

"If so charged, it would just keep Kendall right here." Lorenz smiled at the deputy sheriff.

Wade shrugged. It had already entered his mind that Jackson was about the same age as Kendall. He started to pull out his handcuffs when Lorenz spoke again.

"Why are y'all pulling those out? We were already on our way into town after we discovered there was no one back at Buster's Roost. Just where do y'all think he's going to run when his wife and child are back at the ranch?"

Wade was torn. He detested MacDonald as a damn Yankee, but knew full well who helped the town pay his salary. He also harbored an unspoken love for Mrs. MacDonald. How could such a beautiful, Southern woman tie up with a damn Yankee? Wade was also aware of Mrs. MacDonald's search for her missing son. It was a given in his mind that any Southern lady doted on her sons. Handcuffing Kendall would just anger her. With a shrug he returned the cuffs to the saddlebag and nodded at them.

As they neared town, Wade rode a bit in front of them to stop their progress. "I can't allow you all to stop at the Jackson house. I have to put Kendall in jail and then fetch that other fellow and Mr. Jackson."

"Wade, y'all know that isn't necessary. We'll stay away from Thomas, but we are stopping to say hello to the elder Mrs. Jackson and then we're going to the bank. When y'all have everything set up, just let us know and we'll be there. Y'all will know where we are by where our horses are."

Wade felt bile rising in his throat. He could have objected, but he also knew this town (at least the ones who hired him) would back MacDonald. His mind seemed to clear. Oh, hell, he thought, if this was one of Tillman's kids, he would have thought that a perfect solution.

"Fine, I'll let you all know when we're ready."

They rode past the holding pens for cattle and the small depot. Kendall realized that the town had spread out. The taverns were still by the blacksmith shop where the sounds of a hammer slamming against an anvil rang out, but while Ward rode on into the town proper, Lorenz led the way to the other side where houses had been built.

"There's a doctor's office, town jail, small Justice of the Peace office, a newer bank, Gerald's building a drugstore, there's also a post office, a regular school, and the railroad station with a telegraph. The other new building going up is the library. Gerald and Emily have the biggest two story home, Ernest the next, and the others belong to the people in town. The clerk at the general store rents the house portion over the store."

Kendal remained silent as he followed his father to the front of the Jackson home and up the steps to the opened front door. Lorenz pounded on the jamb.

"Hello, the house," he called out in the old greeting.

Olga appeared wiping her hands on her apron. Her figure was still blocky, and her gradually graying hair pulled into a tight bun. She took one look and swooped down on them.

"Kendall, you're alive."

Ward found them still there thirty minutes later. Olga was plying them with her famous angel food cake and black coffee. Her face was aglow from all the compliments about her baking abilities, and she kept hugging Kendall as they left.

They followed Wade into the Justice of the Peace office set next to the jail. It was a plain one-story room filled with a desk, several chairs, a built-in cabinet, and two men. One man wore a suit that had seen considerable wear and had his arm in a sling. It looked like there was a bulky dressing under his shirt and suit coat. His hair was blond and sparse, his eyes a greenish-blue, and his nose a bit bulbous for his face.

Thomas Jackson was seated behind his desk. His hair was straight and dark. His shoulders and body were enormous from the years of being a black smith, and the brown gabardine suit was under a great strain. One look at Kendall and he was on his feet.

"Kendall, my God man it's good to see y'all."

He was about to come out from behind the desk when he saw the look on Ward's face.

"Don't tell me he's involved in this."

"Here's the extraction warrant, but it looks like I need to take this to a regular judge." The new comer laid the warrant on his desk.

"Shut up and sit down or I'll throw you in jail for contempt. In fact everybody sit down." Thomas banged his fist on the desk top rather than the gravel.

Lorenz's scar pulled up the corner of the right side of his mouth as he tried to keep from smiling and sat. Kendall did likewise. Ward cleared his throat before speaking.

"Mr. Bellingham, this is Texas. A Justice of the Peace has the right to rule on that piece of paper. I'd sit down and speak when spoken to."

"Now then, Kendall, tell me what's going on." Thomas became official.

Kendall explained his situation to Thomas, his voice bitter at the justice received in South Dakota.

"Y'all are charged with kidnapping your own daughter?" Thomas was outraged. "What kind of place is South Dakota?"

Bellingham leaned forward. "Now, look Mr. and Mrs. Jensen are the legal parents of that child; plus, he's got a blind, crazy woman for a wife. What kind of care is that child getting?"

Thomas looked at Lorenz. "Is that true, Uncle?"

Bellingham was on his feet. "Uncle? What kind of law are you people practicing? Give me that warrant back and I'll take it to a real court."

"Mister, if y'all don't sit down, I'll throw y'all in the jail myself. Now let Mr. MacDonald have his say."

Lorenz tried to keep his face solemn as he answered. "Well, I'd say my daughter-in-law is blind and totally exhausted from the hard riding they've done, but little Sarah is just fine. Right now Mrs. MacDonald probably has the whole household fussing over her. I've an extensive list of purchases to make at the store before going back home."

"Which means there are umpteen dozen servants doing her every bidding." Thomas grinned at them and turned to Bellingham.

"Extradition denied." Thomas scribbled across the page, stamped it and signed his name after entering the date.

"Here's your extradition warrant. Y'all can take it anywhere y'all like, but Kendall MacDonald isn't going anywhere. That paper ain't worth the money it cost to print it in Texas. No judge in their right mind will send Kendall back. Y'all can't kidnap your own child.

"Kendall, Uncle, do y'all have time for a drink before y'all go back to the ranch?"

* * *

Antoinette was waiting on the porch as Lorenz and Kendall rode up with their purchases late that afternoon. Kendall was sporting a fancy, new grey Stetson.

"Did y'all bring the material I ordered last night and the cotton stockings?"

Lorenz smiled at her as he rode closer and handed her a wrapped bundle. Antoinette simply presumed he'd overridden any problem about a shooting.

"Of course, and Kendall has another package."

"Mama, how are Alice and Sarah?"

"They're fine. Sarah's taking a nap and Alice is making her way here."

Alice appeared in the doorway. Her blond hair was washed and braided. She was wearing one of Antoinette's old dresses of blue chambray. The dress was a bit long and it hung on her slender form.

"Kendall, is everything all right? Are we leaving? Sarah's sleeping naturally for the first time in ages."

"We aren't leaving, Alice. I've got to help Pawpaw put up the horses, but everything is fine. The Justice of the Peace didn't honor the extradition paper and the deputy sheriff in town doesn't think the sheriff or judge in Arles will bother once they find out the true story. As far as he is concerned, I shot in self-defense last night. We just need to stay in Texas until Pawpaw's lawyers take care of things in South Dakota."

"Dinner is at the usual hour." Antoinette handed the packages to the serving girl behind Alice. "At which time, you all may explain what you all are talking about.

"We have been sewing up a storm. Alice and Sarah may even have some clothes that fit by tonight." With that she led Alice back inside.

"Mama seems to have everything under control."

They'd swung their horses towards the barn. "Surely y'all didn't expect anything different. She's been taking care of things for years. Tomorrow we'll take another ride. There's something I need to show y'all. I had intended to take y'all there on your nineteenth birthday."

It was like a jolt hitting Kendall. All these years it had gnawed at him. His parents hadn't trusted him. "And the explanation of what you two were hiding from me."

"Not hiding, son. We just hadn't explained everything. Do y'all remember Mina's Story?"

"Most of it, but what does a fairy tale have to do with it?"

"It's not a fairy tale. Except for the ending, it's God's truth."

Kendall pulled his horse up, but his father kept riding. He dug his heels in and caught up.

"You're telling a bad joke, right?"

"Nope, but like your mother, y'all aren't going to believe me until y'all see the proof. I've already spent one entire night explaining about ships that can fly and I'm not going to waste another. That will have to wait until tomorrow. We can't talk about it now." They'd reached the barn and Lorenz dismounted.

"Tonight we'll explain to the ladies how things went in town and deliver the various messages, and let your mother know we've invited everybody here for the weekend."

Kendall was left completely baffled. Mina's Story was a fairy tale about creatures that weren't really human. He yanked the saddle off fully intending to ask his father more. It proved impossible. Men were crowding around and from the distance he could see a horse coming at full gallop.

"Son, it looks like August to me. Y'all better go greet him."

Chapter 33

A Visit to the *Golden One*

They rode out next morning shortly before daybreak. Kendall's head was still buzzing. He wasn't accustomed to whiskey any longer. Alice was angry with him for drinking and wanted to leave this vile place. According to her, these people were not teetotalers and therefore not Christians. Leaving, he knew, wouldn't set well with his mother. Alice wasn't placated with the promise of a house of their own on the ranch, plus servants while he took over as foreman. She was certain that his parents were hypocrites. Their professing to be Christians and giving thanks before a meal was meaningless. Everybody knew Lutherans drank and smoked. Even their woman drank. He had no arguments for her strict Methodist ways. Alice was beginning to chaff at the idea of how much they owed his parents. When he explained about their new found wealth, she was dumbfounded.

"But you must return it to them."

"I can't. It's their gift to me. The same gift as they gave my brother and sister."

There was no conversation as they rode to the hills on the East section. They rode past the place where the homesteaders once lived. The small house was now used by line riders and the infrequent traveler.

"Even travelers are disappearing," Lorenz explained. "People don't ride through the country like they once did." He led the way to the other side of the hill that looked out on the plains toward Arles, then doubled back to the midsection through a small canyon, and then upward again. They stopped at a slightly flattened area with shrubs and grass struggling to stay alive. A stunted oak provided shade where it was already shaded by the surrounding rock during the mornings.

"First I have to secure the rope and then we can push and pull." He sailed the wide-looped lasso up and over a boulder and made sure it was snug. "Y'all want to do the same or do y'all want to push?"

Kendall stared at his father. Why would he want to roll that boulder? For what purpose?

"Okay, y'all lead my horse, and I'll push." Lorenz dismounted and his crooked, pulled up smile appeared. He slung his reins over to Kendall and positioned himself behind the boulder.

"Now!"

Kendall started to move forward and behind him he heard the rolling of stones. He looked back and saw an opening. Why would his father hide a cave? And what was a cave doing up here?

"Just think, Papa can move that by himself." Lorenz smiled at the memory. "We can tie the horses to the tree. We shouldn't be too long, unless y'all want to spend a lot of time there. It took your mother two or three trips to become accustomed to it."

Silently, he followed his father into the yawning opening and realized this was far more than a cave. Lorenz reached up and pulled out something hidden behind a rock. From his hand shot a beam of light. The ground sloped downward and was wide enough to accommodate three trains running abreast with room on either side.

"Pawpaw, what the hell is that in your hand?"

"According to your grandfather, it's called a lume. It lights the way until we get down below. The vehicle your grandfather came in is down there with all the information about his people and their universe."

"Wait a minute. What is down there? Why did you say Mina's Story isn't a fairytale?"

"*The Golden One*, the ship that your Grandfather MacDonald arrived in, is down there. He and his people are Thalians, and my biological father is a Justine, the people with two hearts. I have the two hearts; something that Randall and Melissa inherited." He saw the doubtful look on Kendall's face.

"If y'all don't believe me, just listen."

Kendall saw his father's face was solemn, his eyes narrowed as the man unbuttoned the collarless shirt and summer underwear underneath. For a moment he hesitated, then removed his hat, stepped forward, and stooped to lean his head against his father's chest. The sound of two hearts beating was unmistakable and for a moment he was paralyzed by the doubled thumping. He stepped backward looking at his father as though seeing him for the first time.

"Like the Justines, I have the ability to mindspeak with another and to enter the minds of others. The Justines call those who do not possess this skill 'lesser beings.' I do not. It simply means they are different."

Kendall felt empty, but he had to know. "Randall and Melissa can do that too, can't they?"

"Yes, it's why your mother and I tried to make sure you and Randall never fought while growing up. Melissa was a bit more considerate, but equally dangerous."

"Dangerous, how?"

"Either of them could have hurt y'all without intending to or realizing the consequences."

"And they are the ones that will have children like that?"

"It may not work that way, Kendall. According to Papa, the traits can miss a generation, or even several generations, and appear in the next. The Justines and the Thalians call this the recessive genes. That won't mean anything unless y'all study their biology. It's available in the ship below if y'all are interested."

"Are you telling me that Alice and I can have children like you?"

"Yes, it's possible, just not as probable as it is for Melissa and Randall. It's simply the luck of the draw. If y'all do have a child with two hearts, y'all will require help raising that child. Your Aunt Mina did not have such a child."

Kendall was baffled for a moment. "You said Grandpa was Thalian."

"I left out the part about his biological father. Papa does not acknowledge him, but Papa has the two hearts." He smiled at Kendall. "Ready to go down?"

Kendall nodded. He didn't have the least idea where his father was leading him, but this was something everyone in the family had seen. "Why did you tell Mama?"

"Because she heard the two hearts in everyone's chest and she demanded that I explain to her how this could occur."

There was the smell of earth and the air became cooler than outside, but Kendall was beginning to feel queasy and sweaty. The walls seemed to be closer than they actually were. The knowledge that his family was far different than anything he'd ever known added to the desire to leave this place. Ahead Kendall could observe a dim light, almost gray, then gradually gaining strength until they descended into a huge underground cavern. Once they entered the cavern, Kendall stopped short, unable to move.

In front of him sat a huge, monstrous golden ovoid with what looked like a shimmering glass row located along the top of whatever this machine was. It stood three stories tall and was fully as long as ten railroad cars. Kendall had no way to gauge its thickness, but it seemed almost as wide as three trains jammed together. There wasn't any entrance that he could see.

"There it is: *The Golden One.* Papa's and Grandmère's return home vehicle. They are almost ready to move it to a new location."

"Why?" Kendall's voice was barely more than a whisper, and what did he mean "move it?" Also the fact that his great-grandmother could be alive was beyond his comprehension.

Lorenz turned towards his son and saw the sick look on Kendall's face. "I haven't told y'all the true ending to that tale. It was Grandmère who stole a *Golden One*, smashed it into the Justine planet, and escaped using a Krepyon ship. Krepyons are the ones Papa's tale named Kreppies; the mean spirited ones. Their ships don't have the technology this one does, and the support systems started to deteriorate. She landed in the Adirondack Mountains and hid it. They've bought the surrounding land and have had a hunting lodge built. They've a crew working on a basement to house the *Golden One* and the Krepyon vessel underground. They feel it won't be long before this world will have other modes of transportation, and it would be best to have the Krepyon ship loaded into this one. Your Uncle Red will supply any men needed to guard the place. Y'all think you're ready to go inside now."

"Pawpaw, how old are grandpa and his mother?"

Lorenz noted the voice was stronger and color was returning to Kendall's face.

"Remember, in the story that Thalians are long-lived?"

Kendall nodded.

"Papa is about one hundred and twenty and Grandmère is more like two hundred and twenty-five years. It's one of the reasons they are anxious to leave."

"Don't they show their age?"

Lorenz laughed. "Right now they are in their prime. Thalians, according to Papa, do not show their age until about three hundred years. Y'all will find that Papa looks like he has grey hair when he visits, but it's dyed that way. He doesn't stay long as people would eventually figure that out."

"When do you expect him?" Kendall's voice had lowered again. "Is his mother coming with him?"

"Papa will be here within a week or two once he receives that telegram. Grandmère won't be with him as that creates too many questions in people's minds. She couldn't anyway. She's married a sea captain and just had a baby."

It was too much. Kendall made up his mind. "Pawpaw, I'm going back outside where the sky and the sun are where and what they should be." He turned and hurried upward.

Lorenz blew out his breath and shook his head. Kendall was reacting like Daniel. Did that mean that Kendall would take his family and leave? Antoinette would be inconsolable. He walked after Kendall.

When Lorenz stepped outside, Kendall was leaning with his back against the boulder, agony written across his face.

"I'm sorry, Pawpaw, but I don't have the guts to go into that machine."

"Why apologize?" Lorenz's voice was gruff. "I was scared shitless when I first saw it. I was just too stubborn to let the man who would become my father know it. The fear of seeing contempt in his eyes was greater than going inside."

Kendall looked at his father and shook his head. "But you went inside. I couldn't. It's like a lot of things I can't do." His voice became bitter. "You'll just have to admit that your son is a coward. I can't do the things you do. It's the same as when I ran that night Marty died. I couldn't kill a man that just killed my best friend. Frankly, I doubt if I could ever kill a man. It was a fool's dream to even think about joining the army to fight in Cuba."

He started to turn away. Lorenz reached out and grabbed his arm and was suddenly confronted by a cocked fist.

"Whoa, son, y'all reacted just fine on that one. Now calm down a minute and listen.

"Your great-uncle Kasper would never have been able to kill a man, but that didn't mean he was a coward. When he came out here to look for Mama he was a complete tenderfoot. It's a wonder someone didn't kill him. He would stand up against people when he knew they were wrong just like you did by going after your wife and child."

"But I couldn't kill that bounty hunter; nor, could I let him lie there once I had them safe. You would have let the buzzards eat him. There is no way I can go inside that thing—whatever it is, but I'm willing to bet both Randall and Melissa have been inside without any qualms."

"What they do is their business. What y'all do is yours. Your Uncle Daniel wouldn't even get as close as y'all did. He refused to believe anything about us."

"Didn't he hear the two hearts?"

"Yes, but Daniel tended to have his own version of reality. A spaceship and a father from another planet weren't part of it. Personally, I think he did believe us and instinctively knew not to ever have children."

Kendall straightened. "I suppose that will weigh on me too."

"Kendall, aren't y'all interested in how it flies?

"No, it's not humanly possible."

"Wrong, right now the ability to move machines through the air isn't part of Earth's science, but it will be someday.

"I'm not sure how long Alice will be content to stay here, Pawpaw. Right now, I'm not sure if the hands will accept me."

"They will as long as y'all don't do something stupid like try to brand a cow on the wrong end."

Chapter 34

Patriarch of the House

"Where tis the wee one?" The man's voice was as huge as his bulk and filled every corner of the ranch house.

"And where tis that scalawag, Kendall?"

The senior MacDonald had fully matured and weighed in at three hundred and ninety-eight pounds. Every stitch of clothing he owned was tailored and his shoes cobbled, all by the finest of craftsmen. He beamed at Antoinette descending from the upper level.

"Father MacDonald, y'all made record time, but for goodness sake, do lower your voice. Sarah is sleeping."

"Wee one," he greeted her and swept her up into his Thalian embrace, laying his head first on one shoulder and then the other, while he made the "tsk" sound in each ear. Giggling, Toni returned the greeting.

"Now, Father MacDonald, y'all can't expect Alice or Sarah to greet y'all the same way. Alice is upstairs in the sewing room and we've told her that y'all were coming. She'll be down shortly, or did y'all want to ride out and look for Lorenz and Kendall?"

"Mayhap I'd best check on the laddies. Where did they go?"

"They rode out to the northeast section yesterday, and plan to ride back in today. Kendall's becoming reacquainted with the land and is taking over as foreman." There was a pleased purr in her voice.

"They'll have our original house. It's just so exciting. Would y'all like a cup of coffee or a glass of water?"

"I'll have some water later. My valise tis by the door. Which room twill be mine?"

"Why I do believe y'all can take Randall's old room. I doubt if we'll ever have a visit from him and that high society lady he's marrying."

MacDonald bent and kissed her cheek, his brown eyes filled with amusement. Antoinette's voice and words betrayed her thoughts of the cool, perfect Yankee.

"Tell the newest additions to the family that I twill greet them this eve. I have a hunch Lorenz kens I am here and tis now at the corrals." He charged merrily out the door to greet the riders approaching the barn.

Antoinette looked from the door and saw that Lorenz and Kendall had returned. They've been mindspeaking again, she thought while going to the kitchen. Angela would need to increase the amount of food for tonight's meal.

Kendall was almost swept off his feet by the exuberance of his grandfather's greeting. He was caught in a quandary. How could he accept the fact his grandfather wasn't what he thought? And yet this was the man who had given him rides on his shoulders, told wondrous tales, and always brought him gifts when he was little. Right now the elder MacDonald was gripping him by the shoulders.

"Dear Gar, ye look like yere fither."

Lorenz was laughing. "He always has. That's why Antoinette spoiled him rotten."

"Aye, tis true, and now ye are a fither. Ye must introduce me to yere family."

"Uh, Grandpa, Alice is blind. To see you, she needs to run her hand over your face." Kendall was aware that this could make people uncomfortable. How would Grandpa accept this? Worse, Alice had reacted badly to Lorenz. Afterwards she had become more concerned about staying here. What would she think when she "saw" his grandfather? To Kendall's eyes the man hadn't changed. It didn't matter that he'd dyed his hair grey. The man was as rock-hard as he had been when Kendall was little.

MacDonald's brown eyes lit with amusement. He was Thalian, and Alice's way of seeing was the perfect way to greet a new family member. He smiled broadly.

"Tis fine, laddie. Dinna worry, but Antoinette said Alice twas in the sewing room. How does she sew if she tis blind?"

Lorenz had handed the horses over to the hands and grabbed the saddlebags. He then followed the other two to the house.

"She went to a special school in Keokuk, Iowa, Grandpa, and learned to do all sorts of things. She's not helpless like a lot of people think."

"How does she get around?"

"She knows what room she's in and how many steps it takes to go where she wants to be."

MacDonald stopped. "Ye mean she keeps that all in her head?"

"Yes, sir." Kendall realized he'd fallen into his childhood way of responding to his grandfather's questions.

Lorenz had caught up with them. "How about a brew, Papa?" He deliberately used MacDonald's word for beer. "It's not what Mama used to make, but I keep a supply on hand."

"Twould be fine on this warm afternoon."

"Uh, could you two hold your drinking until after Grandpa's met Alice? If you waited until after supper it would be even better."

Both of the older men were staring at him. He tried again.

"Alice is a Methodist. She thinks drinking condemns you to hell. It's one of the reasons she wants to leave."

"Leave? Are y'all out of your mind? Y'all can't leave Texas right now. Not unless the thought of the state of South Dakota arresting y'all, taking Sarah away, and putting Alice in the sanitarium again doesn't bother you two."

"I know, Pawpaw, but she grew up thinking that way and that school just reinforced her thinking. She'll smell the liquor if you have a drink."

"Son, it's my house and if Papa wants a drink, he can have it. Besides it might keep her from figuring out that he's really a young man."

Lorenz was speaking low as they were rapidly approaching the steps to the porch or verandah as Antoinette called it. Comfortable white wicker chairs filled with soft down cushions of muted grey and green were set along the walls.

MacDonald draped his arm over Lorenz's shoulders. "How could she ken that? Did ye go into her mind."

"No, Papa, it was my skin. Yours isn't 'old' and her finger tips will tell her. I saw the look on her face when she traced my features. She made the usual comment about how much Kendall and I look alike, but she made a mistake. She said, 'their skin is identical.' She had a puzzled look on her face, and she's been rather cool to everyone since."

Kendall looked blankly at his father. How could the man sense things like that if he hadn't used his mind? Marty had said that his grandfather Rolfe always knew when people felt something was wrong. Pawpaw hadn't said anything about the elder Rolfe being different.

MacDonald smiled. "In that case, I shall have a brew. She twill nay wish to be near me."

No one was at the front as they entered, but Angela came hurrying from the kitchen. Kendall marveled that his mother always managed to have the people do exactly as she had ordered.

"Do you wish anything, senor?"

"Yes, please bring my father a beer to the office." He smiled at her.

"Papa, this is Angela. I don't believe y'all have met her. She's become head cook since y'all visited last time. Angela this is my father, Mr. MacDonald."

Angela popped a quick curtsy and hurried out of the room. She was slightly alarmed at the sight of such a big man that looked like he might hug her. Those things happened at other ranches, but so far no one had bothered her here. It was said the Patron had forbidden the other hands to go near the Mexican quarter.

They stepped into the office. Lorenz turned and laid his head on MacDonald's shoulders for the Thalian greeting. The older man responded in kind and then ran his hands down Lorenz's back murmuring, "Hello, my laddie."

Kendal stared at them baffled. Somehow, someway this was something almost sexual. He felt the stirring of his manhood. What was this?

Lorenz looked up at MacDonald and grinned. "Hello, my Papa." He turned and read the puzzlement in Kendall's eyes.

"I told y'all, Papa's Thalian. They have their own way of greeting." He poured a whiskey for himself.

"Do y'all want one Papa?"

"Nay, I twill wait for the brew, but what of Kendall?"

Lorenz snorted. "He hasn't had a drink since three nights after he got here. How are Grandmère and Lemont?"

"She tis fine and glorying in the role of motherhood. Melville has accepted the fact that the child tis his." MacDonald grinned. "It seems that the Earth genes match ours. Lemont tis two months old and waxing strong. He screams as loudly as any Thalian for food." The smile on his face broadened.

A discreet knock told them the beer had arrived and Lorenz retrieved the bottle, handed it to his father, and closed the door.

"Lorenz, I need to check on the *Golden One* while I am here. We are about ready to fly it to the new launching port, but Mither wishes to wait until Lemont tis older and Melville tis at sea again."

He turned to Kendall. "Have ye been to the *Golden One*? It twould be my pleasure to introduce ye to the different levels."

Kendall swallowed. "I've seen it and don't want to go any closer." He turned his back and then turned around. "I'm sorry, Grandpa. I can't accept any of this. I'll go see if Alice is ready for dinner."

He walked out of the room.

Llewellyn looked puzzled. "Damn," he finally muttered and turned to Lorenz. "He twill nay accept who we are?"

Lorenz sipped at his whiskey. "He couldn't handle the sight of it, Papa. At least he hasn't told me we're crazy, like Daniel did. Kendall will not go near the ship again."

"That tis a shame. Mayhap curiosity twill lead him to change his mind. His mither accepted it with a certain grace."

"Y'all forget, Papa, Antoinette is not like other women. She's a Texan." Lorenz smiled.

"Bah! What has that to do with it? She simply tis more willing to take risks, and ye are still enthralled with her charms."

"Completely," Lorenz agreed. "Better drink your brew before Antoinette announces dinner is ready."

They assembled at the large, cherry wood table set for six adults and one child as neither Antoinette nor Alice believed in feeding children separately when it was family. Dinner, however, went badly.

Alice wrinkled her nose as she pulled out her chair. Her face assumed a horrified expression when she realized the odor came from her husband's grandfather as well as Lorenz. She had just shook hands with the man and given Sarah to Kendall to put in the highchair. Instead he had boosted her up on his shoulder before sitting.

"Grandpa, this is my daughter Sarah. Sarah, this is your great-grandfather. He gives the most amazing pony rides. In fact, he helped teach me and your Uncle Randall to ride. Can you say, 'hello'?"

Alice froze as she heard Sarah say, "Hello." The word was almost a whisper.

"Hello, my wee one. Ye are a magnificent lassie. Twould ye mind if I held ye?"

Before Alice could intervene, she heard Sarah giggle. "Wee!" The laugh came again and she heard Kendall step to the highchair. She sank into her chair as the swish of Antoinette's skirts announced her arrival.

Antoinette smiled at them all and assumed her place. Then the men sat in their chairs.

"Father MacDonald, this is such a pleasure to have y'all home again." The southern voice was almost syrupy, and Alice felt her stomach clench. "Would y'all like to say the blessing?"

"Tis nay my place, wee one, but I'm sure Kendall remembers the words."

The servants brought the food as soon as Kendall finished saying grace. To Alice the smell of beer seemed to permeate the whole area. Once dinner was over and the Mexican women were clearing the table, she took Sarah by the hand and announced, "It's bedtime." She left as rapidly as possible without the grandparents kissing her baby. How dare they smell of alcohol in front of a child?

Kendall looked at the others. "I'm sorry, but Alice just can't accept your drinking."

"Well, that's too bad, Kendall, but this is our home. Drinks with a meal are firmly anchored in civilized dining as long as drunkenness is not an issue. Frankly, we've never allowed such behavior; nor, would we dream of correcting non-existing faults in someone else's home." Antoinette's tone was icy.

"Y'all are letting that sweet child Sarah believe that her grandparents are evil people."

"I'll agree that this is your home, Mother. When did you wish us to leave?" This was strange. When he was younger his disagreements had been with his father. Now they were with his mother. He could not understand why his mother and wife did not like each other. Before he could respond, Lorenz intervened.

"Kendall, y'all know that mess in South Dakota needs to be straightened out first. The other house will be finished within the week. In fact, you all can move right now. Any work that needs to be completed can be accomplished while you're living there. Agreed, Antoinette? And Toni, that last remark wasn't like y'all."

"Lorenz, I am sick and tired of my sons' selections in women looking down their noses at us; first that skinny snob of Randall's and now Alice. She didn't even have the decency to spend a full hour with our friends that came here to welcome Kendall home. That was not polite; not when our neighbors went to so much trouble to be here on such a short notice."

Kendall sat back down. He was defeated by the truth in his mother's statement and the warning gleam in his grandfather's eyes. Worse, his mother was correct. The drinking hadn't been that much that early in the evening. Of course, the fiddle playing and dancing had upset Alice too.

MacDonald cleared his throat and asked, "Why twould Randall's fiancée find fault?"

"Who knows? She seemed to consider me a robber baron and Antoinette from the worst of the slave owning plantations of the South."

Antoinette sniffed. "She even had the gall to inquire if things had gone badly in France and Italy while we were overseas, and how perhaps we should have hired a translator to accompany us since it had been so very long since I studied French. Fortunately, I was able to inform her that I did just fine and your father speaks both languages fluently."

Kendall stared at his father. "Since when?"

"It seems my mind is able to perform the translation as soon as I identify what some of the words mean. Then I have no problem understanding or speaking it. It was quite enlightening to learn what Europeans really think of the hordes of Americans doing the grand tour."

Kendall picked up his water glass and drained it. He really could have used a shot of whiskey after that statement. "Perhaps you're right, Pawpaw. It would be better if we moved into the other house tomorrow."

"That is probably the best solution." Antoinette smiled. She'd had her say, and her son was not leaving. She turned to her father-in-law.

"Father MacDonald, I want y'all to know that y'all are as welcome as ever. Ah do hope y'all will stay for at least a month. We see so little of y'all and we do need to catch up on all the family gossip. Ah hear y'all have visited Melissa too. Y'all must tell us how she is doing. Her letters can sometimes be so uninformative."

MacDonald leaned back and smiled at her. "Ye, my dear lassie, are a marvel. Melissa tis fine. She claims her stock investments from her New York office twill enrich us all, and I am beginning to believe her. She does fret about having to hire a man to do the actual trading on the floor, but she seems to have found one that tis receptive to her mind telling him when to buy or sell.

"Kendall, how long twill ye stay now that the housing tis settled?"

"Like Pawpaw says, I can't really go anywhere until the legal matters are settled. Pawpaw and Mama want to go to New York for Randall's wedding.

Alice and I have declined as Randall wrote that the reception was at some huge ballroom and that champagne would be served. Alice delivered a sermon that was heard all over the house. She doesn't understand how such 'refined, educated people could be so enmeshed in sin.' Her words, not mine.

"I think I'll go tell her about the move. Grandpa, I'll make sure you see Sarah tomorrow. Goodnight all."

The goodnights were said and the two remaining MacDonald men stepped to the sideboard. Lorenz handed his father another bottle of beer and poured two glasses of wine. He handed one to Antoinette before they resumed their seats.

"Just how long do ye think the laddie and his family twill stay?"

Lorenz grimaced. "Well, until that mess in South Dakota is over and we return from New York, but after that I can't say. It seems all of our children will live far away from us."

"Isn't that what happens in this land? Yere mither and her brither left their home for here."

"Martin's boys have stayed close." Lorenz smiled. "Maybe I should have worked ours harder."

Last Years on Earth
1921 to 1950

Chapter 35

A Death in the Family 1921

Lorenz was at the white board fence looking at the horses while drinking a cup of coffee, and wishing he could ride away his sorrow and forget why he was here. Antoinette had gone to bed with what he suspected was a non-existent headache. She wanted no one to see her weeping; after all, she was a Texan. He really wasn't thinking about one heart, two hearts, or the Schmidt's family history of bad hearts. All his thoughts were focused on losing a child. Such an event aged a man inside no matter what the outside looked like or the length of years that child had lived. Kendall's death at the age of fifty from a heart attack hurt; hurt deeply. Watching Toni grieve for her favorite son hurt, and there was nothing he could do to put things right.

The family had gathered at the MacDonald Lodge after the graveside ceremony for Kendall. He'd asked to be buried up in the mountains if he couldn't be buried in the church cemetery at Schmidt's Corner. Alice refused to consider Texas. She had not spoken to them after the funeral, or at the grave. She rebuffed their attempts to console her and hung onto Sarah or Andrew, sobbing, and using her handkerchief. Sarah would glare at him or Antoinette while supporting her mother. It was as though both blamed them for Kendall's death. According to Alice, Melissa had lured them to New York City with her fancy office and job offer for Kendall. That Alice secured employment reading and writing Braille at the Blind Institute and thoroughly enjoyed the companionship of others there did not matter. Why, Lorenz wondered, had Kendall married her?

For that matter, why did anyone marry another? He'd fallen in love with a pair of smiling, violet eyes at the age of thirteen. Seeing Antoinette again when they were sixteen had only driven the wanting her deeper. Most of the time she was a compliant wife who looked after his comforts, but at other times she was as strong-willed as his mother, Anna. He had never been sure that Alice looked after anything for Kendall. Had Kendall wounded in spirit married someone he considered more wounded than himself?

"Pawpaw, why was Uncle Kendall so different from you, Father, and Aunt Melissa?"

Elizabeth, Randall's tall, slender, auburn-haired fourteen year-old daughter brought his mind back to the now and to the young. She was standing in front of him, physically looking more like Iris than Randall, but she had the same solemn look on her face as Randall did when he was little. Her mouth was in a determined line as though she would be able to understand any adult answer if she were given one. She'd been allowed to dress in black for the funeral and wore two-inch high shoes.

"Elizabeth, hasn't your father explained any of this to you?"

"No, Pawpaw, he hasn't. That's why I came to you." Her words were clearly enunciated.

"Sweetheart, I must have your father's permission. Would y'all mind if I consulted him first? I'm not trying to put y'all off, but it is your father's place to do this."

"It has to do with Mina's Story, doesn't it, Pawpaw?"

He stared at her for a moment. This child realized there was a purpose to the story. It was a concept the adult spouses of his children never grasped, or had they? That wasn't fair to Edward, he decided. Melissa and Edward never had children, but Iris, Randall's wife, had to know. Gary, their firstborn, had two hearts. Amusement flooded his eyes and his mouth twitched.

"Elizabeth, I knew y'all were one smart young woman, I just hadn't realized how smart, but I still need to consult your father."

She pursed her lips. "If he doesn't allow you to tell me, will anyone ever tell me?"

"When you are an adult I will, but I believe he'll agree to the telling it now."

A smile lit her face. "When will you ask Father?"

He returned her smile. "Right now."

She took his hand to walk back to the lodge with him. While they were walking, he used mindspeak.

'Randall, your very intelligent daughter just asked me to explain Mina's Story. Do you wish to do so, or do you prefer Papa and me to give the explanation?'

'It would be preferable for you and Grandfather to do so.'

'Shouldn't your three sons be there? Gary needs to know the full story before he goes off to college again, and so does Wesley if that West Point appointment comes through. Benton, I'll grant is a bit young.'

'Wesley received the confirmation while we were at the cemetery. He's saying his goodbyes right now.'

'Tell him, damnit.'

'I can't. There are too many people. Benton is not mature enough.' Randall ended the mind connection. Unconsciously, Lorenz had increased his stride.

"Pawpaw, I can't walk that rapidly with these shoes and tight skirt."

"Uh, sorry, little lady, we need to go to the great room. It seems Wesley is leaving."

"Pawpaw, how do you…"

Before she could finish speaking, Wesley ran out the back door with his suitcase and the chauffeur trailing him.

"Pawpaw, I was going to look for you. I'm leaving. I have to be at West Point in four days."

He smiled broadly and put out his hand. Lorenz shook the hand when he would have preferred to hug this broad-shouldered, young man with the sandy hair, light brown eyes, and gleaming smile.

"Congratulations, Wes, we're proud of y'all."

"If you have a connection with the departed, let my great-grandfather know I'm following the warrior tradition." With another smile and a hug for Elizabeth he was gone.

"Elizabeth, would you find Gary and your MacDonald cousins for me and then all of you come to the lower conference room? We shouldn't be interrupted there."

She looked at him with puzzled eyes and then her face cleared. "You're like the Justines in the story aren't you, Pawpaw? You just spoke with my father who looks like them." She smiled at him and hurried off.

Her statement startled him, but he needed to contact his father. Mindspeak was the quickest way. 'Papa, we have some explaining to do. Elizabeth has realized the meaning of your fairytale. Meet me in the lower conference room. Ask Grandmère if she wishes to join us.'

He descended to the basement room to wait for his grandchildren. Gary and Elizabeth had followed within minutes and sat in the round chairs at the round table.

"Andrew was saying 'goodbye' to everyone when Elizabeth said you had something to tell us. He went to tell Sarah. It will be a few minutes before they are here," Gary announced before sitting down. Gary was twenty and he shifted in his seat during their wait, his brown eyes puzzled. Elizabeth's brown eyes were smiling and she waited expectantly.

Lorenz nodded and the wait began. LouElla and Llewellyn had decreed this room be done in the manner of a Maca of Don's office on Thalia. To create the illusion of windows, plush royal blue drapes hung over the wall behind him. Filled bookcases and built in cabinets lined two of the walls. The other wall had been lathed and plastered before being painted a lighter shade of blue. The chairs themselves were round, and covered with a navy blue velvet material. It was, thought Lorenz, a little overwhelming and right now, damn depressing. He would have preferred hard, wooden chairs.

Finally, Andrew came running into the room. Although he was only fifteen, he was six-foot tall and broad-shouldered. His straight, strawberry blond hair was parted in the middle and he was still all feet and nose. Lorenz figured Andrew would grow into the nose and feet. Most boys did. Andrew smiled at Lorenz and flopped into a vacant chair next to Elizabeth.

"Sorry I'm late, Pawpaw, Sarah's throwing a fuss."

To prove his words, blond, blue-eyed, petite Sarah came running into the room, her face displaying the same look of disgust as her mother's when around the older MacDonald's. He wondered why she even bothered to answer the summons.

"Andrew, I insist you come with me. Grandfather is an evil, lying hypocrite."

Lorenz stood. "That's enough, Sarah. The good Lord's fourth commandment says that you are to honor your parents. That includes your grandparents. If y'all cannot say anything decent about us in our own quarters, y'all may leave."

Sarah gasped. "How dare you use scriptures? You smoke, you drink alcohol, you have murdered men, and because you pressured my father to work with that vile aunt of mine he's dead."

"Kendall died from a heart attack just like my mother and Uncle Kasper at about the same age. I am not arguing with y'all. Either sit down and shut up, or leave."

Sarah started towards Andrew who was sitting with lips clamped together and staring straight ahead. Lorenz stepped in front of her.

"Not allowed."

"We're leaving now. Andrew must ride home with us."

"Andrew, if y'all wish to stay, we'll see to it that y'all are driven home."

"You are not the head of our family. Mother is. I'll go bring her."

She turned to flounce out, but Lorenz's words made her pause.

"Just remember Mina's Story when y'all have children and the doctors tell y'all that something is abnormal. It won't be. Then y'all will need to talk with me."

Sarah looked at him and shuddered. "I will not listen to you. Mother is correct. You and your father are not natural. You are demons!" She fled the room and the door banged behind her.

Lorenz looked at the other three. Gary was smiling his "I'm just a bit different from the rest of the human race" smile; Elizabeth was shaking her head; and Andrew gave a big sigh and stood.

"Thank you, Pawpaw."

Lorenz smiled. Elizabeth was awed. She rarely saw her grandfather or the smile that drew everyone to him. *My word, he's still a handsome man even if he is old*, she thought.

"By the way, I've asked someone to help clarify certain points. He's here now."

One of the bookcases swung outward and Llewellyn stepped into the room. Surprise, then awe registered on each face. Gary's mouth fell open and both he and Andrew straightened. Andrew had heard tales about how huge his great-grandfather was, but until now had never believed them.

"Hello, Papa, thanks for coming. Let me introduce y'all as they've grown since y'all saw them as babies.

"Everyone, this is your great-grandfather. He is known here as Zebediah L. MacDonald. In his own world he is Llewellyn, Maca of Don.

"Papa, the eldest is Gary, Randall's son," he pointed at Gary, "Elizabeth is his sister, and standing next to her is Kendall's son, Andrew, who I don't believe y'all have seen."

Elizabeth stood and curtseyed. "You would be the Prince from Mina's Story, wouldn't you? She couldn't believe her own courage, but Gary could be so irritating if she didn't beat him at something.

Amusement lighted Llewellyn's brown eyes. "For a wee lassie, ye are as clever as yere great-grandmither, but I am nay a prince."

"However, y'all are right, Elizabeth. He just used the word prince for our language. In his own world he is Maca. That means he rules a continent, if he can reclaim it when we go there."

Lorenz held up his hands. "Now does everyone remember Mina's Story?"

Gary nodded and Andrew looked pensive before speaking. "Isn't that the fairytale my father told me when I was little?"

"Yes, it is, but Mina's Story is basically true. Those that look like your Uncle Randall are the Justines from the planet Justine. Papa's people are called Thalians after their planet. There's another group of people from a different planet called Brendon, and the other enemies are on the planet Krepyon.

"The part that isn't quite true is the ending. The Thalian warrior that destroyed the planet was LouElla, Papa's mother. She is here also. Papa was to be stranded here, but plans went differently as they can on this planet. We have their ship. If you all would like to see it, you all can follow us."

Llewellyn interrupted. "First I need to tell each and every one of ye, that nay tis to be spoken about what tis said and seen outside of these four walls other than with Randall, yere grandfither, or yere Aunt Melissa. If ye find that boarding something so alien is too big a step right now, Lorenz twill remain with ye. Most important tis the fact I want ye all to ken that ye are welcomed in my House and in my heart."

Chapter 36

Smashed Dreams

Margareatha frowned at her ankles. The afternoon was hot and sultry and the air barely moving. The curtains at the bedroom window hung in discouraging stillness. Why would this pregnancy make her ankles swell? This was but one baby, or so "Doctor" Gary had assured her.

"Walk as much as you can, put your feet up every chance you have, drink plenty of water, and take those little tablets every day. Hide them from your husband if necessary."

She smiled in remembrance. Randall's son liked to impress everyone with the knowledge he gained from the Golden One's medical files. She could hear Walter putting away the lawn mower in the shed. It wasn't often he was home since he'd been assigned to the New York area. He'd grown more and more tight-lipped about his work (if it was possible for a Bureau of Investigation agent to become more tight-lipped). Worse, he seemed to be grappling with a problem of insurmountable proportions. Rita assumed it had something to do with the rum running on the high seas, the transfer of spirits in the metropolitan areas, and the different mobs fighting for control over the flow of liquor.

She swung her feet over the side of the bed and pulled on her shoes. The fit was tight and uncomfortable. If the baby didn't arrive when expected she would need to buy new shoes and do it on the sly. Walter had no idea of how wealthy she was. She'd left him with the impression that she had a small family legacy from the stock her family had purchased years ago. With the run-up of the market, he hadn't been too suspicious until last October when the market crashed. Rita had no idea how to tell him that The MacDonald Corporation wasn't listed on the Exchange. The crash would not have affected her stock. Nor could she tell him that part of her income was derived from sporadic lumber or cattle sales from her spread in Nevada. She had intended to tell him, but fear of rejection stilled her tongue.

Rita scooted into the bathroom. She swore she spent more time in there than anywhere in their two bedroom house. Walter had been reluctant to purchase a home, but she assured him it was a commission from Melissa Carson, the wealthy uptown relative, for one of her landscapes. She'd never really gotten around to explaining that Melissa was her niece, not a distant cousin. Right now, the Bureau was demanding to know more about her background. She'd managed to plead not feeling well while pregnant and put off contacting the state of Missouri or a church for a birth certificate. The baby was due within the week. The MacDonald Corporation would need to manufacture some false papers for her. The Bureau hadn't been so picky when she and Walter wed two years ago after a brief courtship. And she was happy, unbelievably happy, but now the pregnancy was her most important concern.

It was time to check the roast. She smiled to herself. Walter loved his meat and potatoes. He was still a Wisconsin farm boy at heart. He'd been surprised that his sophisticated lady from the city fit so well on his family's Wisconsin farm when they visited. Once again, she could not share that part of her life when she visited her grandfather on a Missouri farm in the late1840's. Dear God, how do you tell the one you love that you are old enough to be his great-grandmother? She kept waiting for him to ask about her two hearts, but he had not. The opening for an explanation hadn't occurred.

She pulled open the oven door as Walter stepped inside.

"Is it ready?"

"Yes, I need to pull it out and make the gravy."

"Here, let me do that."

She watched his broad shoulders and blonde head as he bent, his face still red from the sun, his white shirt would need bleaching again from the perspiration stains. Working outside had taken away his grumpiness and strain from his job of fighting the mobs that infiltrated every level of the big cities and brought back his concern for her welfare.

"I'll wash up while you finish."

Rita gave thanks for his change of attitude. He had never spoken about his work, but she knew from the hours he worked and the different routes he would take home that he was deeply involved in some dangerous investigation. She piled the roast and vegetables onto a platter and started the gravy. When the gravy began simmering, she carried the platter to the already set table in the dining area of the small living room. She returned to the kitchen and poured the gravy into the bowl. She was about to pick it up when a radiating pain across the pelvic area hit her and water ran down her legs.

She glanced at the clock. The twins had taken about twenty hours for birthing, but that was no guarantee how long this birth would take. The twins had been born in 1882 almost fifty years ago. She carried the bowl to the table and looked up as Walter entered wearing his suit jacket. He walked to the table.

"Well, that looks fine, Rita." He pulled out her chair for her.

Rita opened her mouth to tell him dinner might be hurried when the kitchen door burst open. Two men with guns pointed at them entered. One moved immediately into the dining area.

"Don't' move. Hands up. Barney, close that door and then go find some blankets."

Rita could see anger turning Walter's face red. "She's expecting."

The man at the doorway laughed, "Maybe a ride will get her over that condition." Then he crumpled to the floor, screaming, holding his head in pain, as he emptied out his stomach on their carpet.

"What the hell?" The other man, who was closer to Rita and the kitchen, looked at the crumpled man and started to take a step forward when Rita's hand shot out and grasped his arm pushing the gun up into the air. She drove her mind into his, searing at his brain. His hand opened and the revolver fell harmlessly to the floor. He stared helplessly at her, unable to move.

Walter was standing with his gun out and pointed directly at the man on his knees. "I need my handcuffs and an extra belt. Once I have them secured, I'll need to call the police." There was a steeliness in his voice that Rita had never heard before, but knew was within him.

She pushed the man away from her like he was a baby, entered the hallway, and quickly went to the bedroom for the cuffs. She could feel the water dripping down her legs. Less than five minutes had passed and the next pain should be at least an hour away. Hurriedly she grabbed the handcuffs and belt. On an impulse, she picked up her purse with the extra car key Walter had made for her. I will need to go to Gary's place, she thought to herself. Walter has to take these two in and write reports. What Walter thought about the incapacitated thugs, he had not said, nor had he asked for an explanation. She had seen the ice in his blue eyes and she knew explanations at this point weren't what he wanted to hear.

The purse she dropped at the edge of the hall before entering the room. The two men were standing by the sofa, hands in the air. The vomit on the floor was reeking, mingling with the smell of roast beef. I cannot be ill, Rita thought to herself. I've smelled worse. She handed the cuffs and belt to Walter.

Walter's next actions proved her suspicions correct. He did not hand the revolver to her, but tucked the belt in his pocket and stepped behind one man.

"Move and I'll just have one live body when the police arrive." He quickly snapped the handcuffs into place. "Turn around, sit on the sofa and do not move. Prove to me how smart you are."

He pulled out the belt and moved behind the other man before tucking the revolver into his waistband.

How stupid, Rita thought.

"Get him!" The handcuffed man launched himself at Walter. Walter whirled to face the man coming off of the couch when the other man jabbed at his shoulder and threw his right fist driving Walter back. Walter recovered and jabbed at the man's jaw and rammed his left fist into the man's belly. The other man threw his body at Walter again and the two went down.

Margareatha had seen enough. She sent her mind into the untied one causing him to scream in pain. Walter grabbed his gun and used the butt to knock the handcuffed one out, and then used it on the man rolling in pain on the floor. As he stood, he pointed the gun at Rita, his face white and drained of color.

"I don't know what you are, but you are not human. I want you to sit in that chair while I tie you."

"You'd do that to your wife, the woman who is carrying your child?"

"That cannot be my child. Now sit."

"Just who do you think the father could possibly be?" Her voice was as cold as her insides.

"That rum and gun running red-head that has the same kind of eyes that you do." He motioned to the chair with the gun. "I'm arresting you."

"Walter, those men had guns and couldn't stop me. Why do you think you can?" Her voice was bitter and she raised her hand to point her right index finger at him. "Toss the revolver towards the hall door."

His face was an interesting study as he tried desperately not to obey her, but his arm and hand moved and the gun flew through the air. Rita waited until it landed, walked to the hall, reached around for her purse, and picked up the gun before she straightened.

"I loved you, Walter, as I have not loved anyone for years. You just destroyed that, but I swear to you, this is your child. I will give birth without worrying about the baby's future or mine. I'm taking the gun and the car. You'll find the gun outside. If you hurry, you might even be able to keep those two confined." Rita felt the tears welling in her eyes and her throat constricting.

"Who is that man?" Walter was shouting at her.

She turned at the archway into the kitchen. "He is my half-brother. He doesn't possess many morals, but committing rape and incest aren't among his sins. Tell your mother I will send her pictures of her grandchild."

He tried to rush after her. Forgive me, she whispered as she entered his mind and stopped him from moving long enough for her to exit the house, open the car door, set the throttle, and turn the crank to start the engine. The effort caused her mind to release him, and he barged out the door. She entered his mind again to stop him and used mindspeak. Perhaps he heard her thinking, 'good bye, Walter, good bye, my love.' She began the drive to Gary's home as a scream of hurt and anger formed in her throat. She fought back the panic and the pain and kept the automobile on the road.

Once she had to pull over for the contractions to subside. By the time she reached Gary's home her clothes and the car seat were drenched, partly from her sweat and partly from her womb. She pulled into his long drive way and parked at the rear of the house. She couldn't tell if he was home or not and she leaned on the horn.

This brought the cook and the handyman running. The handyman kept muttering that she couldn't be here. She needed to leave. Rita was about to go into their minds and direct them to Gary when the cook started screaming.

"She's having a baby. Get Dr. MacDonald."

Gary had started down the steps when he heard the scream and was beside her within seconds. "Help me get her inside of the house."

'We've got to get this car out of here.' Rita had her hands clamped to the wheel. 'Walter will have the police or Bureau agents here. I can't stay here. You haven't seen me.' She used mindspeak rather than risk the servants hearing that the law would be after her.

"There isn't time to take her to the hospital. I'll take her to the office. Mrs. Felton, don't expect me home this evening. I have a prior engagement."

He opened the door. "If you'll lie down in the back seat, you'll be more comfortable."

Rita gritted her teeth. "Just get me some place safe. I'm fine right here. We'll need gas. Walter will be looking for this car."

"We'll go to the office."

He turned to the cook. "Mrs. Felton, would you bring my bag? Quickly, please, as I may need it."

Both the man and woman ran off.

Gary used the opportunity to explain. "Once the baby is born, I'll take you to the lodge. I'll call Aunt Melissa and she can meet us there." His brown eyes were sympathetic as he helped her into the back seat and then he sat in the driver's seat.

Mrs. Felton came running out the house and handed him the bag.

"Thank you, I should return by tomorrow afternoon." He backed out of the driveway.

"I'm serious, Gary, get rid of this car."

"If I don't get you to the office, you'll kill that baby. Nothing is sanitary here."

"Don't you realize I'm from an era that didn't even know there were germs? I'd rather go to the lodge first."

"We may not have time. It's too far to risk it. What happened?"

"Two mobsters broke in and were going to kill us. I stopped them with my mind." She leaned back and closed her eyes, trying to stop the sob in her throat. "Walter accused me of carrying Red's baby and claimed I wasn't human."

Gary was silent, his round face concerned.

"I used my mind to stop Walter from coming after me. He'll have to finish securing the one man before going next door to use a telephone, but he'll have the police looking for me, for this car, and possibly for you. We cannot go to your office."

"Very well, I have a place no one knows about. We should be safe there. I don't want to explain why we both have two hearts."

Chapter 37

Texas: September 1, 1939

"Look, Grandma, it's Uncle Lorenz and he's bringing y'all flowers for your birthday! I'll go get a vase."

Brigetta looked up from the table where she was enthroned in her wheelchair. At ninety-five, her hair was white and thinning, the lashes completely missing from her eyelids, but her eyes still worked well enough to watch as Lorenz approached. He was dressed in a dark grey western suit, his black boots shining beneath the dust, his grey Stetson carefully set on top of his iron grey hair. To her it looked like there was a great blob of white clutched in one hand, but she could see well enough that Lorenz was still walking upright, his broad shoulders swaying with the bowlegged walk of a man more accustomed to riding a horse than to walking, and why, she wondered, was he using that cane. She was certain he did not need the elaborate ebony and gold trimmed stick.

He is still a good looking man, she thought to herself as Lorenz handed her the bouquet and bent to kiss her cheek. The sweet odor of white roses enveloped her.

"I bought these for Martin. He would have brought them for you if he were still with us."

Brigetta smiled to herself remembering that night so long ago. "Lorenz, du sit here beside me.

"Addie," she said to one of the great-nieces sitting on her left side, "du get Uncle Lorenz some lemonade. Make sure there is ice in it."

Lorenz sat in the chair on her right that she had indicated, removed his hat, and carefully set it on his knee. His mouth was almost straight, but the right side still pulled higher from the scar.

He's too thin, thought Brigetta. He is not eating right since Antoinette died. She reached out and patted his hand. "I miss her too, Lorenz. Just think how she vould have loved this party. She always loved parties vhere she could boss everyone around."

Lorenz nodded and smiled softly, and then the mouth tightened. Brigetta bent her head and smelled the roses, the sweet scent evoking more memories.

This time when she spoke she used German. "Ah, this brings back memories. Do you remember our twenty-fifth anniversary?

"Yes, that was quite a party, but there weren't as many people attending. Of course, you weren't ninety-five then and did not have all these descendants to help you celebrate." He too spoke in German.

"I didn't have all these relatives until they discovered oil on our ranch. Now they flock in, but I don't care."

Brigetta sat back, "I've always wanted to tell you. I fell in love with you that night."

"What?"

Brigetta smiled again at the memory. "Ach ja, I was so upset at the thought, I ran to the front porch. Toni followed me and calmed me down. She thought it was something different." Brigetta felt a faint flush for she could not say "the change."

"She insisted I come back for Martin's speech. Somehow I managed to go back and walk up on that stage. Then Martin started telling everyone what a wonderful wife I was and gave me the flowers." She fingered the topaz and pearl broach pinned to the afternoon suit of light blue.

"I fell in love with Martin while he was talking."

Lorenz laughed, his high baritone carrying far enough for some to look at them, and he answered in German. "Brigetta, I never knew you were so fickle."

Brigetta grew pensive. "I need to know. Were the roses Antoinette's or your idea?"

"I swear, Brigetta, it was Martin's idea. He just didn't know where to buy roses. When he asked me, I thought he was crazy. We both had to go to Toni to find out where to buy roses."

"Thank you, Lorenz. She was a good friend." She sat back and closed her eyes.

Lorenz looked at the sleeping Brigetta and shrugged. Her face was relaxed and a slight smile pulled at her lips. She had returned to the stage while Martin told how blessed he was to have her as his wife.

The great-niece returned with the glass of lemonade and the granddaughter followed with a vase filled with water. She smiled at Lorenz while she gently extracted the roses from Brigetta's lap and placed them in the vase.

Lorenz stood with his hat in his hand. "She's asleep."

"Yes, Grandma does that a lot. Y'all should get something to eat, Uncle Lorenz. She may not wake up right away. Sometimes she sleeps for an hour or more."

Lorenz shuddered inside. Antoinette was like that for a year. She had been waiting for death and knew it. Did Brigetta know? The emptiness of grief erupted again. It had been four long years without Antoinette, and the knowledge that Brigetta would soon be in the earth resting beside her Martin was too much. He bowed to the younger women and set the Stetson back on his head.

"Thank y'all for the offer, but I'm a bit tired myself.

He walked back to his automobile and slid in. Once he would have ridden his horse here, but people would wonder at an eighty-nine year-old man still riding a horse everywhere when they believed he was rich as Crocus. Why, he wondered, do the two hearts continue to beat so damn well when his reason for living died four years ago?

He set the choke, pressed the starter, turned the key in the Packard, and heard the motor. It was a powerful car, and he appreciated it the way he appreciated a good horse. He had wanted to join Toni after her funeral, but suicide was out of the question; an act distasteful to him. Perhaps it was too many years of sensing when someone wished to kill him or someone he cared about. Papa had wanted him to join them at the MacDonald Lodge and learn to navigate the stars before they left for Thalia.

"I can learn that on the way there."

"Even ye are nay that clever."

"I'll come when I'm ready," he had growled. He did not like the East. The smells were wrong, the winters too long and cold, and the food too bland. "We can't go anywhere until Rity finishes raising her girl and Randall won't leave his Iris anymore than I would have left Antoinette. Since Iris is only about fifty, she'll probably live another twenty years, Papa."

The sound of annoyance in MacDonald's voice told him that Papa might not wait that long. He still had to find someone they could trust to manage their funds and run the various MacDonald enterprises. Lorenz thought he had found the ranch manager in Pinky's husband, Bruce Tillman. Now he wasn't so sure. So far the man performed well, but there were mutterings among the Mexican hands. They did not like him.

All too soon he was back at the Rearing Bear Ranch and pulling into his garage. He walked into the house debating whether to drink too much or study the math his father had sent.

"Hello, Pawpaw." Pinky used the greeting that all the grandchildren and great-nieces and great-nephews used. "I didn't expect you back so soon." Her ivory skin, framed by strawberry blond hair, flushed with pleasure. "The cook was just going to prepare a light supper as we thought you'd be eating at the Rolfes."

"I'm not hungry." He smiled back at her. Except for the much lighter hair, she reminded him of his sister, her grandmother, Mina.

"Now Pawpaw, you simply must eat. Would you like to come for supper at our house tonight? I can make the salad bigger and have the cook come over to my place."

"No, whatever Maria is making here is fine with me." It was beginning to annoy him that Pinky kept referring to the Mexican help by title instead of their name. It was as though she was denying their existence as human beings.

Pinky almost frowned, and then her light-brown eyes brightened. "I have something to tell you, Pawpaw. I was going to tell you the next time I saw you and that's now." She gave a self-conscious giggle and blushed. "Bruce and I, well, we're expecting again."

He stared at her stunned. She had arrived for Antoinette's funeral from St. Louis with Tillman's grandson, Bruce, and their two-year-old son. Pinky was so ill from miscarrying that he ordered her to bed and the nurse for Antoinette rehired. Bruce had thanked him profusely and asked for a job since the Tillman ranch was run by his uncle who had enough sons of his own to keep busy.

"Y'all can start as a regular hand as long as Pinky stays here until she's well. If it works out, I may need a new foreman or manager."

At first things went well. Bruce offered no objections when Lorenz told him that he had to pay for someone to care for their son until Pinky was well enough to care for him.

The six months it took Pinky to recover made up for the quiet without the bustle of Antoinette. As Mina's granddaughter, Pinky had every right to consider the Rearing Bear her ancestral home. His father's feelings about House were quite clear. Everyone was his, the Maca's, responsibility. That so few of the family knew he was the Maca of Don and still alive, did not concern him. The elder MacDonald had sent Gary MacDonald to Texas find out why Pinky was having medical problems in birthing.

"I've told her not to have any more children." Gary had sat in Lorenz's office nursing a whiskey, the door firmly closed against intruders and too thick for someone to hear through. "My problem is that I can't tell her that my knowledge comes from a machine in a spaceship for God's sake." He brushed his overly long hair back off his brow.

Lorenz noted his grandson's added weight made him appear soft, but held his tongue. To Lorenz, most people from the East looked soft. He was sure Iris would berate her son about excesses of any kind.

"What causes the problem?"

"It's probably the same thing that afflicted so many of the people in our family. It's a matter of RH negative and RH positive blood. The cure is quite simple, but, unfortunately, that doesn't exist in Earth's medical lore. I can't even tell Pinky how I determined this. If I make a medical discovery and share it with this world, it's sharing knowledge from another culture and bringing attention to me and the whole MacDonald clan. Grandpa Mac, Great-great-grandmother LouElla, and my father turn absolutely livid at the idea." Gary had left the next morning.

Lorenz finally found his voice to answer Pinky. "Are y'all sure? Remember what Gary told y'all. No more children." He was considering calling Gary to return and put a stop to this insanity.

"Of course, I'm sure, Pawpaw. I'm fine. It's been four months now and, well, I thought you had noticed already." She frowned slightly and then smiled again. "I need to run home now Pawpaw. Bruce doesn't like it when I neglect the family."

Lorenz watched with a sour mouth as she ran down the steps and toward the foreman's house where they were living. What the hell did she mean neglect the family? And why was she running if she was pregnant. He could not recall Toni ever running when she was expecting, but then people did things differently now.

Chapter 38

House Call

Lorenz woke suddenly and realized the dark of night still surrounded the house. He was slightly surprised that he'd slept at all. There had been another argument that evening with the elder MacDonald about Lorenz rejuvenating himself. Lorenz had installed a ham radio system in his office to conceal a communication device from the *Golden One* that he actually used to talk with his father. The argument had deteriorated into both of them yelling and ending the conversation abruptly. He realized that the man was apt to pay a visit here. Bad idea! Papa was hard to miss. What if someone realized that he was the original MacDonald?

After the argument, he'd turned on the radio and heard the news that Germany had invaded Poland. He knew it meant the beginning of another war. If they were going to leave, it would need to be before actual war broke out. If they didn't, he was sure half the men Red had started to train would join the service. Unsure of what to do, he had paced the floor before retiring.

Lorenz listened for a moment and then realized a faint light intruded under the door. Who was in his house and at this time of night? He pulled on his Levis and boots and grabbed the shirt hanging on the wooden valet.

He found Pinky and her six-year-old son, Bob, in the kitchen. Pinky was holding a washcloth filled with ice to her bloodied nose. When she looked at him, she hurriedly turned away. Both of her eyes were blackened and her lower lip was split.

"What happened? Have y'all called the doctor?"

"No, don't, Pawpaw. No doctor, please, it will only make Bruce madder." Her voice was terror stricken. "I'll be fine, really I will." She started to rise, but sank back down.

"The hell, sorry, Pinky, but y'all can't even stand up. Where is that no-good man of yours?"

Bob stared at him. "You can't talk about my daddy like that."

"Your daddy is a coward." Lorenz spat the words out and stalked to his office where he called the doctor, and then returned to the kitchen.

"Y'all are going to bed. I've called the doctor and he'll be here in twenty minutes. Now where is that worthless man of yours?"

"I don't know, Pawpaw." Pinky was sobbing, the words a mumbled mess coming out of jumbled lips. "It's not his fault. I haven't been able to be a wife. We had a fight just before he left, and I can't say anything more in front of my child. I just need you to get someone to watch him. I can't let the help see me like this."

"Up, and into bed." Lorenz helped her up and walked her through the dining room and huge foyer into his bedroom.

"Now y'all stay in bed. I'll get Maria and her daughter in here."

By the time he returned to the house after waking Maria, he realized his father was right. He had let himself become weaker in body and mind. He should have realized what was going on. He walked into his bedroom and noted that Bob was sleeping in the bed too. He pulled out his white shirt and grey suit. He knew where that bastard had gone.

Within minutes he was speeding down the road towards Arles, but swung off near one of the places where they used to camp along the river. Now the oaks, cottonwoods, and willows helped to conceal a neat, white two-story house. The front porch was flanked by two Grecian columns that looked out of place on the plains of Texas. The parking lot held an assortment of newer and used autos. He turned his car toward the road, parked, put the key in his pocket, and took his cane. Anger drove him after a man that had hurt someone in his family.

Lorenz was ready to bring his cane down on the door when it was thrown open. Thelma, or Mrs. Patterson as she liked to be called by her clients, wore an orange-red smile on her face. Her orange dress was one of the tightest, lowest cut gowns Lorenz had ever seen on an aging, well padded body.

"Why, Mr. MacDonald, y'all just come right on in. This is such an honor." Her husky voice was purring. She turned just enough to yell at someone. "Mickey, y'all open a bottle of our best bourbon for our guest." She turned to Lorenz again and her smile faded. There was no mistaking the tight mouth pulled slightly to the right side and the cold, smoky eyes looking at her, seeing her, but not caring about her. This was an angry man and an angry man could mess up a good night's business.

"Which room is Bruce Tillman in?"

"Why, Mr. MacDonald, what on earth do y'all mean?" She started to twitter, when her brown eyes widened and she whispered, "He's in the room with the blue door. That's on the second floor." Her hand flew to her mouth as he pushed past her and took the steps two at a time, his mind thwarting her ability to move or speak.

At the blue door he tried the knob: locked. He raised his cane and rapped loudly on the door not caring whether he dented the gold knob or not.

"Go away." An angry male voice shouted.

"Open the damn door, Bruce, or I'll shoot my way in."

A naked Bruce yanked the door open. "Go away, Pawpaw…" The words stopped as the cane smashed into his midsection. The brunette on the bed screamed.

Bruce grabbed for the cane and missed. Lorenz rammed the gold knob into Bruce's face knocking him backwards.

Lorenz followed him into the room and his next blow caught Bruce square on his head. He swung the cane over and over, rapidly striking at every vulnerable point until Bruce was on his knees, whimpering, holding his hands over his head in a futile effort to avoid the blows. Lorenz looked up when he heard the people at the door. The woman on the bed was cowering in the corner in fear, a sheet clutched up to her chin.

"Let me through, damn it."

Probably a bouncer, Lorenz thought and jammed the cane into Bruce's ribs one last time. Then he turned and started for the door.

"You all are in my way. Move!"

The women and men moved back, their eyes filled with awe, some had open mouths. Many of them had known him for years. They thought of him as old, a broken legend, no longer the dangerous man he might have been.

Lorenz shouldered past them and was almost at the stairs when a hand reached out and grabbed his right arm holding the cane.

"Mr…"

The man wasn't able to say more. Lorenz spun, his left fist smashing into the man's stomach and driving him to his knees. It would forever blow his cover as a normal almost eighty-nine-year-old-man, but he allowed no one put their hands on him. He went down the stairs with a slight swagger, the cane resting on his right shoulder. He was MacDonald again.

"Mr. MacDonald, y'all will have to wait here. I've called the sheriff." It was Thelma bleating at him like some sheep afraid to irritate the ram.

"Fine, he can arrest that son-of-a-bitchin' wife beater when he gets here."

He yanked the door open and walked out into the fresh air. He would need to call Papa again and tell him to expect him as soon as he made the arrangements for a new foreman and housing for Pinky. Bruce Tillman would never set foot on the Rearing Bear Ranch again.

Chapter 39

The Organization Investigates

"I know that is the same man." Walter Andresen tossed the five by seven inch picture of Red O'Neal standing by the *Colombia Queen* onto the desk. Twenty years had added twenty pounds to Walter's body and his blond hair was laced with white streaks.

"It can't be."

"And it's my guess that he's still running booze, women, guns, and God knows what else on that boat and others." Walter finished his sentence. He looked across the desk at Creighton. "You know it's him. Why else would you ask me to come out of the cellar if not to come in and confirm your identification?"

The man at the desk frowned, swiveled in his chair and looked out the window. Abruptly, he swiveled back and withdrew another photograph from the folder.

"Bear with me. I have one more photograph to show you and it may be a shock."

Both men wore dark suits and white shirts. Walter studied Creighton's face. The dark eyes were set in a lean face that matched his thinning dark hair and slender build. The white shirt was immaculate, the dark suit tailored to a perfect fit. All of the agents on this level seemed to be slender, but then they were successful or young, and he—he brought his mind back to Creighton, watching him. Creighton was uneasy about something.

"We all know how, well, how difficult it was for you when your wife left." Creighton left unsaid the part about how no one in the organization every really trusted him again. None had accused him of embellishing what occurred when his wife left or the tale of a long-lived man, but they almost fired him. They did not because they were short of good men during the gangland years and the Bureau's reorganization into the Federal Bureau of Investigation.

"Did you ever hear from her again?"

"Not directly. She has sent my mother pictures of her daughter." Walter left out the part that it couldn't be his daughter; yet the pictures looked like a younger version of himself or his mother. He did not understand, nor did he wish to. "There were no return addresses and the pictures were postmarked from different states. I suspect many of the pictures were taken in the West."

"Why?" Creighton's voice was too sharp.

Walter smiled. "I really don't believe that would matter. You said you had another photograph?"

Creighton's face became harder. "This is not to be discussed anywhere else. Do you understand?"

Walter's own blue eyes hardened and he nodded his head. Creighton turned the photograph and placed it in front of him.

"This was taken four weeks ago at a small port on Long Island."

The colored photograph showed Margareatha, Red O'Neal, and a very tall, muscular, dark-haired woman (or maybe it was a man? Walter couldn't decide) standing in front the *Colombia Queen*, the words clearly painted on the prow. Walter's sharply indrawn breath told Creighton his hunch was correct.

"Would you like to explain her youthful appearance, Walter?"

"I can't."

"Humor me and venture a guess."

"If I tell you my hunch, I'm out of the Bureau." Worry and agony were written across his face. "For God's sake, man, I've only five years left and I will have my thirty years as an agent."

"You claim you have had no contact with her, yet we can prove your mother has." Creighton's voice had grown cold. "We need to know where these people are hiding, and why they are in this country. No one can trace their origin. The *Columbia Queen* has disappeared into the Atlantic again, but as far as we can determine that man," he jabbed his index finger down at the picture of Red, "is still in this country. All three," he pointed at Red and the two women, "disembarked the day the *Columbia Queen* docked. They went somewhere, but where? Our man lost them. We think we know where they went, but the man we have posted there didn't see them arrive, nor has he seen them since. There are no hotel records, no taxi driver, or ferry boat crew that recognizes them. We're not even positive what names they are using.

"Now, tell me why you think she looks so young. That way I won't submit a report about your insubordination."

Walter stood, leaned forward, and put his knuckled fists down on the desk edge in front of him. "Very well, but I am not crazy. I have not spoken to her or seen her since she walked out the door. Without her physical presence there is no way I can prove what I am about to say. It is the reason I have not told anyone. If for some reason you use this to muster me out, I'll deny ever saying it. I am not going to be labeled as one of those loonies who have seen a UFO or been contacted by aliens. Is that understood?"

Creighton nodded yes, his brown eyes carefully gauging Walter.

Walter took a deep breath and started, almost like he'd rehearsed the speech over and over. "I was young, and I thought we were both in love. Strange, when you love a woman that much, it can sap your innate common sense. I never had the courage to ask her why or how it was possible, but she has two hearts."

Creighton's face hardened and he leaned forward. "You were married for almost two years. Do you have any idea why they would use a New York State port other than to dispose of booze, guns, or South American artifacts?"

Walter considered as he turned over the thought of divulging what he'd learned on his vacations.

"She used to visit a woman called Melissa Carson in New York City. This Carson woman was older and Margareatha claimed she was a distant relative. Just how distant she never elucidated. I had the feeling that Mrs. Carson was somehow handling financial arrangements for my wife. Once again, I have no proof." He sat back down.

"Where did this Mrs. Carson live?"

"I never went with Margareatha to the woman's home so that will remain another unknown in my wife's mysterious background. She and Margareatha would meet for lunch. She would come to our house when I wasn't there. I tried to locate Margareatha through the doctor she went to, but his office refused to let me talk with him. When I tried to investigate him, he disappeared for awhile. Strange, as he is the son of an upper New York state judge who was later appointed to the New York Supreme Court. The judge has two other sons; one in the military and the other is a lawyer. As far as I know, neither the judge nor the other sons had any contact with Margareatha. The judge has a daughter. She's a high society lady and O'Neal never went near any of the venues she visits."

Creighton sat back. "What was this doctor's name and where was he located?"

"His name is Gary MacDonald. I've forgotten the exact street, but it was somewhere in the borough of Brooklyn.

"How much time did you spend trying to locate her?"

"About six months, but I backed off when the agent who was hot on O'Neal's or Neal's trail felt I was stepping on his toes. He never found O'Neal. He wouldn't interrogate anyone connected with Melissa Carson. Her brother is Judge MacDonald, now retired New York Supreme Court Justice. The man felt Judge MacDonald was too well-respected and wealthy to bother with gunrunners. Yet he is also the father of the doctor my wife went to."

Creighton noticed bitterness had crept into Walter's voice. "Did your wife ever show any signs of extreme wealth?"

"No, she just mentioned that she had insurance money, some property out West, and a few family stocks inherited from her mother. It was enough for her to live on, but that was the late 1920's. Why are you interested in her now?"

"You should have surmised why. We've no idea of the origins of those three, or why they are here; plus, she's in that picture with O'Neal. Do you recognize the other woman?"

Walter frowned and picked the photograph up and studied the cropped hair and build. "No, I never saw her. Are you sure that's a woman? Look at those biceps and thigh muscles." His guesses he kept to himself.

"You're still married to her, aren't you?"

Walter looked up and his eyes hardened. "So, that's why you called me in here. You know the answer to that. You have a whole field of investigators at your command. Since you want reassurance, yes, technically we are still married. I never filed for divorce. It would have meant instantaneous dismissal in 1930. Later it didn't seem worth the effort."

"You never met anyone else? Are you still in love with the woman?"

"The answer is no to both questions. I simply saw no reason to endanger my retirement. Have you arrested her already and need to know whether I can testify against her?"

Creighton shifted. "We haven't arrested anyone yet, but we expect to wrap things up within six weeks to six months, however, two to three months is more likely. We need for you to file for divorce now using abandonment as the reason. Yesterday would have been better. Reno will do it quicker than New York or Virginia."

Walter leaned forward again. "You've tracked them to the MacDonald Lodge in upper New York State and you're planning a raid."

"I thought you said you dropped your investigation."

"I did, but what I do on my vacation is my business. I don't think you're going to find anything there. O'Neal doesn't take his goods inland. He goes up there whenever he's in the East, or at least he used to. I gave it up when I never spotted Rita in town or going towards the grounds."

He watched Creighton's face. The man showed nothing.

"What amazes me is that you didn't protest when I told you how she was different. O'Neal hasn't aged any in the last twenty years either." He smiled at Creighton. "You haven't been honest about what you know. I think you traced Melissa Carson to the MacDonald family and tried to find out about the MacDonald Corporation. I'm betting without the IRS it would have been a dead-end."

Creighton's face looked as if it were carved from marble.

"What did you find out about the MacDonald that started the ranch in Texas? That he probably looks like that so-called woman?" Walter couldn't resist proving his knowledge.

Creighton's eyes finally looked at him. "How did you find all that information? How do you know about the original MacDonald?"

"It took time, but I'm a farm boy. I can go in a western tavern and be accepted. Small towns love folktales about the old days. Once I found out the doctor's father was originally from Schmidt's Corner, Texas, I went there. No one is sure when the original MacDonald died, and his son, the Judges' father, disappeared about ten years ago after nearly beating a man to death. He did this while in his late eighties or early nineties. I don't believe they're dead. I just haven't been able to tie them to Margareatha. How did you do it?"

Creighton relaxed. "Through Melissa, the Judge, and the marriage licenses in Arles County and the state capital repository. The original MacDonald's daughter married a Rolfe from the neighboring ranch. As a Lutheran minister he left all sorts of tracks. We traced them back to Missouri where his synod is located and their children led us to her." He pointed at LouElla. "She's part of the MacDonald Corporation according to the initial corporation filings in

Texas and their tax returns. Originally, it was a LouElla MacDonald. Now it's LouElla Polk. Have you ever heard of her?"

Walter shook his head no. How had he missed her?

"What about the name Rolfe? Did your wife mention that one?"

"She did not, but they're still out there in Texas close to the MacDonald ranch."

"Not all of them. I'm referring to the descendents of the one that married the original MacDonald's daughter. Two or more are employees of various Mac-Donald subsidiaries and a third owns a small steel milling factory. In fact, one member of that branch has been seen with your daughter."

Walter straightened. "My God, what are they doing? Interbreeding?"

"We checked with a doctor. If there is a family connection, there are too many generations separating them. It wouldn't matter. We did find out from the corporation filings in Texas, a Jeremiah O'Neal brought in a ranch, ships based in Galveston, and a separate subsidiary of gambling houses and houses of prostitution."

"What?"

"Even more interesting, a Margareatha Buckley was the first Treasurer and added a ranch and logging firm from Nevada. I suspected you knew that when you said the pictures were taken out West. A LouElla MacDonald added a boarding house in St. Louis. Somehow this entitled her to be Vice President."

"My God, are they all that old?"

"We're not sure. Margarcatha and her daughter, Brianna Andresen, have been living on the ranch until about two years ago. My man missed your wife by weeks. The daughter is at college and goes to the MacDonald Lodge in the summer. This Margareatha claimed to be a descendant of the original. We were unable to find any other records; except one."

There was a puzzled look on Walter's face.

"Don't worry it wasn't something you were looking for. We tried to find the original MacDonald's marriage license, but the older journals were moldy, faded, and unreadable. What we did find was a marriage license for a Lorenz Adolf MacDonald and an Antoinette Theresa Josephine O'Neal issued in 1869."

"So they are inter-related. What else did you find? What about the IRS tax reports? Why haven't you arrested them?"

"So far we haven't found much. We can't arrest them for longevity and they have been meticulous about reporting their income. It's their out-of-country corporations that are subsidiaries that we can't verify income for tax evasion. Those are run by O'Neal. If we can catch him at their lodge, we can move in. We've a man watching them now. That's why you need to get that divorce."

"I'll get that divorce if I can go along on the raid. If you want to ruin my retirement over insubordination, you go right ahead."

Creighton drummed his fingers on the oak arm rest. "You're a little old for that type of exercise. They brought in some real toughs these last couple of years, but nobody sees them once they're at the place. I need men capable of fighting."

"I'm still in great shape, and if necessary, I am a marksman."

"This is not for your revenge."

"It's not about revenge. Whatever she is, she can't pass O'Neal's spawn off as mine. I'm not sure she's really human—her or all the others that haven't died."

"Another agent saw a picture of your daughter. She looks remarkably like your mother."

"You son-of-a-bitch! You had agents questioning my mother?"

"No, he posed as a magazine salesman and showed her a picture of his granddaughter. Your mother showed him a picture of a very normal looking Mid-Western farm girl and said it was her granddaughter." Creighton smiled. "The subscriptions she ordered are all legit. She wasn't cheated.

"Now back to Margareatha's looks. I don't believe that two hearts are possible. Something else determines their resistance to aging. Would you like to explain that in other terms?"

"How do you explain that O'Neal hasn't changed in appearance?" He took advantage of Creighton's scowl to continue.

"I'm curious though as to how you connected them to the MacDonald Lodge."

"We discovered that O'Neal and the other female visited Melissa Carson in New York City. Mrs. Carson spends the hottest part of the summer up at the MacDonald Lodge. According to the locals, she's very rich and a daughter of a Texas rancher named MacDonald. It simply tied everything together. Then we found the birth certificate for a Melissa Angelique MacDonald born to Lorenz and Antoinette MacDonald. We're not sure about the exact relationship of LouElla Polk as we don't know if these are the same people or their descendants."

"Yes," Walter agreed, "the Carson woman could be more than a distant cousin. It was no coincidence that Margareatha chose a MacDonald as her doctor. Any other doctor would have detected the two hearts and reported it.

"And I still go on that raid or no divorce."

"I can't promise that."

"Then no divorce." Walter sat back. He would win this one.

Chapter 40

Time to Leave

Lorenz bent down and inspected where the man had been. He nodded with satisfaction as his finger air traced where the man had shifted positions. The place was perfect for watching any incoming and outgoing traffic at the MacDonald Lodge or the out buildings, but the trees, hillocks, and the rock formations of the mountain hid most of the complex. The man was close, no more than several yards ahead. He knew it, he could sense it. Why was someone spying on the MacDonald Lodge? They'd been here so long the locals ignored them. Lorenz doubted that this man was local. The prints said shoes, not the boots or heavy brogans worn in the mountains. Plus, locals only came into this area to hunt, and hunting season wasn't until fall. It was one of the reasons they had chosen to have the family reunion and corporate meeting now. He had risen early and ridden out to clear his mind. Now it looked as though events would go faster than anyone planned.

He had taken the draught of the Justine elixir ten years ago. Llewellyn and Gary had approximated the needed dosage, but the *Golden One* had no data for the reaction on a Justine Earth mutant his age. It was almost too much. Something in his Justine genes restarted and at first he was weak and the amount of food was never enough. Plates of roast beef and gallons of ice cream had disappeared into his mouth. It took six months to recover. To his astonishment he had grown and now stood six foot three: the same height as what Daniel had been. His hair was dark again with no trace of grey.

"Mayhap the Justine genes are fighting to override the Earth genes as they can grow when they take the first three or four rejuvenating draughts." Llewellyn's speculation did little to cheer him.

"I like my earth genes," he had growled back. At least the extreme hunger had dissipated and his appetite was normal.

Gary speculated that his body had required that amount of food to repair the cells that had been damaged from aging and his rapid re-growth.

"I recommend you take the elixir like a medicine every 50 years, certainly no longer than 60 years apart. That should forestall any or most of the side effects. It's the regime that Margareatha and Red employ."

If they had been discovered, it looked like he would be drinking the elixir on Thalia. Taking the potion now would be too soon and too risky.

Lorenz remounted his horse and looked at the ground. This was almost too easy. The man made no attempt to hide his footsteps or step lightly. The sounds of his horse must have spooked the man. Did he do this like a human or with his mind? Lorenz decided on the mind. A local might have been a challenge to track, but this man was a city dude and he didn't belong.

He sent his mind searching, first one direction and then another, until he located the man slightly downhill. The man was not moving. *Probably hoping I'll ride the other way*, thought Lorenz. He wheeled his horse and went loping down the hill, easily avoiding the small bushes. These trees were old and their branches and leaves formed a canopy that prevented huge shrubs like those growing in the logged forests of the Pacific Northwest. Lorenz had ridden but a few yards when he saw the man huddled behind a tree peering out at him.

The man stepped out, holding his hands in front, palms outward, and a smile on his face.

"I'm a bit lost. I wonder if you could direct me back to town." Inside Prentice was wondering what this cowboy was doing in the woods of New York. His smile died. He realized he could not move.

"What's your name and what are y'all doing here?"

"I'm Michael Prentice, and I'm observing the house, the grounds, and the people below."

"Why?"

"I've been assigned to do so." The man was sweating, his face contorting as he tried vainly to keep his lips from moving.

"Who are you doing this for?"

Prentice tried to bite his tongue, but the words tumbled out. "The Federal Bureau of Investigation."

Lorenz sat back in the saddle and observed the man. "Did they tell you why?"

"No."

"Who are you looking for?"

The man tried to move, to turn away from those grey eyes boring into his and the names and descriptions came tumbling out. When he finished, Lorenz's eyes were like flint.

"I'm not going to kill y'all, but when y'all get back to town, you're not going to remember too well. Y'all will leave town by morning."

Lorenz rode behind as the man started down the hill. He walked Prentice the almost four miles into town. Once there, he stayed in the man's mind long enough to leave fear: a fear so deep Prentice fled town that day. He did not stop until nightfall.

* * *

MacDonald was practicing fighting moves with LouElla in the exercise room of the *Golden One* when Lorenz entered. Some of the selected crew, men and women, were trying to emulate the two Thalians. Another group was watching them while lifting weights.

'Papa, we need to have a conference.' He used mindspeak rather than try to yell over the noise.

MacDonald grasped the arms of his mother, and spoke softly into her ear. "The laddie says we need to hold a conference."

LouElla looked around, sweat pouring down her chest and back. She had lifted weights prior to the practice with Llewellyn. She scowled at Lorenz.

"Canna it wait till after we finish?"

Lorenz smiled. "No, Grandmère, it can't. I've already alerted Melissa and Margareatha. They're on their way. You all can shower later."

* * *

Lorenz sat down after giving a quick explanation of what had occurred in the woods earlier. He did not use mindspeak as LouElla and his grandson Andrew were at the captain's command table. Neither one would have heard him.

"Thank ye, laddie, it seems we are compromised." Llewellyn's lips gave a slight twitch, but it was not a smile and the amusement had fled from his dark eyes.

"Since the man twas from the FBI, they must be ready to launch a physical inspection of this area. Everything can be hidden, but I suggest we leave now."

He swiveled in the captain's chair and looked at Red. "Are the supplies sufficient for five years?"

Red shrugged. "According to my calculations, yes. I've included everything that would be needed for a sailing trip of four to five years with the amount of personnel we have, plus extra flour, rice, and beans. Our biggest worry will be the canned fruits, meats, vegetables, and water. If they go bad and we cannot replenish our supply, we're in trouble. Even vitamin tablets won't change that. We don't have anyone here with the knowledge to run the bio-garden level. It's possible we could use some of the equipment, but the resulting mass may or may not be palatable."

LouElla's face was one of contentment as she looked up. She was going home after urging Llewellyn and Lorenz for years. "I have done what I could in that level, but we twould need four or more fully trained crew members to maintain the correct temperature, water content, humidity level, and rotate the type of plant materials growing there. I have nay of those skills. Mine are but basic to keep it running should the bio personnel suffer a mishap. The water I can keep recycling." She watched in amusement as distaste flicked across Margareatha's and Lorenz's face before she continued.

"Howe'er, I believe ye are all forgetting something. We twill be picking up Toma from the Ayana's Dominion. He twill nay wish to starve if he tis on his way home, and he kens how to run the system."

"Then it's agreed, we twill leave Elizabeth and Benton in charge until Priscilla, Charles, and Jerry are old enough to begin sharing in the responsibilities. Gary has trained Matthew Rolfe, Jerry's older brother to take over as the family doctor. David, Kendall's great-grandson, tis far too young to consider at this time. The others twill make the decisions about his care and training till he tis of age." MacDonald looked at Randall.

"Do ye object?"

"No, Grandfather, Elizabeth may not be Justine or Thalian, but she was the only one clever enough to ask questions and connect Mina's Story to her family. Benton also realized there was a deeper meaning." Randall at eighty was still slender, his red hair white and considerably thinned, but his face was unlined.

"Mayhap, it twould be best if ye took the Justine liquid after we adjourn, Randall. We are still here and yere hunger twill nay deplete our resources."

Randall nodded. Since Iris died, he really did not care whether he was old or young, but his body continued to live. He was startled to discover that he and his father were alike. Without the women they loved, neither considered remaining on Earth.

Margareatha was grim faced. Her emotions were ambiguous. Bianna was only nineteen. True, she was in college and would marry Jerry Rolfe as soon as she graduated. She had already started a life of her own. Rita wasn't sure she wanted to miss the wedding. Then again, Rita didn't relish the idea of becoming a grandmother, nor did she wish to remain and hide her true identity.

Melissa, almost four years younger than Randall, was slender; her step youthful, but her shoulder length hair, styled into a pageboy, was grey. She had taken the Justine elixir months ago, but her hair did not darken. Like her Great-grandmother LouElla, she was looking forward to the trip.

Andrew was an accountant with a penchant for starting new companies. He had no fear of the unknown. He had defied his mother to read Jules Vern and Edgar Rice Burroughs while still in his teens. The first time he visited the Golden One, he was filled with awe and the desire to see the stars and new worlds. At forty-five that desire burned as strong as when he was fifteen.

"They are old worlds." Lorenz had pointed out when Andrew told him of his passion.

"It doesn't matter, Pawpaw. It's something that most men will never experience. I'm going."

Lorenz quit his musing and listened to his father.

"That leaves the matter of smoking. Tis agreed that one area, and one area only, tis to be used. One of the double access doors twill remain closed and sealed. We canna scrub or recycle that air. It twould gum up the ventilation system. Have all the members of the crew agreed?" MacDonald looked at Red.

Red grinned. "They have, and everyone realizes I'll confiscate their smokes if they don't. They've been going outside the *Golden One* or using that room now.

"Then we have two more nights. We twill say our good-byes to those that are here and ken us. The rest dinna ken that we are here and twill nay miss us."

Gary stood. He was still stocky and his jowls full, but he worked diligently to keep his body fit. His hair, like most of the MacDonald's at forty-nine, was rapidly graying. The dose of elixir had not halted its advance. Vanity made him use hair dye, often having one of his lovers apply it for him. "If that's all, I need to check over the list of the medical supplies. I've added some of the remedies we're familiar with. I don't believe the medical area was stocked for as large a crew as we are. There were only eight aboard when Grandpa Mac came here. Krepyons are smaller than most Earthmen and have different physical requirements."

"They are Kreppies." LouElla spat the word out. "We have nay finished. Ye have checked those supplies twenty times."

Gary smiled at her and Llewellyn before sitting back down. It wouldn't do to walk out if LouElla was already upset. He was sure his great-grandparent's world would be more accepting of who he was. He had to be part of the command sector to impress the members of their hardened crew. That appointment with Darryl would have to wait.

Chapter 41

Plans

Michael Prentice dialed his contact the next morning. "I can't go back there. They've seen me."

"Who was it, O'Neal?"

"I don't know who it was. He was unreal, like some cowboy out of a bad western movie."

"How close was he? Who did he look like?"

"I can't remember."

"Why not? Did you talk to him?"

"I can't remember." Prentice groaned. "I was on the mountain watching the road into the Lodge, and then I was in town. I don't know how I got there, and the man was gone. I'd seen him riding once or twice, but if I try to remember more than that I feel like I need to get in the car and drive far away from here. His grey eyes are looking straight into me. That's all I remember. I can't go back there." Desperation and hysteria cracked his voice.

"Wait, don't say anything more. Just tell me where you are and stay there."

* * *

Creighton looked at the agents assembled before speaking. "You have all seen the files on the MacDonald family, their cohorts, and the location of where they are. They were able to get to the man we had posted there. How much they know, we can't be certain. We can be certain that they have added to their security. We need to go in now before any of them leave." He studied them again. At least Andresen wasn't smirking over the fact that he, Creighton, had capitulated, and Andresen did add stability to the younger agents.

"The two agents stationed in Albany to watch Judge MacDonald's movements reported two months ago that Mrs. MacDonald had passed away and the Judge had moved to the MacDonald Lodge. His daughter and her child live at the Judge's home, but four days ago they went to the lodge. It is likely that the family is gathering there as General MacDonald and his family have also arrived at the town a few miles from the lodge.

We'll take six cars with four men to each car. We will all take turns driving and sleeping in the car. We want to hit them before they know we're there. Any questions?"

"How many are there?"

"We estimate at least twenty to fifty. Since they discovered the man we had posted there, we haven't had any new reports. His previous reports tell of seeing about twenty to thirty men at different times, but they rarely leave or even show themselves. There also were over twelve hard looking women there, but we can't say how long they stayed. This makes it difficult to achieve an accurate count. The staff and visitors fluctuate any time of the year. We think there could be as high as sixty or as few as twenty. If the family is gathering, many of them will be women and younger people."

Creighton looked at each one. "We prefer to take them alive, but if necessary, every one of you has permission to use your revolver. Our office is getting a search warrant right now. It will be ready before we leave.

"Go home, get some rest, and meet tomorrow morning at six a.m. sharp. Take a change of clothes and a traveling kit."

Chapter 42

General MacDonald

Creighton led his men up to the front door. Bailey was at the rear of the house with four others in case someone tried to run, and two more teams were sent to either side. Andresen was in his group. Once the door chimes stopped the door was opened by the maid.

"We're from the FBI and my name is Creighton. I have a warrant to search this place and arrest warrants for some of the people here. Please step aside. You will need to answer questions later."

The maid stood there staring at them, and they pushed their way in. It was five days after the MacDonald conference aboard the *Golden One*. The foyer turned directly into an informal sitting room equipped with a rosewood desk. The chair in front of the desk contained a slender woman and she stood to face them.

Creighton noticed her high boned cheeks, a finely chiseled nose, and medium curly, beginning to turn grey, brown-red hair cropped in the shorter modern style. She was clad in a green riding habit and white blouse. About forty or forty-five, thought Creighton.

"I'm Mrs. Elizabeth Chadwell. May I see the search warrant, please?"

"The one to search the house is right here. Please be seated. We'll have questions once we're through."

Two people dressed in bathing suits entered the room from the dining area and Creighton swung to look at them while keeping a firm grip on the warrant. The young woman looked at them. When she saw Walter, she gasped.

"You're my father. Why are you doing this?"

Walter was at a loss for words. It was one thing for his mother to tell him this was his child and that she looked like him, but it was a shock to see how true the assessment rang.

The young man with her was huge, a good six feet five inches tall, his chest massive, and muscles rippled down his torso and thighs. He put his arm around her and drew her close.

More people started filing into the room. Some entered from the dining room and others were coming down the stairs. A tall, graying, red-headed man dressed in a military uniform came forward.

"What is going on, Elizabeth?"

"It seems these are FBI agents and they wish to arrest someone or several some ones, Wesley."

"In that case, I believe we should call a lawyer."

"You can do that after we leave." Creighton stepped forward. Something was wrong. He wasn't recognizing any of them other than the two bathing suit clad young people and Randall's children, Wesley and Elizabeth.

"Where is your mother?" Creighton stepped closer to Brianna. "I have an arrest warrant for her."

"She left three days ago." Brianna seemed to move closer under Jerry's protective arm.

"We'll see about that. Everybody have a seat in this room. If there isn't a chair, I suggest you sit on the floor. No one leaves until we're through."

Creighton and four men went up the stairs, two guarded those in the room and two others stood by the open front door, watching for any fleeing man or woman.

The lodge was huge: eight bedrooms and three baths were on the second floor, the third floor had more bedrooms and bathrooms. The attic held a sleeping loft and several trunks of old clothes. The ground floor consisted of a sitting room, music room, formal parlor, informal living room, a powder room, two dining rooms, a conference room with a round table and ten chairs, and a kitchen large enough for two stoves and two refrigerators. The basement level contained a gym, showers, two bathrooms, and another meeting room.

They opened closet doors, pulled out drawers, pounded on walls, and looked for a hiding place. They found nothing.

"Did you find any paperwork?" He asked the man coming out of the lower conference room.

"Nothing, except the MacDonald Corporation minutes and some paid invoices; otherwise, it's been stripped clean."

Creighton hurried back upstairs. The papers he would save to compare with what the IRS provided next year. It looked like he was going to need to take some of these people in for questioning, but he needed some pretext. He also needed more warrants for Randall's adult children, the company auditor and the lawyer. Those might be difficult to come by. What made it worse, he knew Wesley MacDonald was a two star general assigned to the United Nations. If he took him in, there'd better be a good reason or his career was over. He walked through the kitchen and opened the back door to give orders to the men outside.

"Start searching all those outbuildings. Look for anything that might not belong."

The men looked puzzled, but hurried off. Creighton narrowed his eyes as he watched them. Where had those people gone?

He walked over towards the rocky cliff that ascended to the northwest. Just below the crest was a shadowed opening to a cave. Prentice had claimed there was radiation in there, but whatever had been there was taken out years ago. Creighton rocked back and forth on his heels staring at the mountains and outbuildings. They had proof that men and trucks of supplies arrived here. But where were the men and the truck loads of supplies? They had made certain that the trucks that left the mountain town were empty and no humans or other cargo inside.

It was eleven a.m. when one of the men at the gate came into the yard looking for Creighton. He found him outside staring at the timbered lodge with a slate roof. There was an outdoor swimming pool and modern bathhouse on this side. The bathhouse held towels and extra suits, but nothing to indicate illegal activities.

"Sir, I've got the local sheriff telling me that his people are complaining about not being able to get to their jobs. He's also threatening to call his congressman if we don't let these people alone."

"Do you think he's on the MacDonald payroll?"

"No, sir, I think he's related to half the people that work here. They won't be paid if they don't work. The whole town thinks the MacDonald's do a lot for the community. They don't want any problems; plus, they are all jumpy since that report of a flying saucer three days ago. All sorts of reporters are in town questioning people."

Creighton's face flushed. He didn't need a bunch of reporters up here interviewing people about nonexistent space craft and then asking the people why the FBI was here. Without proof, he couldn't afford publicity.

"Tell him this shouldn't take much longer." He stalked back into the house and entered the sitting room where the members of the MacDonald clan were seated.

Wesley stood. "This has gone on long enough. We're becoming hungry and we're expecting more guests. Either you tell us why you are here, arrest someone, or leave this place."

"General, we have reason to believe certain people connected with this lodge and your family corporation are bringing in contraband and may be plotting treason."

Wesley's lips thinned and his face flushed. He was always ramrod straight and he stood at least three inches taller than Creighton. "In that case, I suggest you name that person or persons right now."

"Margareatha Andresen, a certain "Red" O'Neal or Neal, and two other people we cannot identify. They were seen coming onto this property or on it. Where are they?"

When no one answered, Creighton turned to Brianna. "Where did your mother go?"

"She didn't say."

It was Creighton's turn to flush. "Get dressed. You'll be coming with us."

"No, she isn't." Jerry stood like a rock; his blue eyes were hard and cold. He sent his mind into Creighton's to forbid Brianna leaving, but he spoke aloud. "You have nothing against her or her mother. It's a bluff."

Creighton wanted to smash his fist into the young man's face, but that one he knew was clean.

"She also knows about that O'Neal person. He's a dangerous man. She'll be interrogated and if, and when, we're satisfied, she'll be released. If you try to interfere, there will be federal charges against you."

Jerry's blue eyes lit with amusement. "I don't believe you listened to General MacDonald. He is not happy with your accusations." With his mind he kept forbidding Creighton to take Brianna. No one noticed his eyes blink. He took time to look across the room at Priscilla, Elizabeth's red-haired daughter. She winked at him. He was right. His cousin from the other side of the family could enter minds too.

General MacDonald walked to the desk and picked up the telephone.

"Put that down," commanded Creighton.

The General dialed the operator. "Connect me to the Pentagon, please."

Creighton's mouth dropped. "Didn't you hear me?" He had his revolver on Wesley.

Wesley stood staring at him, the telephone held firmly to his ear. "Mister, I defy you to shoot me or anyone else in this room. I will still be dying for the freedoms of my country."

"You're in cahoots with a gunrunner." Creighton was desperate to control the situation. Others in the room were edging away, but his men had all the exits blocked.

Wesley turned his back on him. "This is General MacDonald. Connect me with my office." There was a slight pause.

"Delores, get in touch with the State Department and tell them that the FBI are at the MacDonald Lodge trying to arrest us all. I need someone to tell them to back off." He slammed the telephone back into the cradle, turned, and faced them.

"Well, it's your move."

"General, someone in this room knows where Red O'Neal and Margareatha Andresen are. They were here. We have not observed them leaving."

Silence hung over the room. "You see, even you won't admit to knowing them."

"I have never met either of them."

Creighton took a deep breath. "Are you claiming you have never met a tall, well-built red-haired woman on this property?"

"I am. I am not claiming that for anyone else other than my wife and family. Frankly, I don't believe you are able to produce one bit of evidence that anyone in this room is engaged in illegal activities."

Creighton turned to face Brianna. "How often was your mother with O'Neal?"

"She was never "with" him. He came to visit us on the ranch because he's her half-brother. We never knew where he was or when he would arrive. Sometimes years would go by."

Walter wondered what his daughter thought about New York after living on a ranch. It did not occur to him that he had just thought of her as his daughter.

"And, of course, he brought you all sorts of things." Creighton's voice was a sneer. "Or else he'd ask for a place to hide. Isn't that correct? Your mother would store illegal guns and South American artifacts there. Do you deny that?"

Brianna looked at him with distaste. "Uncle Red never kept anything there but his suitcase. Once he brought me a pony, and he certainly never hid anywhere. He would go into town even if we didn't."

"That's enough." Wesley was disgusted. "I'm not even sure how Miss Andresen or her mother are related to our side of the family, but if they are, this young lady will have a lawyer before she answers another question."

Creighton ignored him, but for some reason his throat tightened. He turned back to the group. Why wouldn't words come out of his mouth? The General was glaring at him. Was he lying? He didn't have any reason to arrest the General. The others were looking at them with the distaste of someone looking at lower, ugly creations. Finally, the words came.

"The FBI doesn't need to provide a lawyer during an investigation. You, General, must be aware of that."

It did not matter to Wesley that Creighton was correct. Wesley was the grandchild that idolized his "Pawpaw" and wanted to emulate him. To his parents dismay, he had found any excuse he could to visit his grandfather and grandmother in Texas. The tales of early Texas and his great-grandfather's rescue of his great-grandmother and other exploits as a scout in the Second Cavalry and later with the Eighth U.S. Infantry during the Civil War had inspired his own application to West Point. He considered the military as a way to uphold the visions of those long-ago-Western ideals. Wesley had become the patriarch of the family. They were his responsibility.

"Miss Andresen will have a lawyer or she shall not go with you. She will also have the opportunity to dress in proper attire."

Creighton ignored the dictum. "We have reason to believe that your grandfather interfered with our investigation. That's obstructing justice. Where is he?"

"You have taken leave of your senses. Grandfather would be almost 100 years old if he were still alive."

"If he is dead, where is he buried? Frankly, somehow both he and his father have avoided death and the grave."

All eyes were staring at him like an insane person. Several shrugged their shoulders and amused contempt settled on Wesley's face.

"There's one thing wrong with your premise. They are not biologically re-lated. Pawpaw was adopted. MacDonald is our name because a big man with a big heart took in a half-starved vagabond."

Creighton felt like a blow had hit his stomach. All these years wasted looking for records without one of the crucial surnames. Before he could speak the telephone rang. Creighton nodded at Bailey to take it and motioned the rest to be silent.

"MacDonald Lodge, Bailey speaking." There was a pause. "Uh, yes sir, right here, sir." He held the telephone towards Creighton. "It's for you, sir." The awe in his voice was unmistakable.

Creighton frowned and stepped to the desk. "Creighton here." The voice of cold fury in his ear shook him to his core.

"Yes, sir, we'll leave immediately." He replaced the telephone, his face an ashen color.

"I don't know how you accomplished that, General, but you have your wish. We'll be leaving. If any of you try to leave the country, believe me, I will and can stop that." He motioned to his men to follow him.

Creighton was angrier than he had ever been in his life. Never had he been so thwarted in an investigation. Who had that kind of power over the old man? No one but the President his mind told him. This United Nations thing couldn't be that important could it?

Epilogue

"Any regrets, laddie?"

Lorenz was standing by the silver-colored panel that functioned as a screen looking out into the blackness of space. "A few, Papa, but right now Earth can't be anymore alien than Thalia. The prairies are fenced little squares, the longhorns are gone, and Antoinette is gone. There's nothing left of the life I once knew. I am an old man by Earth's reckoning, but my body is young."

MacDonald looked at his son lounging against the rail. Physically Lorenz was in great shape, but somehow the grieving for Antoinette had not stopped. Had Lorenz even bothered to spend time with another female? He doubted it. The man was a complete contradiction. He wondered if Thalia was ready for Lorenz.

Lorenz turned his back to the surrounding blackness. "Now that Toma's aboard, how long do y'all reckon this will take?"

"Oh a good three to five years, but more like a little over three or so before we land at the Justine Refuge. Mither tis quite good at mapping the way through the stars. She kens when tis the time to use a warp aisle and how far it takes us. I find I seem to have a facility for it also. Mayhap ye twill discover the same for yereself."

Lorenz shrugged and then that smile broke out: the smile that was Anna's. "At least this time y'all don't have to threaten to hogtie me and drag me all the way home."

The End

About the Author

Mari Collier was born on a farm in Iowa, and has lived in Arizona, Washington, and Southern California. She and her husband, Lanny, met in high school and were married for forty-five years. She is Co-Coordinator of the Desert Writers Guild of Twentynine Palms and serves on the Board of Directors for the Twentynine Palms Historical Society. She has worked as a collector, bookkeeper, receptionist, and Advanced Super Agent for Nintendo of America. Several of her short stories have appeared in print and electronically, plus three anthologies. Twisted Tales From The Desert, Twisted Tales From The Northwest, and Twisted Tales From The Universe. Earthbound is the first of the Chronicles of the Maca series.

Author Contact Information

Website: http://www.maricollier.com
Twitter: https://twitter.com/child7mari